A Prince at First

"There is not a more corrupting thing
this side of Hell than baseball."
—Sam Jones, Evangelist

A Prince at First

The Fictional Autobiography of Baseball's Hal Chase

by ED DINGER

McFarland & Company, Inc., Publishers
Jefferson, North Carolina, and London

ISBN 0-7864-1330-1 (softcover : 50# alkaline paper)

Library of Congress cataloguing data are available

British Library cataloguing data are available

On the cover: Hal Chase circa 1912
(National Baseball Hall of Fame Library, Cooperstown, N.Y.)

Manufactured in the United States of America

*McFarland & Company, Inc., Publishers
Box 611, Jefferson, North Carolina 28640
www.mcfarlandpub.com*

Chapter 1

My big brother John was considered the real baseball player in the family and he never made a dime out of the game. He played purely as a testimony to the Lord. John Chase was as handsome as a collar ad in a magazine and had every girl in town angling for his attention and every young man hanging around hoping to maybe pick up his castoffs. But there were none, because John took no interest in the delights of the flesh. He never knew drink nor tobacco, and if he cussed nobody ever heard it.

None of these fine personal traits would have mattered as much if he hadn't also been the best damn baseball player that anybody had ever seen. Hell, if he acted like a complete rake he would have still been considered a local treasure. Because of him our little town of Alviso, California, could take on and whip burgs five times our size. Town ball was *the* game back in the 1890s and it was a matter of civic pride to root for the neighbor boys, not to mention slap a few dollars on the barrelhead to show that you really meant it. Some fine baseballers were forged in the heat of a local affair. When you know every last body sitting in those rickety country grandstands or perched on the back of a buckboard grazing in the outfield, and the men have been drinking heavy and got as much money on the outcome as to their names, you can't help but feel some pressure. If you get the yips on an easy roller, heave the old apple into the nickel seats and it costs your side the game, then, mister, you might as well just pack your grip and emigrate to Australia to join the other outcasts of society.

My brother John never got the yips. Cool as buttermilk he turned every play no matter what the score or how near the ninth. At the plate he swung so free and easy it was like he was casting for trout, but you should have seen the way the ball shot off his bat. And damn could he run, smooth and regular like an antelope, yet determined like some kind of wild hound. Watching him stretch out a triple or a home run made your heart jump. And no matter how close the play he always beat the ball to the base. Then he'd just slap off the dust, palm back his hair and not even favor a breath. He did this all without boasting because he was also the perfect example of good sportsmanship. The guy would beat the hell out of you all afternoon and there was nothing you could do but hang your head and take it.

I admired my big brother, I loved him a lot, but there was something about the way the entire community held him up as a shining example that could rub a guy the wrong way. I mean, wasn't it a boy's right to pick his own heroes?

What with the Civil War long past and the Wild West tamed, instead of generals and gun slingers we boys in the market for heroes took our commerce out on big league baseball players. King Kelly was our man, though we didn't have much to go on other than stories from *The Sporting Life* and the color cigar cards we begged off the loafers at the barber shop. It was taken as Gospel that nobody played a brainier brand of ball than King Kelly. He was a regular whiz at cheating and doping out the edge. And after the game the King and his court lived a life that we boys couldn't help but envy. They were the hell-raising, skirt-chasing, booze-guzzling darlings of the sporting crowd, from Boston to Chicago.

Of course our folks didn't see much to admire in King Kelly. To them professional baseball playing was right up there with horse stealing and street walking. That's when they'd shove my big brother in our faces. *Why can't you aspire to be like him? He teaches Sunday School.* John caused more than one copy of *The Sporting Life* or cigar card of the King to be consigned to the flames of a kitchen stove.

The ones that took the most offense were the four Mayo brothers: Matthew, Mark, Luke and John. Their father, a circuit preacher, had abandoned the family, leaving them to care for their spirit-broken mother. They were big King Kelly boosters and didn't care to have their morality questioned, being preachers' kids and consecrated.

"Say it," insisted Matthew the oldest.

"I can't." They had me cornered against the backstop of the town ball field.

"Ah, he's as soft as his brother." John Mayo, the youngest, a couple of years older than I was, always seemed to have it in for me.

The twins, Mark and Luke, spat tobacco juice, balled their fists and looked ready to weigh in.

"Take it easy, boys," Matthew said. "Hal just needs a minute." Then he shoved my face against the sharp wire backstop. I felt like a block of cheese.

I gave in and said the words they wanted to hear. "I hate my brother. He stinks."

"And?"

"I hope he dies."

"And?"

"He eats shit with a spoon."

I didn't mean it. I was just a kid. Not more than ten years old. But wouldn't you know it, a couple days later my big brother contracts the polio.

Polio had spread like a wildfire from the East Coast to the West over the last couple of years so its arrival in California came as no surprise— except that it struck down John Chase. Everybody knew how deadly the disease could be, but surely a strong young man like him would shake it off. And with all of his fine works it made no sense for the Almighty to call him home so soon. Yet John didn't shake off the polio, he kept sinking lower and lower, to the point that the entire town began to doubt its faith.

John was considered infectious, confined to a sick room in our house, and I was forbidden to enter. That only made me more determined to get inside.

One night, the night that the doctor declared to be the crisis, I stayed up until two in the morning waiting for my mother to leave John's side for a spell so I could sneak in. I slowly opened the door to keep it from creaking and found him tossing in bed, moaning quietly. I crept up to see that he was feverish and beading with sweat. He was crying and muttering to himself, "I'm sorry. I didn't mean it. Whatever I did, I'm sorry." Then he opened his eyes and looked at the ceiling. "What do you want from me?"

He turned his head and caught me gawking at him. "Hal, hey kid. You're not supposed to be here."

"Doc Lowry said it was all right."

"*Doc Lowry.*" The way John said the name it was like something sour. "The old fraud couldn't cure an upset stomach. He wants me dead, Hal. They all want me dead."

"I don't."

"Dead!" he shouted, clutched the top sheet pulled over his chest and tried to tear it apart. He was too weak and only managed to wrinkle it a little.

"I gave my life for this town. And they want me dead."

"That's not true."

"Oh, I can see it now. I can see it all."

"No, John."

"They look at me and see what they aren't. I upset all their little apple-carts."

"I should get back to bed." I started to close the door to go.

"Don't leave me alone, Hal. Please," he said, "could you—could you mop my brow?"

He'd been there for days, there was this smell in the room of stale clothing and the bedpan in the corner, and I start to think, *The guy's contagious!*

"Please, Hal."

So I pick up the washcloth that was scented with rose water and, sitting as far away as possible, I begin to dab the sweat from his face and wait for him to drift off to sleep. Then I stand up, only to have the squealing bed springs wake him.

"Don't leave me," he says. "Just five more minutes."

I go back to mopping his brow with rose water, listening to his wheezy, rattling breath and keeping a sharp eye out for a chance to slip away. Too bad I was the first one to nod off.

John startled me awake with a jerk on the wrist. He was propped up on one elbow, looking off into space. "I'm not ready," he cried.

"For what?"

"I've been an abomination. I know that now. I've been so blind with pride. I've been so lost."

Then he turned to look at me.

"But you still have a chance, Hal. I want you to do something for me. I want you to make me an oath. Say you'll swear me an oath."

"Just name it."

"Say you'll swear."

"I will. I swear."

"And no fibbing?"

"No fibbing."

A calm spreads over the room and this contented look comes over his face. John lays back down and his grip on my wrist begins to loosen— but not enough to let me go. The candlelight in the room is all screwy and dreamlike, and even though our house is set back in the woods it sounds like ocean waves are rolling up on a shore.

"Promise me," he said, "that you won't waste your life on baseball."

His hand began to fall off my wrist.

"Do you swear to it, Hal?"

It was like I could see his spirit starting to clear out of the body.

"Do you swear to it on your soul?"

I knew I had to answer.

"Do you swear to it?"

"Yes," I said. "Yes, I swear to it on my soul."

"Then kiss me on the cheek."

I leaned down and kissed my brother on the cheek. His hand dropped away. He had barely enough strength to smile, as the light in his eyes began to melt away.

Chapter 2

When I got back to my room I couldn't sleep. A little later I heard my Mom climbing the stairs, a door shutting quietly then opening up quick again, excited footsteps, the rumble of my old man's voice, and a few minutes later the whinny of a pissed-off horse in the barn wanting to know what in the hell the big deal was.

A couple hours later my Mom peeks in my room. "Are you awake, honey?" I made her ask a second time before I rolled over and cracked an eyelid.

"It's your brother," she said.

"Huh?"

"He's been taken from us." She rushed over to comfort me, pressing my face to her bosom and rocking me back and forth.

"Don't cry, honey," she said. So now I had no choice but to.

Now the old man comes into the room, not happy to see his youngest working the tear ducts. "Well," he says to Mom, "I got Doc Lowry for you, not that he can do much now."

Mom pets my hair one last time and leaves me and the old man alone together. The truth of the matter is my father and me never got on much. After having John and five girls, I guess by the time I showed he had his fill of fatherhood. He just lingered in the doorway, looking like he might actually have something to say to me. He was especially proud of John and his reputation in town, acting like all of my big brother's attributes were just chips off his own block. But the way he's eyeing me I begin to feel like a player who's been sitting at the end of the bench for so long he can't recall what position I play.

"Your brother was a fine young man," was all he said, then went out and got stinking drunk.

My old man had originally come out to California to catch the gold rush of 1849. Too bad by the time he got there it was 1860. He went to Nevada to take over a claim, but after working it for a few weeks all he had to show for his effort was a lot of blue mud. He was just thankful to unload that claim for a couple bucks on some newer fool than him. That fool turned out to be a geologist, that blue mud turned out to be silver ore, and that claim turned out to be a piece of the Comstock Lode. And so for the rest of his life my old man brooded on how close he had come to striking it big. He opened up a saw mill in Alviso and did all right for himself—most folks considered him a successful man—but none of that eased the sting of missing out on something glorious.

The news of John's death troubled the entire community. People either took to drink like my father or religion like my mother and sisters. Drunk or sober, everybody came to the funeral.

As for me, I was in sort of a fog that didn't begin to lift until the eulogy. A preacher from San Jose had been brought in special to bury John. Nobody had personally heard the man preach but he came with excellent references. He certainly offered plenty of words for the dollar, going on so long that he numbed the folks who weren't already numb enough from John's death. Then he said something that shook me out of my daze.

"No matter what good works John Chase may have done in this world," said the preacher, "all he takes with him on his final journey is his immoral soul."

Something sounded wrong.

"That's the simple truth, friends. All he takes with him is his immoral soul."

I looked around at my family and half the county, and everybody just nodded their heads. Didn't they hear the man just call John's soul immoral–not *immortal* but *immoral*?

I figure maybe my ears were playing tricks, but at the gravesite it happened again. The preacher leads us in one last prayer before lowering John's body into the ground, again droning on so long I'm almost asleep on my feet.

"Therefore, Father," he says, "we now *condemn* this boy into your keeping."

Again I look around. I mean, the man said *condemn*.

But no one seemed to notice. Was I the only one in the world with ears that could hear? Was I the only one with eyes that could see?

"Amen," says the preacher.

And it's time for chicken and biscuits in the church basement. So much for the town hero.

◈

Our family went into an extended period of mourning, which meant I couldn't go out of the house. A couple days of dead-slow boredom had me on the verge, so I was glad to hear a pebble ring off of my bedroom window and look outside to see the Mayo brothers urging me to sneak out to join in a ballgame.

Only when I had a bat in my hands and cracked a single did I feel I was coming out of my funk. *That's it,* I'm thinking at first base, *just a little dose of baseball to get me back on the black squares.*

And so I'm taking my lead off the bag, just daring the pitcher to toss one my way, when it felt like an ice pick stabbed me in the head. It was my brother's voice.

Promise me that you won't waste your life on baseball.

The pitcher twirled and pegged the ball over. I didn't even make a try at getting back to first. I walked off the diamond and straight home, in such a state that I could hardly hear the Mayo boys asking what the hell was the matter with me.

I didn't have the heart to play ball, and to get out of the house began to keep company with my old man, who for the first time seemed to want me around. He got this idea that he should become mayor of Alviso and he took me along on his campaign jaunts. Mostly it was standing for drinks at a saloon, handing out cigars and swapping stories with the no-accounts. To tell the truth he was kind of stiff around other men. He smiled the whole time and snorted a laugh every so often, always told the same two jokes, and since he was buying, everybody laughed every time and promised not to forget his hospitality come election day.

My father always had dreams about John's prospects in the world. He liked to think that his calling was to mold John's calling, always offering what he thought were pearls of wisdom, blind to the fact that the reason John was respected in the community was his ability to play baseball. Sure, my brother was pious, but no more than a bunch of other young men in town.

My old man did appreciate the value of baseball in helping John to get ahead, but overall he considered it a frivolous thing. He simply couldn't comprehend why a grown man would want to run around in circles wearing pajamas. Play some town ball and make some friends who might help you later—that was his advice. But don't even think about playing for money in the new California State League, because why sully your reputation for a hundred bucks a month? The real game was in big business or big politics.

"I'll guarantee you one thing, son," I remember him declaring. "No baseball player or stage actor is ever going to stay in the best hotels or get himself elected President of the United States."

"I don't want to be President of the United States," John said. "I just want to serve the Lord."

"There you go. That's the angle. You don't want to appear pushy."

That was the real hope my old man had for John. Politics. And no office less than President of the United States would do. Of course that would make him the father of the President, the man who groomed his boy for greatness, because surely John would be the greatest president that ever was or would be. And to thank him for his invaluable service to the nation, the American people would repay my old man by burying him in Arlington Cemetery and slapping his profile on a postage stamp.

With John taken by the polio where did that leave my old man's chance for the White House? With me? No, he'd just have to finish the job himself. But in spite of springing for all that whiskey and tobacco my old man got beat out for the job of town mayor by a barber. If a man holds a cold razor to your throat who are you going to vote for?

That's when the old man really began to brood over what might have been. And me? I went back to playing baseball. I didn't forget the promise I made to my brother, but I had gotten over the shock of his death and started to think clear. I was just a kid, so why shouldn't I play a kid's game? I figured I still had plenty of time to do something worthwhile in life.

So I played a lot of baseball and started to show I had some of the same tools as my brother. It looked like another Chase boy was coming along and the older players on the town club kept close watch on my progress. I tried out and made the junior town team and in no time made the jump to the big club. I was only fourteen when I became the starting second baseman, even though I was a lefty, playing against some men twenty years older than me. Maybe part of it was due to the legend of my brother and how it pleased folks to have another Chase in the batting order, but I showed I could play. I was one of the guys. Too bad a lot of the guys were up to no good.

Chapter 3

When my teammates invited me along to a fandango I didn't have the nerve to say no. They called it a fandango, but it wasn't the kind of family affair the Mexicans hold. This fandango turned out to be a barn, a banjo, a barrel of rye and two fat logging camp whores. Everybody seemed to be having a swell enough time, especially those whores who every few minutes gave someone a tour of the hayloft.

"Here's something to wet your whistle," said Matthew Mayo, handing me a tin cup brimming with rye whiskey. I was sitting on some bales of hay with the other Mayo boys.

Matthew was now a pretty fair pitcher on the town team, the twins Mark and Luke played the outfield, and John was a utility man looking for a starting job. He was sixteen and made no secret that he couldn't see how a runt like me could have been tapped over him for second base.

I took a sip of that whiskey and just about twisted up.

"Get the baby some milk," said John.

"That's okay, Hal," Matthew said. "Just throw it back quick."

After a few tries I got the hang of it. Not to mention as drunk as a boiled owl.

Soon Mark and Luke pushed me out onto the floor to cut in for a dance with one of those whores. Then they forced me up to the hayloft, a huge whore's ass hanging over my head and the ladder creaking like it's ready to collapse.

In the loft a circle of hay was flattened and covered by a couple of ratty horse blankets. The whore, laughing like crazy, dropped on her back, spread her legs and fell right to sleep. I stayed up there a spell, stared at her matching mole and mustache and tried to remember what they said her name was, then I climbed back down to a hearty roar from the boys and a bunch of slaps on the back.

◆

Conduct had gone to blazes since the influence of my big brother vacated the town team. And there was certainly no lack of opportunity to go wrong in a northern California that wasn't too far removed from the Wild West, with enough loggers, miners, cowboys, card sharps, old gun fighters, fallen women and shiftless drifters around to make life pretty interesting on a Saturday night. Or a Tuesday morning, for that matter.

The better players on the town team were given more sufferance than other young men, because in a small town only .200 hitters go to jail. Bat .300 and the gun has to be found smoking in your hand before you get charged with murder—that is, unless the victim was batting .400, in which case everybody looks the other way because *now* they really need your bat in the lineup.

Just trying to fit in with my older teammates I soon landed myself in the same bind. Your wild ways are tolerated so long as you deliver the goods on the field, but the better you play the more temptation comes your way. You had to play even better to stay square with respectable society, until either you retired and settled down to a quiet life—something few could accomplish—or you went into an extended hitting slump and got yourself jailed. Maybe hung.

My sisters who were overly concerned about their personal reputations told my mother that I was straying down the wrong path. She was determined to save me, convinced that if only she had been a bit more religious God would have spared John.

One morning when I was still dizzy from drink the night before, they trapped me in the kitchen. The girls blocked every door and passage. My Mom sat at the table, ready with her Bible, and asked me to take a chair.

"What am I going to do with you, Harold?" she said.

I hated to be called Harold. Only an eastern dandy would go by a handle like that. John Mayo liked to call me Harold, mostly when I was at the bat and he was sitting in his usual spot on the bench. "Try to put some sock into it, *Harold!*" He made it seem like he was rooting for me when he was just trying to throw me off my game and get an edge at taking away the second base job.

"The *entire* town is talking!" cried the girls just like the church choir. Hell, they pretty much *were* the church choir.

"A bunch of gossiping old biddies ain't the entire town," I said, and you should have seen them gape in horror.

"I want the truth now." Mom fingered her Bible. "Have you begun to smoke cigarettes?"

I rolled my eyes—the way only bad boys can do it.

"Am I to take that as a denial?"

"I wouldn't be caught dead smoking a cigarette."

"Is that the truth, *John*?"

"I smoke cigars, all right?" *The name was Hal! Not Harold. And certainly not John.*

"And what about shooting pool?"

"Never tried it."

"That's not what we heard," said the girls.

"I imagine that you are confusing pool with billiards, which happens to be the second best way to develop your brain, the angles and possibilities being so great and complex."

"And what about playing poker?" asked Mom.

"That happens to be the best way to develop your brain."

"Like fun!" said my sisters.

"It's scientific."

"Girls, please," said Mom. "Harold, I know this isn't you talking."

"I'd like to know who it is then."

"Those ballplayer friends of yours."

"Oh, cheese and crackers! God all muddy!"

That did it. The girls let out a wail to wake the dead and Mom started up the water works. I felt like such a skate I pledged to go to church and straighten up my life. My Mom and sisters were so pleased they doted on me the way they did when I was little and the girls' favorite doll. I felt like a new creature, certain that my brother John couldn't have been any more pure and sanctified than me at that moment. The problem was that a couple days later, and certainly by Saturday night, I managed to find myself in the company of the Mayo brothers.

The Mayo boys, being consecrated as they were, had no doubts they were heaven bound. They'd want to go off drinking at some logging camp and when I tried to resist they'd look to scripture to convince me otherwise.

"What's the good book say about drinking spirits?" Matthew turned to the twins.

"'Drink a little for your stomach ache,'" replied Mark.

"I thought that was wine," I said.

"Wine's the same thing as whiskey in the Bible," Matthew explained.

So it seemed that I was always giving in, one thing would lead to another and come Sunday morning I'd be in no condition to attend church. On Monday, Mom and the girls would gang up on me, I'd repent and we'd go through the same routine, only the stakes kept mounting as my mother grew more worried over the perilous state of my soul.

And she had no doubts that the root of all my troubles was the pursuit of that little white orb with the fiery-red seams down the side.

Chapter 4

I t wasn't just me. It seemed that America itself couldn't get enough baseball. In addition to town teams and minor leagues cropping up all over
the map, any self-respecting factory, orphanage or prison had to field a nine
or look pretty miserable. This created a ripe market for visiting opposition, and there was no lack of fellows ready to take the road for weeks at
a time to grapple with any club that had a chicken-wire backstop and some
of the actual to plunk down on the outcome of the game. There was also
no shortage of locals willing to pony up a coin to watch the proceedings.

To take advantage of the need for fresh opposition the Mayo brothers created their own independent baseball team and invited me to go
barnstorming with them. Representing your hometown was one thing,
but playing the game for nothing more than adventure and filthy lucre
was definitely going over the line of respectability. After four seasons of
playing for the town team I had already become something of a disappointment to my folks, and if it wasn't for the intervention of community boosters who urged them to let me keep playing I would have been
forced to quit. I could only imagine what they'd have to say if I announced
I was turning semi-pro. No, I had to draw the line.

"Can't you think about your friends for once?" asked Matthew. We
were eating saltine crackers from a huge barrel on the porch of a general
store. So long as the town team won we could have all the crackers we
wanted. Soda pops cost extra.

"You don't want to let us down, do you?" said Mark.

"Where are your morals?" added Luke.

"Ah, forget about him," John said. "He's just scared he can't cut the
buck in the big time." Of course the main reason John was so anxious to
form up an independent team was so he could land a starting berth.

"I only play for my hometown," I said. "I ain't gonna be no professional."

"We respect your stand," Matthew said. "Hell, we're preachers' kids! We're just asking that you help us out at second base until we find someone. Just go on the first trip with us, Hal. That way the word will get around about the ball club, we'll be able to land some better players and take on the bigger towns."

"I wish I could help, I really do."

"What does the good book say, Mark?"

"You mean about letting down your brother?"

"That's it?"

"'Woe betide the man who fails to keep his brother's promise.'"

"What promise?" I said.

"He's just a chicken liver," says John.

"If he's just going to deny us three times, what's the point?" says Luke.

But Matthew was never one to give up easy. "Mark, what's the Book say about backstabbers?"

"Backstabbers? Lemme see, there's 'Let the backstabber look before he leap, lest he be devoured.'"

"Backstabber!" I cry. "That's not fair."

"Ah, who needs him?" John slams the lid on the cracker barrel and hops off the porch.

"I guess there's no reasoning with the guy." And Luke jumps off the porch, too.

"Now hold on there," I said, and just like that all four of them have leapt off the porch and are walking away from the store. I ran after them, pleading that they hear me out. "I don't mean to let nobody down. You just want a player to tie you over until you find a replacement, right?"

"No need to trouble yourself," Matthew said.

"I'll do it."

"We can always play with eight."

"Hopefully we won't embarrass ourselves too much," said Luke.

"You went and made your decision," said Matthew. "It's no good going back and forth on your word."

"'Verily,'" says Mark, "'He who looks in two directions shall break his neck.'"

It took some effort but I finally convinced them to let me come along. I was only doing it as a favor to a bunch of fatherless boys; still, I couldn't help getting a bit excited over the prospect of playing a tougher brand of ball and seeing the world in the process—not that we planned on getting any further than fifty miles from home.

I guess I should have explained things to my folks, but I was afraid they wouldn't understand, so one day I just disappeared. I figured they'd learn what became of me soon enough, since my sisters made a point of knowing everybody's business in town. I'd just explain myself when we got back. As Mark Mayo said, "'For every season there is a reasonable explanation.'"

I found out that it was a good idea for us to stick fairly close to home. It was no mean task beating a local team when they provided the umpire and all the shotguns necessary to back up his rotten calls. You also had to accustom yourself to all manner of playing conditions. Left field might be little more than a swamp, hitting the old oak tree on the fly in right might be ruled an automatic double, maybe the infield is laid out wrong and the sun is facing the batter instead of the fielders, and, of course, some kid thinks he invented the trick of flashing a mirror in your eyes. And on every pop-up the crowd starts to yell, "Watch out for that wheelbarrow!" There's at least one drunk cowboy who, just as you're about to field an easy one, fires off his peacemaker. Bottles, pennies, rocks—if it can be thrown you can be sure it's coming in your direction at some point in the game. Wagers, whiskey and firearms make a first-class recipe for a riot, so plenty of times the smart play for a barnstorming outfit was to just lose to the home side with as much grace as possible, pay off the bets and thank the good Lord you got out of that burg still wearing your own skin.

Matthew Mayo made sure we played in places where some of us had relations, and he made a point of delivering a prayer to the crowd before the first pitch. After that people didn't feel quite right about screwing their own kin, let alone doing them violence, so we actually won more than our share of ballgames and managed to pile up a little cash. We figured we were prized china and had a grand time knocking around the countryside. There was just the nine of us, no subs, and we shared everything: the same bumpy ground to bed on, the same roadside apples for breakfast, the same case of dysentery. Even John Mayo and me got on better, especially since he finally had his own position to play.

No effort was made along the way to find a replacement for me and I didn't bother to remind Matthew. After a month or so, the other guys wanted a break from the road and we headed home to Alviso. Baseball playing was pretty much done for the year, anyway.

I didn't really want to go home, not just because I was having such a swell time, but because the longer we stayed away the worse it was going to be explaining myself. The Mayo brothers tried to reassure me with the Bible story about the prodigal son. It didn't help. I had a feeling that when I showed up at the door grubby and foul-smelling, my folks weren't about to slaughter no fatted cat in my honor.

Chapter 5

My old man raised his hand to hit me, but even though he was drunk he never pulled the trigger. I was a strapping boy of nineteen and he had gone soft. It was my Mom who really killed me. She didn't have to say anything, just look brokenhearted, but she managed a few words anyway. She hoped I recognized the slippery slope I was on. Many a boy had thrown away a chance at an honest living by kicking around playing baseball; no employer would want such an unreliable character. It got too late in life too quick, and one day you'd find yourself broken and worthless.

So I swore off baseball for good, only to have another delegation of community leaders call to plead with my folks. I was needed on the town team more than ever, what with all the defections to the Mayo brothers.

Luckily I had told the boys I was only good for that first season of barnstorming. I avoided their company, figuring I didn't even owe them a reminder that I wouldn't be joining the team when it hit the road again. That didn't prevent the Mayo brothers from tracking me down one day with a mail order catalog in hand. They were ordering actual baseball uniforms that cost a buck apiece and boasted a large, bright blue shield that buttoned over a white blouse. For a cap, instead of the usual beanie, they picked out something that looked like what a Swiss mountaineer might wear.

"We figured you're the same size as John," Matthew said. "So we used his measurements for your outfit."

"My outfit?"

"Don't worry. You can pay us later."

"Who told you to order me a uniform?"

"We had to do it all at once. To get the discount."

I pointed out that I wasn't really a member of the team, that I had just been helping them in a pinch.

"Didn't I tell you he'd try to weasel out," said John. "Who cares if he plays or not?"

"Hal's a fine ballplayer and everybody knows it." Matthew laid his arm over my shoulder. "I wouldn't advance money to Sears and Roebuck for just anybody."

I pulled his arm off of me. "I hope you find someone the same size, because I promised my folks that my semi-pro days are through and I wouldn't have anything more to do with you pack of strays."

"Strays is it?" said John. That's when he took a poke at me and the twins had to hold him back.

"Come on, boys. We should be going home," Matthew says. "Sorry to trouble you, Hal. Sorry to upset your fine parents. It's time for our Bible reading, anyway. Mom'll be waiting on us. Oh, did I tell you, she's dying of the consumption?"

They left me feeling like a regular heel, and the rest of the winter they gave me the icy treatment. But I kept my word to my parents. I even made it to church more often than not. In a way it felt good it be pious, but hymn singing and potluck dinners didn't quite stimulate the blood like a fandango. Piety turned out to be so tame I had to wonder if it wasn't an acquired taste.

Well before spring arrived the bats and gloves came out of the closets all over the county. I started to practice with the town team, but we didn't have much of a collection of talent anymore. The Mayo brothers had picked us clean. Civic pride and all the crackers you can eat are one thing, actual cash another. We took the field and were trounced by villages that we once thought we were doing a favor by putting on the schedule. Now it was other towns that didn't see the need to accept our challenges.

The Mayo brothers in the meantime were storming the sticks and earning a reputation as a side that was pretty tough to beat. I pretended not to notice, but it wasn't easy when people insisted on filling me in on their latest exploits. After a couple months the club came home for a break and I ran into the brothers as I was stepping out of the general store. They were wearing their uniforms and Swiss caps, even though they weren't scheduled to play a game, and I had to admit to myself that the flannels looked even better than in the catalog.

"How's the crackers?" asked John.

"It's good to see you, Hal." Matthew offered his hand to give mine a good shake. The twins took their turns, then John gave me the point of his shoulder as he bumped me on his way inside the store.

"I hope you were able to unload that uniform you ordered for me."

"We still got it," Matthew said. "To tell you the truth, Hal, we didn't just run into you by accident. We're in a situation again. Our second baseman turned an ankle and we got a game over in Los Gatos tomorrow. You think you could help us out?"

I tried to beg off, really I did, but after a half-dozen Bible verses I was beaten down and agreed to play one game with them as a matter of Christian charity. Still, I couldn't wait to try on that mail order uniform and Swiss cap. And the next day I was so happy to be playing on a decent club for a change that I played like an absolute demon. The spectators were raving about my play. Too bad they raved so much that word got back to Alviso sooner than I did. I was still wearing my new uniform when I ran into a couple of my sisters. The look they gave me—it was like they caught me covered in our folks' blood with the ax still warm in my hands. They spun on their heels and bolted without so much as a word.

I was just being a Good Samaritan, trying to help out some unfortunates, but I knew that my folks would never see it that way. I was working myself into a regular lather over being misunderstood, when Matthew asked me if I'd consider joining the club on their next trip. They were leaving that night. Mark was about to quote some scripture at me, but I cut him off.

"I'm your man," I said. "Just lend me some clothes. I don't want to go back home."

I felt perfectly miserable as we rode the wagon to the next contest, but as soon as I took the field I forgot about everything but the game. I would have preferred to stay on the road forever, but after a couple of months my teammates needed to go home for a rest. That's when a man came up to me after a game and asked if I might be interested in *matriculating* at Santa Clara College. Hell, I figured he was asking for a handout so I brushed him off.

"You got me all wrong, son," he says. "We want to pay *you* to go to college."

Now that was something I had never considered. Fielding a winning baseball team was important to any school, from elementary on up. A college team had as crazy a following back then as football got to be, and the pressure to win was so great that nobody was overly delicate about bending a few rules. *You ain't got a high school diploma? Well, there's no need to get sticky on the fine points.* When we got back to Alviso in a couple days

I didn't hesitate to march on home. You bet the folks and the girls changed their tune when I showed them a letter from Santa Clara offering to make me a college boy. I mean, out came the robe and the ring. I was finally on the path to respectability and making something of my life. Even the Mayo brothers were too much in awe of the prospect of me getting a college degree to try and interfere. They wished me the best of luck—except for John.

"You'll be back soon enough," he said.

My old man was the one who took the keenest interest in my college studies. You'd think he was the one going off to matriculate, considering how excited he was with the notion of me someday becoming a civil engineer. For some reason the prospect of me traveling this great land damming up every stream that dared to flow provided him the greatest satisfaction. To me it sounded as worthy as anything else I could do.

He gave me a wad of dough and sent me to San Jose to buy college clothes. I returned wearing a new suit with a vest and watch fob, spats and a derby that I pulled down to one corner. Not exactly college-looking material—more like carny—but in our small town everybody was so impressed by my ring it was like the heavens had parted to let me descend. When I finally left for college everyone turned out. The only thing missing at the train crossing was a brass band. But hell, I had enough brass all by myself to kettle half the world.

Chapter 6

Dressed as I was, I stood out at Santa Clara like a blackjack at a tea party. A couple of my new teammates were assigned to show me around the campus, and they kept trying to put distance between us. They ran into some pals and started to yapping, acting like I was invisible. I would have been more welcomed at school if I had been holding a tin cup and chained to an organ grinder.

They showed me the dining hall and dropped these broad hints that it would be a good idea if I tried to use all the utensils at my place setting, like I was some kind of hick sword swallower, you know, the kind to eat everything using a butter knife then wash it all down with the finger bowl.

Next the boys showed me to my room, a single tucked under the stairs, and that was the grand tour.

"What about classes?" I said. "When's school start?"

They looked at each other, sharing a little smile, before one of them answers, "*We* begin studies on Monday."

"What about me?"

"You don't."

"Well, when do I start?"

"*You don't.*"

I felt kind of foolish. I should have understood that I was only brought in to bolster the baseball squad. I'd have no business in the classroom—I wasn't supposed to go anywhere near a classroom—but so long as I didn't publicly embarrass the school I'd be treated just fine. I'd get room, board and maybe some folding money now and then—what more could somebody like me want?

I would have left the college right then if it wasn't for the humiliating prospect of slinking back home to have the likes of John Mayo needle me. No, I had to gut it out for at least a couple of months.

After the first practice, when I proved I was at least a ringer worth the cheating, my new teammates began to thaw a little—not that I would ever be good enough to associate with them off the field. And it's not like they were my kind, anyway. I quickly gravitated to the billiard parlors and beaneries to find locals I could chum with. I even began to step out with a young waitress. I was making the best of the situation, and that dormitory closet became just a place to bed down at night. Of course, there were times after baseball practice I'd see a bunch of students on the verandah chatting, maybe vocalizing together, when I wished I could be part of it.

I must have been feeling glum about things, because my baseball coach noticed and pulled me aside one day after practice. His name was Joe Corbett, the younger brother of the famous prize fighter, Gentleman Jim Corbett. Joe was a pretty fair athlete himself, having once won twenty-four games in a season pitching for one of those great Baltimore Orioles teams. After he developed a glass arm he had to turn to coaching, though he wasn't yet thirty years old.

"It's just I thought I was going to study engineering," I confessed. "I want to make something of my life."

"Yeah, I know how it feels to be treated like a field dog."

Joe was a good egg. He said he'd talk to somebody about getting me a chance to take some classes to see if I could make the cut, but in the meanwhile he wanted me to concentrate on playing baseball for the school. That was my ticket to better things.

So I go home to the dormitory, feeling better about my prospects. Some of the boys were on the verandah again, their legs crossed like society ladies, and singing to a ukulele. The sight was a little corny but I couldn't help feeling that I wanted to belong, that one day soon I would belong—not that it wouldn't take some getting used to. It was tough to see me lounging around with a bunch of kid bankers, singing pie-in-the-sky love songs and laying my head on some guy's lap.

I decided to make an effort, be sociable and comment on the weather. That always worked wonders in Alviso. I had plans for the evening—I was stepping out with that waitress—but I could spare a few moments to discuss the temperature.

I waited for the boys to finish up a sad song, something about somebody dying at the end of some fancy-ass party.

"Nice night out," I said.

"Isn't it about time for Heathcliff to be bedding down in the stables?"

says one of them by the name of Stanton. Judging by how his pals snickered I figured he had made a smart one at my expense.

I don't know if Stanton was his first name or his last, but I do remember what the snotty bastard looked like: hawk nose, real high forehead, twenty years old and already his hair was thinned out at the temples. He had it slicked back and curled in front of his ears in what was called the fish hook effect. I knew he considered himself to be something of a sensation because I had watched him run track near the ball diamond. He was tall enough and boasted some speed, but I chalked him up as a scratch. He was too scrawny and a little too satisfied with just making a good showing to ever be anything more than a college boy who dabbled in sports. More than anyone else on the verandah Stanton looked like a future banker, maybe because I knew that his family owned two or three of them already.

"Was that crack intended for me?" I said.

He tosses the cigarette he's blowing and grinds it under his heel. "I was talking *about* you, not *to* you."

The ukulele playing comes to a dead stop.

I'm starting to bristle but I can't see much advantage in challenging Little Lord Fauntleroy to a fistfight, so I try to strike a reasonable note.

"Maybe we don't come from the same side of town—"

"We don't even come from the same town," he butts in, making his pals snicker some more.

So now I'm ready to spill some of the red. I'm armed with a baseball bat and his crew's got nothing more dangerous than a pint-size guitar, and even if they pooled all their blood they'd still come up a gallon short. I gave Stanton a smile to let him know he was fooling with the wrong rube.

"I wonder what it is that tramp Melody sees in you," he says, and in a flash I divine the full situation.

The waitress I was seeing, the one I kept calling Melanie by mistake, must have pulled this boy's chain. The banker's boy was looking to plow the tenant's daughter, then I show up and she's getting it good from someone who wasn't ashamed to have her seen on his elbow. You could wager your mail order teeth that if brother Stanton ever brought her home to papa it'd be to scrub the laundry or do the windows.

"Whatever she sees in me," I said, "she must not see in you."

Stanton's only answer to that was to look up and give me the tip of his nose.

"Where I come from," I said, "when a man talks the way you do it means he's itching for a fight."

"How positively provincial."

"So are you itching?"

"What about your club, caveman?"

I dropped the bat and it clattered on the cement.

He stands up and begins to pull off his jacket. "I do believe I'm in a scratching mood."

Double-quick a ring forms up as the Vienna Boys Choir turns into an instant pack of bloodthirsty young men. It doesn't matter if it's a college dorm or a gin mill, a mob of men will generally act like a mob of men. They urge on their boy as he pops off his collar and cuffs and carefully rolls up his shirt sleeves.

"There," he says.

"What do you think I want to do, Sugar?" I reply. "Bang you?"

The boys laugh at that one, causing Stanton's cheeks to ruby up. Mobs don't really back anyone, so long as at least one of the parties supplies blood for the party. I was prepared for a charge, figuring Stanton to be steamed, and I'm ready to answer with a boot to his family fortune.

Where I came from fighting was not considered an intercollegiate sport, so I was surprised when Stanton bit his lip, gathered himself and assumed a boxing position that he must have learned in ballet class. He lined up his fists in front of his chin, elbows tucked close to his chest, left foot forward. He just holds the pose, waiting for me to do the same.

I just let my dukes hang by my side. "Don't wait for me, honey."

Now Stanton doesn't care if my guard is up or not, he pops this puny jab three feet from my kisser and starts hopping in. I just kept smiling and let him circle me around. He starts to snort from nerves and every few seconds has to jerk that fish hook hair out of his eyes. He's jab, jab, jabbing, following me around the circle of boys screaming for action. I allow Stanton to step into range and with my hands still by my side I slide my head to dodge his patty-cake blows. His friends are practically howling and he's already winded and dropping his jaw to suck in some air, when quick as a snake I spring out with my right hand, snag his left shirt sleeve that's come unfurled, yank him forward and deliver a straight left fist to his beak. A slight variation on the Marquis of Queensbury rules.

Stanton's nose snapped like a dry twig and he began to spout the claret all over his fresh, white shirt. He crumpled to his knees, clutching his face, yelping like a puppy dog. Back home a guy would have kept after me until he couldn't stand up no more, but this was college—our little set-to was done.

"Anybody else with an itch?"

It got awful solemn awful quick on that dormitory verandah. The boys quickly opened up a lane to let me pass.

Vocalizing was done for the evening.

Chapter 7

In a way it would be nice to report that after the fight Stanton and me became the best of pals. You know, a couple days later he sticks out his paw and says that any man who can lick him is all right in his book. But that's not even the sort of thing a bumpkin would do. A bumpkin would lay in the weeds to kill you. Bankers' boys like Stanton are content to wait until later in life when they can take their revenge on widows and orphans.

Word of the fracas spread pretty quickly. It must not have been considered sporting to inform the administration, but that didn't prevent Joe Corbett from getting wind of it.

"You dumb hick," he said, and I mean he was boiling over. "Didn't I just tell you to stay out of trouble?"

"The guy was giving me the business."

"Do you know how much dough his father gives to this school?"

"I'm sorry, Joe. I wasn't thinking. I couldn't help myself."

"Ah, hell." He calmed down a little. "I saw the kid this morning. You must have nailed him pretty good. The little bastard looked like a pelican."

The upshot was that I was on probation with Joe. My chance for getting an education depended on how well I behaved myself off the field and how well I performed on it. And it's not like I had anything better to do than concentrate on baseball, since nobody on campus would now talk to me.

Joe really took me under his wing, teaching me the inside game of baseball that those Baltimore Orioles had pioneered, what they liked to call "scientific baseball." Taking a science angle was all the rage—scientific investing, scientific child raising, scientific stamp collecting—you name it and somebody was apt to put a scientific tag on it.

Scientific baseball meant brain over brawn. Because the game was played with a dead ball (not that we'd know it was dead until years later when the rabbit ball came into play) the fielders would bunch in, and you were forced to be conniving to score runs. Rather than whale away at the ball you tried to place your hits, work the hurler for a walk, maybe get that baggy uniform in the way of the pitch and try to cheat your way onto first base. Then it was push the man over to scoring position with the sacrifice bunt, the hit and run, or maybe the slam and steal, because scientific ball was played from station to station, you moved runners to third, then did anything necessary to plate the run, even if it meant stealing home. Once you made a tally or two you concentrated on tough pitching and solid fielding to pickle away the win.

So I actually was getting an education at Santa Clara, only it wasn't the kind my folks had in mind. When I went home I lied about my classes and my professors, I even picked up some secondhand books to show. Mostly I tried to act modest, although you can bet if I really was a college boy I wouldn't have been above letting certain parties, like John Mayo, know all about it. Him and his brothers were losing some steam with their barnstorming. Their mail order uniforms had lost their sheen and I heard that Matthew had dropped a foot or two on his speed ball. The twins were the stars now, batting three and four. John was still buried at the end of the lineup and as sour as ever. I watched a game and was shocked to see how they played. When I was on the club I thought we delivered pretty good, but now I knew better. They played dumb, brute baseball. Hardly scientific.

When I returned to Santa Clara I had a little more appreciation for what Joe Corbett was teaching me, so I was finally open to his idea that my best position was first base, not second. He had to admit that for a lefty I was pretty crafty finding a way to make the plays, but he said if I concentrated on playing first, where being a lefty was an advantage, I could become something really special.

"You could make them all forget about Charlie Comiskey," he said.

That was a huge compliment, considering how Comiskey was one of the all-time greats when he played for the old St. Louie Browns. He was the first man to play off the bag and not anchor himself on the line to leave the right side of the infield open for a batter to poke a ball through. But Joe also made it clear that I still had a lot to learn before I'd start making anybody notice Hal Chase, let alone forget Charlie Comiskey.

Joe taught me how to watch a game so I could make a book in my head for future reference. He taught me to study a pitcher. Maybe the straight ball looked like it came over the top of his head while the curve came out of his ear. Maybe he fanned out his glove to get a grip for the slow ball. Maybe his catcher would give away the pitch or the infielders would. I watched the shortstop to see if he was picking up the catcher's signals and might shift his position one way or the other.

Baseball was becoming a lot like poker to me: plenty of bluff and guile and less luck involved than the average person might think. I got into the habit of always doping out an edge. My teammates, all of them true college boys, respected Joe, but they didn't really listen and never caught on to what he had to teach them about inside baseball.

When I came back to Santa Clara for a second year Joe taught me how to play tough. He showed me plays they pulled off regular in the fast company: where the fielders stood to force a runner to take an extra wide berth, how to decoy a guy into thinking the ball was coming in when it wasn't or not coming in when it was. He showed me how to run the bases, how to spot the decoys that he just showed me how to make, when and where to take a peek at the fielders, when to rely on my coaches and when to rely on my own judgment, and if necessary how to spike a foot or dig an elbow to the ribs of anybody who got in my way. On top of that Joe insisted that I hustle on every play, that I always run the bases as far as I could, just in case a fielder mishandled a ball so I'd be in a position to take advantage. I didn't fully appreciate it but I was being groomed on the most up-to-date way to play the game in the big time by a guy who knew every knot and stitch of it.

Just to round off my education and make me familiar with the game from every angle, Joe took to playing me all over the diamond. I was the catcher the day I got "discovered."

It was one of the first games of the season, against St. Vincent College in Los Angeles. The year was 1903 so L.A. was still just another sleepy little burg, more Mexican than Anglo, a few years before anyone got the bright idea of making moving pictures there. I made this one play that got everybody's attention. It was a bunt situation with a runner on first and nobody out. At that time catchers stood bent over several feet behind the plate, not crouched and tucked in close to the batter. I knew that St. Vincent's had their best bunter at the plate, the best in our league, so I figured he'd get a piece of the ball. Even as our pitcher began his delivery I was edging forward to skirt the plate at the same time the hitter would drop the bunt. I pounced on it, almost snagging the ball right off the bat, spun to tag out the hitter, then pegged the ball down to second for one of your snappier double plays.

A scout for the Los Angeles Angels of the new Pacific Coast League was there to witness the trick. He had a pretty good view too, considering how he was the umpire. The next day he's pushing a contract under my nose and offering a fountain pen. I begged off, saying I needed to talk things over with Joe Corbett.

"What's there to talk about?" Joe said. "Take the money."

"But what about my education? My degree?"

"I thought you forgot all about that applesauce."

"I never said I changed my mind."

"Don't you get it, kid?" he said. "Guys like you and me aren't cut out for books. We're ballplayers. There's a lot worse places to start your professional career than the Pacific Coast League."

"But that's not a respectable life, Joe. College is one thing…"

"Hal, you really are a lefty. You already play for dough, you already are a professional, so you may as well take a raise in pay."

"It's just that I made a promise to somebody."

"To do what?" he says. "To go back home to work in the family saw mill? To turn out planks to someday make your own coffin? Wise up, kid. I've been grooming you for this. You're the best damn prospect I'll ever turn out, and that's the goddamn truth."

I just stood there, shaking my head and looking like I was incapable of making a decision.

"I'm sorry I have to do this, Hal, but I'm kicking you off the ball club."

"Why?"

"For punching a student in the nose."

"That happened last year!"

"I'll see that you're expelled, too, so you better clear out of your hotel room. I can't have you mixing with the other boys."

"I'm broke, Joe. I don't know anybody in Los Angeles. Where am I supposed to go?"

"Well, if I were you I'd look up that scout."

So what choice did I have in the matter?

Chapter 8

People in the West didn't draw much distinction between professional leagues. The major leagues, the National and the new American, were called the "eastern leagues" and not thought to be any better than the circuits we had. The Pacific Coast League looked like it was destined to become a dandy one, so I assumed I was now standing on top of the baseball world. The contract I signed with the Angels called for $125 a month, a nice wage for a boy of twenty-one, especially when your average working stiff slaving away six days a weeks, twelve hours per, was happy to pull in maybe 500 bucks a year. And because of our good weather the season on the West Coast ran from March through Thanksgiving, some 200 games, which meant nine months of pay instead of the six that ballplayers got back east.

The Angels gave me some advance money and I was able to buy a train ticket home to Alviso, supposedly so I could get my things together then report back to Los Angeles for the start of the regular season. But I wasn't so sure I'd be returning.

Of course, showing up unexpected the way I did upset my folks. I told them I had decided to drop out of school, and they insisted that I return at once to finish taking my degree.

"I can't go back," I said. "I was kicked off the baseball team."

"Baseball again!" cried Mom.

"Now you can just concentrate on your engineering classes," my old man said.

I really did my best to level with them. I confessed that I never had attended classes.

"You couldn't wait to sign that contract with the Angels." My old man was turning purple he was so angry.

"Angels!" My mother said the word like she was sucking on something sour. "They play that wicked game and have the nerve to call themselves 'angels'!"

"You signed your name, boy. You gave your word to play for those people."

"So I'll just return the advance money," I said.

"What good is a man who can't keep his word?"

I explained that I only signed that contract because I was stuck in Los Angeles and didn't want to wire them for train fare. What could I say by telegram? HAVE BEEN LYING THROUGH TEETH STOP. They just didn't want to hear me out, convinced I was just twisting everything to get my way.

I had to go out for a walk to cool off. I wasn't paying attention to where I was going and before long found myself near the cemetery where my brother John was buried. I hadn't been to his grave for the longest time, so I decided to pay a visit.

It had been ten years since his passing away, yet there were fresh flowers decked around the headstone. My mom and sisters kept his memory alive. Hell, I thought, the entire town keeps it alive, the way they like to recollect the good old days when the town baseball team was the talk of the county because of the Chase boy.

Although John's headstone was showing the weather around the edges, the granite was still glassy enough to reflect your image. I stared at my own glum face and talked out loud.

"How do I get myself into these scrapes?" I mumbled. "What would you do, John?"

But I didn't need any signs from Heaven to supply the answer. I knew what John would have done. He would have kept his word and honored the paper he signed his name to.

The next morning I returned to Los Angeles with as much enthusiasm as if I were heading to prison. And my family didn't encourage me to think otherwise. I would serve out my term and hope when I had paid my debt that decent society might accept me back.

I was still down in the dumps when I played my first game in a professional league. I had barely stepped into the box for my first at bat when zip! the ball cracked the leather of the catcher's mitt and the umpire barked, "Steeeeriiiikeee oneeeee!"

"I wasn't ready, sir," I said, politely.

The ump ignored me but the catcher growled, "Tough shit, kid," and fired the ball back to the pitcher who fired it right back to the plate.

"Steeeeriiiikeeee twooooo!"

"If you wanna talk, run for Congress." Then the catcher skins my nose on his peg back to the mound. All the ump does is to look at his indicator and rack up that second strike.

I jump out of the batter's box before I get another quick pitch, and try to get my bearings. The other team is in a ruckus as they start to razz me. "What's the matter, little sis, don't you wanna play?" Then they chant, sing-song like, "Un-cle Char-lie's got him!"

"Batter!" shouts the umpire, sounding like he's in a hurry to be somewhere else. So I take a deep breath, keep my eye on the pitcher and hop into the box ready to swing the bat. Only, now the big bastard just stands on the slab and grins at me.

"What's the rush, busher?" says the catcher.

Only when he's ready does the pitcher go into an eighteen-carat windup and kick. Just as he releases the ball a handful of dirt lands on my spikes, courtesy of my pal the catcher, so I'm lucky to swing the bat and dribble a foul down the first base line.

"You cheating bastard," I say. I meant it to sound tough but the words came out a little too squeaky.

"Such language." Then, like he's pointing a pistol, the catcher motions to the pitcher who's already got back the ball. He skips the windup, slides his foot and gives me the old burnt offering aimed right for my bean. I'm lucky to spin out of the way and land face-first in the dirt. My heart is racing like a locomotive on a down grade, I'm spitting out half the infield, and right away the umpire says, "One-two count, batter. Let's go."

My coacher at third starts in on me. "Jesus Christ, kid," he yells. As I get to my feet I look over to him for some guidance, maybe a little encouragement, but all he does is give me this sour look, like he's disgusted with how unmanly I'm handling the situation, turns his back and walks up the line a couple of steps.

And it's not like I notice any peppy chatter coming from the bench on my behalf. All I can hear are the patrons in the box seats howling like mad ghouls, urging me to catch the next train home. And these were our hometown fans!

"I'm warning you, batter!" says the ump.

I'm not close to having regained my composure but I step into the box, ready to swing at anything, because I figure the ump is willing to give the veteran pitcher the benefit of the doubt on any ball close to the northern hemisphere. So here we go again with the grin and the stall, the fancy windup, a double pump, then a bender that after the previous knockdown pitch looks for sure to be aimed right for my ear but is really ticketed for the heart of the plate. My brain knows where the ball is going, but my ass hasn't gotten the word and is bailing the hell out of there, so it's all I can manage to wave the stick and poke a hopper. It has eyes and squeezes between first and second for a safety.

As I scamper down the line, everybody in the yard starts to groan. If this kid is going to get a hit then surely the end of the world is near.

So I find myself perched on first, I still haven't recovered from seeing my life flash before my eyes, and now I have to put up with my first base coach who sneaks up behind me and snarls, "There ain't no outs and if you get your ass picked off, I swear I'll murder you, busher."

The first baseman takes up his position to hold me close and turns out to be just as neighborly as the catcher.

"Lucky hit." He spits a glob of tobacco juice on my ankle.

I step away from the bag to take my lead, as the pitcher gives me the old I.C. over his shoulder. I could tell that he was none too pleased to have me occupying that pillow—I've become a fly in his ointment—but instead of throwing my way all he does is glare. And wait. And wait. It feels like an hour goes by. Eventually I lean back towards first. That's when he delivers home.

Steeeeriiiikeee oneeeee!

The coacher who had just warned me against getting picked off is now yelling, "Get a decent lead, goddamn it." He keeps yapping at me until I edge so far off the bag I feel like I'm in the middle of a lake and I haven't a clue how to swim. I don't care what the guy says, I know I'm too far off, and just as I begin to creep back the pitcher spins and pegs the ball over. The baseman sticks out his foot to block me off, forcing me to dive and reach between his legs to get back safe. The play's not really that close but he still smacks me in the nose with the ball. Then, even though I'm still on the ground hugging the base, he fakes the toss back to the pitcher just so he can lay another knock on me.

While I'm checking to see if my nose is bleeding, my coacher is hissing like a regular menace, "I kid you not, college boy, if you get picked off I will kill you with my own bare hands."

I'm still dusting myself off when the pitcher delivers his next one, because my teammate at the plate didn't bother to step out to give me a chance to reset. No, he's a hoary old veteran, having been with the club the last two weeks of the previous season and is not about to cut any slack to a lowly rookie. Luckily he takes a swipe and comes up empty, because if he soaks a grounder anywhere I'm a Christmas goose at second.

"Take a lead, kid. TAKE A LEAD!"

I say the hell with my coacher, I'm only straying as far off the bag as I feel comfortable. This time when the pitcher goes into his stalling act I'm determined to wait him out. He's the one who finally gets antsy and delivers a pitch that comes in too fat and the batter cracks a gapper. Suddenly I'm on my horse and looking to score on the play. I'm so eager to run as fast as I can that I drop my head and it's only out of habit, the kind that Joe Corbett stuck in my brain, that I glance up as I'm about to round second to check on the basemen and see that the shortstop is standing on the inside corner of the sack. It's either bowl him over or touch the upper corner of the base and swing wide into left field, which is what I do, not to mention leap over the foot of the second baseman that's appeared out of nowhere. The outfielders are just tracking down the ball as I near third, where that fielder is standing well off his base and acting like he knows there's no chance to keep me from scoring. Just as I cut the angle to round the base he sidesteps, gives me the old hip and sends me somersaulting in front of my third base coach who was waving me in but is now walking away and shaking his head in disgust.

As I roll to my feet the ball is shooting in from the outfield and I figure the batter is hell-bent for a triple so I have no choice but to try and score. I spy the catcher tossing his mask in my path and planting himself squarely in front of the dish. The crowd is yelling like a bunch of Romans out for blood, the on-deck hitter doesn't seem inclined to fill me in on how close the play is likely to be, so I just lower my shoulder and prepare to drive that catcher into the third row of box seats. The ball, me, the catcher's mask—everything converges on home plate. I'm in the middle of an explosion, blinded by a cloud of dirt. I don't touch the plate so much as flop on top of it, all tangled up with the catcher like a pair of wrecked trains. In a heartbeat the roar of the crowd turns completely quiet, all eyes are on the umpire who's standing with hands on knees, bug-eyed, measuring the situation as the dust settles. Then his finger points out the baseball spinning in the dirt and he shouts, "The man is safeeeee!"

The on-deck batter drags me to my feet, slaps me on the ass, the crowd now loves me, and both my coaches are yelling, "Attaway to score, boy, attaway!" The catcher has trouble getting to his feet, the pitcher is kicking at the ground and cussing himself, as my teammates begin to ride him awful fierce.

I'm happy. Hell, I'm exhilarated. But I'm also relieved and winded and bruised, and the thought runs through my brain, *How am I going to keep this up for 200 games?*

Chapter 9

I didn't play all 200 games that season. I only got into 173. Not counting exhibition contests. Just to survive I had to give up feeling sorry for myself. The Pacific Coast League was a real fighting loop, with every club well-stocked with fire-eaters, and a few outright criminals. Plenty of balls were intended for a batter's head, and in reply more than a few bats went skipping back through the pitcher's box. So I just didn't have the luxury of being sensitive.

After a couple of weeks I got accustomed to the fast pace and hard-nosed tactics, so that every play wasn't nearly so hellacious as my first at-bat. I started to keep a book on the league just like Joe Corbett taught me. But it was the daily grind that you could never really get used to. We had teams in that loop as far north as Portland and Seattle, which made for some pretty long road trips. We spent a good portion of the season riding coach on coal-burning trains, eating cinders all night, lucky to catch any sleep. Once we made town, of course, it was straight out to the ballpark since we usually arrived the day of the game and the club owners weren't about to give up a paying date just so the players could get some rest. You'd take the field feeling stiff from the train, pretty much dead on the vine, and the home side wasted no time trying to run you into the ground. Even if they had a big lead they'd kick you to make sure you'd still be exhausted the next day. And it wasn't just business; they'd take pure pleasure in the beating, since it was likely that you had done the same thing to them when they visited your park a couple weeks earlier. You play every team in the league like that 30 times a year and you develop some grudges.

After a road game we would retire to one of those cheap bowl and pitcher hotels, sleep four to a room and fight each other for the use of the one bathroom on the floor. Then we'd fight all over again at the dinner table where we ate family style on the American Plan and the ballplayers always outnumbered the chops and potatoes. There were as many squabbles on the team over the tub and the grub as to who got to play regular. Sometimes you had it in for your own teammates as much as you did the opposing players.

It felt like I was always packing or unpacking, at the ballpark or on my way to it. I felt tired and half-starved, healing up from one nick or another and forever feuding with somebody on my side or the other. I was in a foul mood for half the season when I woke up one morning, a catcher and a pitcher curled up to either side of me in bed, and I realized how much I loved it all. For the first time in my life I was getting my fill of playing baseball. And at the same time I was keeping my word, honoring my contract, so I didn't even have to feel rotten about it. When the year was over I could leave the game knowing that I had done something a lot of guys dreamed of and few had achieved.

What made it even more satisfying is that I *showed*. I was one of the top hitters and base stealers on the club, and developed into one of the league's best men with the leather. Turning the same plays day after day, getting to know the opposition and filling in my book, I began to anticipate situations like Joe Corbett taught me, instead of just reacting to what happened. I blossomed into a special ballplayer and everybody recognized it.

My manager, Jim Morley, was pleased pink by my progress and eager to take a lion's share of the credit. He was a solid baseball man and generally a good guy, except in matters of money where he was known to have one-way pockets. I didn't tell him that I had no plans to re-sign with the Angels, that I had other obligations in life. He began to pave the way for negotiating a new contract with me. He said he wasn't overly optimistic about my chances my sophomore year in the league. I knew that he was just setting me up, but I didn't care. I wasn't coming back, anyway.

So it's the last week of the season and Morley calls me into the little closet he used as an office at the ballpark. He looked kind of dejected as he told me to sit down on a trunk. He had a letter in front of him.

"I have some terrible news, lad," he says. "You've been drafted."

I had to confess that I didn't even know there was a war on. Morley had to explain that he was talking about the baseball draft. The New York team in the American League, the Highlanders, had put in a draft for my services and were set to pay the Los Angeles Angels $2,700 in return.

"I told them," he said. "The bastards are going to steal all our best prospects."

"Who will?"

"The major leagues, son. The goddamn major leagues."

Since my days of following King Kelly I hadn't paid much attention to the eastern leagues. Joe Corbett had taught me the game, not the politics. I didn't know how the baseball owners operated like a bunch of Chinese bandits, and that just a couple of years earlier a major war between the American and National leagues had ended with the signing of the National Agreement, which basically settled all their differences by agreeing to divide the loot. The major leagues declared that for a fee, which they would set themselves, they could "draft" players from any of the "minor leagues"—any league other than themselves—that had also signed the National Agreement. The kicker was that any league refusing to sign on would be considered an "outlaw league" and anybody associated with it in any way would be banned from "Organized Baseball" for the rest of their natural lives.

The minor leagues weren't happy to have the gun put to their heads and the major leagues didn't make matters any more agreeable by the way they lorded over their new partners. The minor league teams would develop players only to have the majors pick them off the tree as soon as they showed signs of coming ripe. The transfer fee paid to compensate for the loss of the player seemed hardly worth the loss in talent. And it wasn't unusual to wait a few months before the major league club got around to actually writing the check. Raise a fuss and you might see that player farmed back to your biggest rival, purely out of spite, so not only would you be out the draft money, you'd have to battle against the very player you discovered and developed.

The Pacific Coast League considered challenging the easterners by declaring themselves a major league on the West Coast, but matters had already gone too far for that. Just about every league of any size in the country had already given in, making it almost impossible to do business as an outlaw circuit. When the Pacific Coast League finally surrendered and signed, they weren't happy about it, especially the way the majors ignored our longer season and began to draft our players when their season was over but ours still had two months to run. Pennant-contending clubs could have their best players taken away from them. The major leagues had no need for the players until the next year but didn't want to take the chance on having their new property damaged. So the hell with the pennant race in the Pacific Coast League.

"I told them it would come to this," Morley said, pulling out a bottle of whiskey from a desk drawer.

"Gee, Skip," I said. "I feel like a blue ribbon pig."

"You're a twenty-seven-hundred dollar pig, my boy." He poured himself a stiff one and proceeded to get good and starched.

I had never even heard about the New York Americans—the Highlanders—or suspected that anybody outside of the Pacific Coast League even knew I was alive, yet here I was coveted by strangers 3,000 miles away. That kind of thing can't help but go to your head a little bit. Then I began to think that if these major leagues could pluck the best players from all the circuits across the entire country, didn't it stand to reason that they would have to produce a superior brand of ball?

Jesus, I'm thinking, New York wants me. And it wasn't just the ball club, it felt like the entire town was giving me the wink.

Chapter 10

N ew York could go straight to Hell. That's what I told myself as I rode the train home to Alviso at the close of the baseball season. It was flattering to have the New York Americans draft my rights, but I decided I had my fill of the game. I was bruised and drained and down ten pounds after playing nine months in the Pacific Coast League. Besides, it was time to get on with my life. I had honored the letter of my contract to Los Angeles; now I had to honor my word to my brother. Anyway, I told myself, I'm a westerner, New York is my natural enemy. Many a boy a lot purer than me had been corrupted by that stinking cesspool on the Hudson. I should consider myself blessed to avoid it.

I wasn't really sure what to do with the rest of my life, but I had some dough, I could rest up, enjoy Christmas at home, and think about the big picture later. I didn't tell anyone about the New York Highlanders drafting my rights. I kept that to myself and sometimes, when I couldn't resist, I'd wondered what it would be like to play in the East. In Alviso I found myself treated like some kind of conquering hero for just playing a year in the Pacific Coast League. I had small boys and large dogs following me everywhere I went. Pretty girls gave me long looks. Men want to buy me a shot and a beer. I could only wonder what it would be like to be the cock of the walk in a town the size of New York City.

Most people assumed that I would return to Los Angeles for another season. I probably should have announced right then that I was through with the professional game, but I just enjoyed all the attention too much. I figured there was no harm in basking in the glow for just a little longer.

I spent a day in San Francisco and spent a wad of dough on Christmas presents for my family. By now my sisters were all married and trying to outbid each other in the number of babies they could bear, so home during the holidays was as crowded as a train station waiting room. Nobody was common enough to bring up the subject of baseball and risk offending my folks, but I could tell some of the new husbands were busting to ask about my season.

All in all, everybody was in a grand mood on Christmas day—except for the old man. He had drifted into a funk. Even the grandkids crawling all over his lap couldn't pull him out of it. Every so often he'd wander outside to the wood pile for a pull of whiskey.

I handed out my presents and everybody couldn't wait to see the next wonder that would emerge from one of those fancy wrapped packages I brought from San Francisco. At the end I handed a small box to my old man. He just set it aside on a small side table.

"Open it!" the girls cried.

So he began to tear at the packaging.

"Don't rip it, Daddy. We want to save the paper."

But he mangled it anyway, quickly opened the box underneath and removed a ivory-handled hunting knife.

"Oooooh!" sighed the girls.

Their husbands agreed among themselves that it was one sweetheart of a knife.

My old man didn't thank me, just stared at the knife, then began to press the tip of the blade into his index finger so hard it was a wonder he didn't draw blood.

"It comes with a certificate," I said.

Still he didn't say anything.

"Guaranteed for life."

The entire room is quiet, there's not even one baby crying for attention, when suddenly he raises that knife and WHAM! buries the blade a good two inches into the side table. It was like he set off a fire alarm. Babies began to wail and my sisters were quick to answer the bell.

"Who do you think you are!" He struggles to stand up. He's a little too drunk and drops back into his chair. "You think your baseball money can buy you respect?"

"It's just a Christmas present," I said.

"I'm no fool." This time he manages to get to his feet. He marches out of the house, scattering the dogs on the porch, and heads in the direction of the saw mill he owned.

Everyone tried acting like nothing happened. The babies finally calmed down, and Mom went to the kitchen to fix some punch and cookies. I followed after her.

"I didn't mean to upset him," I said.

"Maybe you shouldn't have spent so much money."

"I thought that was the decent thing to do."

"I'm sure your heart was in the right place." She turned her back to fetch some glasses. "You didn't mean to show off."

"I can't do nothing right, can I?"

"To some people it might seem like you were trying to make your baseball playing more acceptable by buying us things."

"It's Christmas! Isn't that what you're supposed to do? Buy things?"

Just to prove that my intentions were pure I told her about the chance I had to play baseball in New York and how I refused to accept, no matter how rare an opportunity and prized a compliment it was for a young man in the West.

"I suppose they pay even more in the East," she says. "I can only imagine what kind of presents you'll buy us next year."

"Didn't I just say I don't want to play in New York?"

"Please, Hal, I don't want to have this discussion on Christmas day."

I didn't hang around for punch and cookies. I left the house, not in a huff like the old man, but I was pretty sore. In my folks' eyes I was always trying to pull the fast one.

I wandered to the saw mill where I found one of the hired men turning a bat on a lathe for his little boy. He told me that my father had gone upstream to check on some beavers.

I wasn't really looking for him but now I decided to. I followed the stream that powered the saw mill until I caught up to my father who was drinking rye and watching some beavers swim branches and trash to build a dam where a tree had fallen across the water. He wasn't angry anymore. As I approached him he held out his bottle of budge. I guess I should have recognized the gesture as a peace offering, but I shook my head no.

"Suit yourself."

We stood there the longest time just watching those beavers work and listening to that boiling stream.

"I was just telling Mom," I said, "that it appears I have a business opportunity back east."

"What's that supposed to mean?"

"Some ball club wants my services pretty bad."

"Congratulations." He takes a long pull of whiskey. "An eastern ball club, you say? What, some outfit in Idaho offers you ten bucks more a month and you're ready to pee yourself for joy?"

"It's New York City for your information. And they seem to think my rights are worth three thousand dollars."

"So I guess you didn't hike out here for the scenery." He drains the bottle, drops it at his feet and watches as it slides down the bank into the water. "You're a big shot now. You come to throw it in my face."

"Do you have to take everything as an insult?"

"A man works hard all his life and for what? To watch his oldest boy die for nothing and his youngest live for nothing."

"Too bad I didn't know how much you were sacrificing for me."

"Well, I know one thing." He stooped down to pick up a rock. "When you go to New York I'll be back here with some dynamite and blow the hell out of that dam."

He wings the rock at those beavers and it fell short by ten feet. The old man threw like a girl.

"When did I say I was going to New York? Did you ever think to ask me if I might want to stay here and maybe help you run the saw mill?"

"Why waste my breath?"

"Have it your own way then." I turn to walk away.

"Tell me one thing, boy," he yells after me. "How much of that money New York is paying for your rights do you see?"

"I'm through talking with you."

"You don't get one cent, do you?"

I wheeled around and stepped right up to him. "Why don't you just shut your stupid trap?"

"They're selling your ass from coast to coast like some kind of nigger slave."

I took a sock at him. Knocked him down, too.

"Don't you ever think you got something to say about how I run my life." I spit the words at him on the ground. "None of you!"

I left him there in the dirt. Caught the next train to San Jose, holed up in a room, and waited for that contract from the New York team to arrive.

If my folks wanted a baseball man in the family so bad, they could have one.

Chapter 11

The more I thought about it the more I resented being sold to the New York Highlanders. I wanted my cut of the transfer fee. It wasn't a matter of greed but respect.

While I waited for my New York contract to arrive I wrote to Morley in Los Angeles, telling him that my family was experiencing some financial difficulties and I wasn't sure that I'd be able to report to the Highlanders. His answer was that I should take up the matter with my new employers. Then I wrote to explain that, to be honest, it wasn't my family so much as it was that I really wanted to stay in the West and play for him and the Angels. He warmed to that approach, sympathizing to my plight and regretting how those eastern bastards were in a position to call any tune they desired. There must be some way, I replied, to make a rotten situation a little more tolerable to a young man who only wanted to do right by everyone, hinting that a few hundred bucks might do wonders for my pain.

Now I had Morley's sympathy but I was no closer to his purse. He wrote back to declare how thoroughly fed up he was with the National Agreement and that if a youngster like me wanted to play for the Los Angeles Angels that should be my decision. He said it was high time that somebody challenged those Shylocks in Chicago and New York and if that meant another baseball war, so be it!

That was when the New York Americans sent me a warm letter welcoming me to the fold, along with a contract that in their words called for a generous sum. When I returned a signed copy they'd wire me $200 in advance of salary plus travel money to spring training in Montgomery, Alabama. I decided to give up on Morley and the Angels, and signed my contract to get the easy dough. Too bad when I got it, I promptly lost it all plus every dollar I had in the bank in a crooked card game.

Next a contract from the Angels arrived. It seems that Morley hadn't been idle. He had contacted his friends throughout the minor leagues and found plenty of like-minded men who now regretted knuckling under to the majors and were ready to rally around my cause to play for the Angels.

I knew it was wrong to sign with two ball clubs, but the way I figured it the Angels still owed me part of that transfer fee. Knowing Morley I doubted he was about to send New York a refund. So I signed again and Los Angeles wired me some more advance money and train fare.

My plan was to report to the Highlanders in Alabama, only I ran into those card sharps again. I thought I had them figured out and would win back my dough. I was wrong.

All I had left to my name was enough for the train to Los Angeles, not Alabama. I was about to pawn my pocket watch to make up the difference when one of my Angels teammates showed up by Morley's request to make sure nothing happened to me on the train. So what choice did I have but to go along peacefully?

Jim Morley met us at the train depot in Los Angeles, pie-eyed from drink and excited to see me.

"There he is! There's my spunky lad! There's my ginger snap!" He hugged me so hard he almost crushed my breast bone. "By God, Hal, we'll show them big league sons of bitches. They may have started the fight but we'll finish it. Am I right, you sweet chestnut of a boy? Am I right?"

"I hope it isn't a bad time to mention this," I said as Morley picked up my bag, "but my mother just went into the hospital in San Francisco."

"That's a horrible shame, lad."

"And all the advance money you sent me had to go towards the operation."

"Don't worry none about your room and board. I'll just deduct the expense from your first paycheck."

"That's awful swell of you, Skip. Still ... it would be nice to have something to jingle in my pocket."

"Say no more." Morley reached into his own pocket and cheerfully handed me a fifty cent piece. "And don't be shy about coming back for more in a week or two."

I figured that if in a week or two I didn't come up with the train fare to Alabama, the New York club would be getting a little suspicious about their new player. So far, thankfully, they didn't know what was brewing in the Class A minor leagues on my behalf.

From reading *The Sporting News* I learned that the Highlanders were counting on me. They were having a problem with their regular first baseman, John Ganzel, who had saved enough dough to buy the Grand Rapids minor league team and planned on playing for it. The only problem was that despite owning the club he didn't own the rights to himself. New York claimed to own him and didn't care for his fat nerve in thinking that he could deprive them of their lawful property. Ganzel didn't do himself any favors then by telling the Highlanders where they could plant a good-bye kiss.

The National Commission declared that if John Ganzel so much as stepped on the field in a Grand Rapids uniform every player, coach and hot dog vendor in the entire league would be banned from Organized Baseball for life, and they already had Pinkertons contracted to see if he tried. That threat sobered Ganzel, so now he *requested* his release from the Highlanders. Matters, though, had gone too far for that, and New York ordered him to report to Alabama for spring training. Ganzel offered to buy himself out of captivity, which didn't fly either, because now he was to be made an example to all potential renegades. New York would settle for nothing less than his unconditional surrender. Everybody knew, of course, that as soon as Ganzel broke down and reported to camp he'd be traded away for a song to another club that would take a turn at giving him the treatment.

Whatever happened to the poor bastard the New York ball club would be needing a first baseman. I was the only prospect they had available, and the last thing they wanted to hear was that some rookie was not only defying them but leading a revolt against Organized Baseball.

A week after my reporting date, the Highlanders tracked me down and the telegrams began to fly.

EXPECTED FRIDAY PLEASE INFORM PLANS COLLECT

AM SICK WILL LEAVE TOMORROW

NO ARRIVAL PLEASE INFORM

MOM SICK WILL LEAVE TOMORROW

STILL NO ARRIVAL PLEASE INFORM

TRAIN ACCIDENT WILL LEAVE TOMORROW

I showed Morley the cables I received. I never told him about the ones I sent. Some local newspapermen got wind of things and asked Morley for an explanation and he obliged with a whiskey speech about the draft system being an insult to any true American. The Southern League, Eastern League, Western League and American Association were then quick to publicly stand by the Pacific Coast League, declaring to be just as committed to the right of Hal Chase to play for the Angels.

I never knew I had so many friends.

Chapter 12

N ow that it looked like we're in a war together, Morley is feeling young and vital again and loves me like the son he never had. He invites me home to Sunday dinner to introduce me to the family: his wife and an unmarried daughter of age named Emily. The girl was on the quiet side and looked like she had every right to be. Her hair was cut too short and her glasses too big for her face. Her lips, round and thin, made her look like a fish. But according to Morley she could throw a ball pretty good.

Conversation at the dinner table consisted mostly of Morley bragging to his wife what a splendid bully boy I was, and his wife assuring him what a prize catch Emily was. I didn't need a hammer to tell me I was a nail.

After dessert Morley and the wife contrived for Emily to give me the tour of their dog patch garden. The girl had uttered maybe two words all night but as soon as we step outside she says, "I'd like to apologize for my parents. I suppose they seem rather common to a college man such as yourself. Mother, the poor thing, never intended to marry a baseball man. And Father, alas, there's someone who's never dared to be himself."

"What kind of flowers are these?" I asked, uncomfortable with the way the tour of the garden had started.

"Five o'clocks, because they come back year after year like clockwork. About as exciting as raising weeds, but it makes Mother feel genteel … and me want to cry."

"I guess you read a lot of books."

"I try to keep up. Nothing like you, I'm sure."

"I don't know about that." I was starting to sound like a farm hand.

"May I be honest with you, Harold? You don't mind if I call you Harold, do you?"

"Of course not, Miss Emily."

"My parents have fixed my cap for you. I prefer, however, to fix my own cap. I must confess that I assumed you would be like the other ball-players Father has brought home to our happy web. *Common.*"

"Oh, I'm common enough."

"*Au contraire.*"

"Common as dirt."

"No, you're actually quite sensual."

"I'm just another no-account baseballer."

"People grow."

"Not me. When the old batting eye goes I probably won't be as lucky as your Dad and find a club to manage. I'll wind up tending bar some place, or more likely a tramp."

"A noble tramp."

"A dirty tramp."

"A forlorn, misunderstood tramp."

"A tramp who'll probably die on the dole."

"And that's why," she said, her eyes misting, "that I think I love you already."

I didn't have the heart to tell her I thought she was out of her mind. Hell, she probably would have found it a charming declaration. I just fudged and fidgeted and by the end of the evening we could have been engaged for all I knew.

The next day at practice Morley gave me a wink and told me what a fine impression I had made on the wife and daughter. Before he had a chance to invite me over to complete my conquest of the girl I handed him the latest telegram I got from New York.

EXPECT OUR REPRESENTATIVE

"Representative is it?" Morley was instantly up to pressure. "Let 'em send their plug uglies. We'll send 'em all home dressed in pine. Am I right, my plucky boy? Am I right, my game young son of a buck?"

"You're right, Skip. You're always right," I said. "But maybe things have gone far enough. For everyone's sake, maybe I should just swallow my pride and report to the Highlanders."

"Never!"

"You've got a family to think about."

"You're all but family to me, too, lad. You know I'd do anything for you, give anything to you, including my own dear, sweet—"

"Then could I get an advance on my salary?"

"Anything but that, Hal," he said quickly. "I've got to think of team harmony, you understand."

It looked like I'd have to wait until the first payday of the season before I would have enough train fare for Alabama, but by then a base-ball war would be raging and I had a suspicion on who would be the first casualty. After practice I'm walking back to my room giving serious con-sideration to hopping an eastbound freight train when a man standing on the corner asks me for a light to his cigar. He was a little taller than me and about twice my weight with strawberry-dotted cheeks and a waxed mustache. A sport overdressed for Los Angeles.

"The name's Jack Delaney," he said, firing up this expensive stogie from the match I lent him. "My friends call me Fat Jack Delaney. It might also be of interest to you to know that New York sent me to see ya."

"The whole town or anyone in particular?"

"None other than Frank Farrell himself."

"And who the hell is he?"

"A question I've often asked myself, now that Frank's become quite the muck-a-muck since buying a baseball team. I don't know, maybe you seen the name Joe Gordon printed on the letterhead, but it's Frank who pulls the strings for the Highlanders."

"Well, be sure to give him my regards."

"I plan on giving him more than that, kid. You took some of his dough. You were supposed to report to the ball club. You don't show. That's the kind of thing Frank does to other people. A chisler don't like to be chiseled, you know what I mean?"

"In case you haven't heard, I play ball for the Los Angeles Angels."

"Aw, what's so special about this place?" he says, dropping the tough guy act. "I showed up to town yesterday and I already got my fill. Why should I waste away eating in these local chop suey joints when there's cherry stone clams waiting for me at the Waldorf-Astoria?"

He reaches inside his coat and pulls a cigar that he holds out to me.

"Have one of my dollar Havanas. Go on, take it, kid. Get used to it. When you run with Frank Farrell's crowd you won't think how many of these you burn in a day."

So I accept this long tom, looking tan and sweet.

"I watched you practice this morning." It turns out he had matches on him all along, because he puts a light to the cigar for me. "You just might have the goods. Do you realize, kid, what it means to be a big time player in a big time town like New York?"

"Ever hear about loyalty?" That cigar tasted smooth. It tasted like the big leagues.

"I get it." Fat Jack reaches inside his coat again, this time removing his pocket book. "How much does it take to ease your conscience?"

"You're wasting your breath."

"Ten bucks?"

"The manager is like a father to me."

"Twenty?"

"I'm practically engaged to his only daughter."

"Okay, fifty bucks. What do you say?" He begins to count out the bank notes.

"I wish I had a horse whip right now."

"Fifty easy clams. Not against your salary or anything. Just for cooperating with Jack."

"You ought to be ashamed of yourself."

He fans out the bills in front of my nose. "There's a train leaving in an hour."

I waited for a few more seconds then snatched the dough out of his hands, folded and slipped it into my trouser pocket. "Just give me twenty minutes to pack, you rotten bastard."

Chapter 13

A few more seasons would pass before the New York American League baseball team would become known as the Yankees. When I joined them they were called the Highlanders after the famous Scottish fighting troops commanded by Joe Gordon, which happened to be the same name as the president of the ball club. Because of the Scottish angle some of the newspapermen liked to call the team the Kilties, and playing at Hilltop Park up in Washington Heights got them called the Hilltoppers. Giants fans, partial to their National League, referred to the team as the Invaders, because the Giants were *the* baseball team in New York. Of course Brooklyn had a team, but as far as anyone in Manhattan was concerned the Dodgers may as well have played in Philadelphia.

It wasn't easy to squeeze a second ball club on Manhattan island. When Ban Johnson announced in 1901 that his Western League was changing its name and meant to challenge the Nationals, he knew that to be taken seriously as a big league he'd have to field a nine in Manhattan. The major problem was that the Giants had been owned by Andrew Freedman, who still held a stake in the club and was in thick with the Tammany Hall thieves who had been running City Hall since before the "War Between the States." The new owner, John Brush, was a bigwig in real estate and held options on every parcel of land on the island large enough to fit a ballpark. If anything should free up, with Freedman's connections Johnson knew that the city would quickly find some compelling reason to cut a street through the property.

The prospects looked dim for the American League when another Tammany Hall hack, Frank Farrell, decided he wanted a piece of the action. Farrell had worked for Tammany boss Tim Sullivan and was part of the syndicate that ran all the gambling in the city. Besides maintaining a string of race horses, Farrell owned a couple hundred pool halls where the small fries could wager on the ponies as well as baseball games and prize fights. He also held a major interest in one of the posh gambling dens near the theaters and hotels that catered to the carriage trade, one of those joints that everybody but the cops seemed to know about. Farrell's partner, Big Jim Devery, made sure that the authorities stayed stupid, a job made to order considering how he was once the police commissioner.

But Farrell and Devery were not quite the management team Ban Johnson would have preferred. He had been billing his new league as the champions of clean baseball, making out the Nationals as the rowdy circuit where gambling flourished and hard liquor was sold at rundown ballparks in the seediest parts of town. The only ladies that ventured to their games, he declared, were of the sporting variety looking to line up some trade for the cheap rooming houses nearby. Johnson doubled the admission price to fifty cents to drive away some of the undesirable elements. So part of the deal with Farrell was to come up with a more respectable front man to serve as president of the ball club. Joe Gordon was the answer, a coal merchant who nobody had ever heard of or had reason to.

Before the Giants got wind of the deal the old Baltimore Orioles franchise was transferred to New York and Farrell closed on a tract of land at 168th and Broadway where a new subway line was going in. Right away construction began on Hilltop Park. It was the last of the all-wood firetraps that the majors would see, just slapped together in weeks, never maintained and pretty much thrown away ten years later.

Freedman and Brush used all their influence to cut a street through Hilltop but Farrell was too well connected for that trick to work. When the season opened Brush sent thugs to the new park to pick fights with the players and spectators. Farrell brought in his own uglies to keep the peace, and patrons kept coming out to Hilltop, so it wasn't long before the Giants had to admit defeat. The American League had won the battle of New York—a major skirmish in the baseball war—giving the Nationals no choice but to go broke buying back players who began to jump from league to league to whatever club offered the most money. That's when the robber barons came to the bargaining table and hammered out the National Agreement. To everyone's surprise, business picked up for both leagues, and the owners wasted no time putting the screws to the players to get salaries back in line.

When I arrived the Highlanders were beginning their third year. On the last day of the previous season the club had barely missed out on nabbing the pennant, so a lot of people figured us to win it this time out. The only major change was at first base where the defection of John Ganzel left some young kid expected to fill the job.

I was more than just another rookie, of course. I had almost sparked another baseball war. I caught up to the Highlanders in Jackson, Mississippi, after the club broke camp and began to make its way to Atlanta for a series of barnstorming games before taking the train north to begin the new season. The idea was to play local minor league clubs along the way—not so much to get into condition as to pay off training expenses. A Southern town would close up shop, declare a holiday, and pack the ballyard where a band would play and dignitaries in search of votes would work the crowd.

On the day I arrived, just minutes before the game was to begin, I found the governor of Mississippi making an appearance. All the players toed the foul lines so this walrus could inspect our ranks like he was some kind of general. The veterans on the team who had seen plenty of politicians before were generally more interested in me. They spat tobacco juice and glared at me, while the governor delivered a few off-the-cuff remarks to the local voters and the newspapermen that knelt before him.

"Let me assure the great people of the great state of Mississippi that so long as you allow me to be your humble servant and I have breath in this mortal vessel," he blared to all parts of the yard, "never shall I compromise on our shared spiritual values and allow baseball to be played on Sunday. Let my political adversaries take note that I make this solemn pledge before God and you, the voters."

Playing baseball on a Sunday was as much a political hot potato as giving women the vote or prohibiting liquor. Some areas of the country supported Sunday ball, especially in St. Louis and Cincinnati, where a lot of the German immigrants had been raised to drink beer on their one day off from work and wanted something to watch while doing it. Older towns like New York and Philadelphia were dead set against the practice. Every week in the East young boys were pinched playing baseball on Sunday, because not only was charging admission against the law, it was a crime to even play the game.

Then the governor said he had pressing business in the capital but lingered long enough to freeze for the flash cameras and gladhand a few citizens as he made his way to a touring car idling at the gate. One last wave of his fat hand and flash of his teeth and we were allowed to get on with the game.

None of my new teammates seemed inclined to introduce themselves to me. After an inning or two the manager, Clark Griffith, sat down at the end of the bench with me, clapped my knee and gave a smile. Well, it wasn't exactly a smile, but at least it wasn't a sneer, which under the circumstance was as much as I could expect.

Only thirty-six years old, Griff was completely gray. He had been a fine pitcher in the National League when it was a twelve-team circuit, and even though his arm was pretty much shot he punched his own ticket every couple of weeks. In spot duty, he could still be as tough as anybody in the league.

He told me to take it easy, I'd see action soon enough, then he talked me around the diamond to fill me in on my new teammates.

Chapter 14

G riff didn't waste time, starting the tour at first base with my main competition for a job, John Anderson. With Ganzel gone and me late to report, Anderson had been moved in from the outfield. He had been in the big leagues for a dozen seasons and had played some first base over the years, but I could tell right away that he hadn't picked up much skill over there. He stuck so close to the bag you could drive a team of cattle through the hole he left between himself and the second baseman. Maybe I was a little brash but I already dismissed the guy as no serious challenge.

Playing second we had "Homerun" Jimmy Williams, who was just a little guy with not much pop in his bat. He got the nickname in Pittsburgh one year when he topped the league in homers with nine. In the dead ball days with the fences set back 400 to 500 feet from the plate, it was mostly the little guys with speed who could hit the gaps and circle the bases that led the league in the big knocks. Over all, Jimmy was a patty-cake hitter. What made him an asset was his steady field game.

Over at short we had Kid Elberfeld, called "The Tabasco Kid" because he had such a short fuse, especially with umpires. Even on a routine grounder when he nailed the runner by ten feet he'd manage to antagonize the ump with some kind of comment like, "I guess even a dumb-ass Chinaman couldn't have missed that call." He never got wise to the fact that "Blind Tom" always gets even. Hardly a month would pass when Kid didn't go belly to belly and maybe take a poke at an umpire, forcing Ban Johnson to give him an unpaid vacation. But judging the way he turned the double play when one of those Mississippi boys spiked him in the shin I could see he was a tough little egg. He just spit some tobacco juice on the cut and between innings cauterized it with medicinal whiskey. He didn't even flinch from the sting.

At third was "Little Joe" Yeager who wasn't much taller than Elber-feld or Williams. "He's another pepper pot," Griff told me. And the guy sure was lively, yapping it up, boosting our side and razzing the other. What Griff didn't tell me, but wouldn't take long to learn, was that Little Joe knew every red light district south of the Mason-Dixon Line. "Going down the line" they called it, and even the married men on the club would tag along to at least have a drink and joke with the Madam. Little Joe might have had a longer career in the fast company if he wasn't always battling a fresh outbreak of "malaria." It wasn't malaria, of course, but along with rheumatism that was what the newspapers called the VD to spare public sensibilities.

In left field we had Patrick Henry Dougherty, a big rough and tum-ble Irishman everybody called Patsy. His first two seasons with the Boston Americans he had been near the top in batting; then the pitchers caught up to him and Patsy wasn't smart enough to adjust and became pretty much a middle-of-the-road player. When he was sober, Patsy was quite the brawler, but get him stewed, which didn't take much convincing, and he'd turn weepy and start in about the Irish Republic. It was kind of touch-ing really to watch a bruiser like Patsy Dougherty cry over a country that on a world map he'd confuse with Scotland.

In center we had Dave Fultz, one of the fastest and smartest men to ever play the game. After graduating from Brown University he earned a law degree at Columbia. He was also the most religious man in the game since Billy Sunday left to preach on the sawdust trail. Dave did a bit of inspirational speaking himself. I caught his act later in my rookie year when he invited me to dinner, only he didn't bother to tell me it was at the YMCA with 500 other people.

Playing right field we had one of the most famous ballplayers of all time—Wee Willie Keeler. Most people only remember the reason he gave for being such a good hitter: "I just hit 'em where they ain't." Be-sides batting .340 for twenty years he was a feisty little guy who could steal bases and play the field. He didn't have more than a rubber band for an arm but he knew how to play in tight, charge the ball and unload it in a hurry.

Pitching for us that afternoon in Mississippi was Jack Chesbro, the first great spitball artist. He was called Happy Jack because he was any-thing but. Jack was always on the sour side, especially on the mound where nothing an umpire decided could satisfy him. Even when he got the strike call Jack would grumble, like he expected the ump to lift his mask, turn to the crowd and announce, "Ladies and gentlemen, never in all my years in baseball have I seen as swell a strike as the last delivery of Mr. Chesbro. Game awarded to New York. Good day."

In addition to Happy Jack, our pitching staff boasted Red Powell, who had won twenty for the club the year before, Buffalo Bill Hogg, and Smiling Al Orth, "The Curveless Wonder." It wasn't so much that Al pitched so good without having to resort to a crook, it was that no matter how hard he tried he couldn't make the ball break so much as an inch, a fact that left him feeling somewhat inadequate, which is why they called him Smiling Al. Because he didn't. He and Chesbro were a matching set, and in more ways than one. Orth picked up Chesbro's spitter and it was that ball movement that made him a big winner.

The spring I joined the team was the season after Chesbro set the league on its ear with forty-one wins, so every player and the ushers were trying to throw his spitball. A lot of people objected to the pitch on sanitary grounds as well as delicacy. Some suggested that the pitch should be called the slideball or the thumbball. Neither stuck, so it remained the spitball and perfectly legal to throw for the next fifteen years.

If you weren't learning to throw the spitter that spring you were looking to invent your own pitch. Rumors of new deliveries were reported in the papers like secret weapons designed to destroy the earth. Happy Jack, to stay ahead of the competition, asked for the patent on the jumpball, called that because as it neared the plate the ball would take a sudden hop over the bat. Hogg was boosting the wave ball, intended to rise and slide in either direction, depending on Bill's desire. Somebody else laid claim to the stopball, a pitch that would pause just before home plate then zip past the confused batter who wasn't sure if he was facing the spitball, jumpball or waveball. All of it was pure gas, of course, the writers knew it, but that fact didn't stop the special dispatches or discourage pitchers from twisting their arms like pretzels in the hope of making the ball do impossible tricks. Mostly guys just wore out their wings so that the only thing they could serve up to home plate was the meatball. And that pitch had been around a long time.

Catching all that junk for the Highlanders was Red Kleinow, who couldn't hit his foot with a sledgehammer but was solid and durable behind the plate. Just being able to log a lot of innings was an asset for a catcher, especially since it would be a couple more years before Breshnahan with the Giants took to wearing cricket pads to protect his shins. Backing up Red we had a real wonder of baseball, Deacon McGuire, a catcher for twenty years in the major leagues. His fingers looked like branches off an old apple tree, so shaking hands with him was an experience not soon forgotten. He had so many creepy knots and valleys that you couldn't help but pull away like you'd been shocked.

And finally on that New York club we had our utility man, Wid Conroy. Wid was short for Widow, a name he got because of his unusual concern for the plight of young boys. To save dough most clubs left the utility man behind on road trips, so like an old woman with nothing better to do Wid visited the sandlots and taught the kids how to play, keeping a close eye on the troubled ones. A few times he even brought them out to Hilltop to meet the players which, other than Dave Fultz, nobody appreciated much. If Wid had brought by a string of chorus girls that would have been a different story. But kids? And unhappy ones at that?

"Well, that's the hand we've been dealt to give Boston and Philadelphia a run for the flag," Griff said. "And you're my hole card. Think you're ready to play up here, son?"

"Yes, sir," I answered. "You can count on me."

Like, what else could I say?

Chapter 15

We took the overnight train to Atlanta and around two or three in the morning, as I was plowing the deep in my Pullman upper, Kid Elberfeld and Willie Keeler shook me awake.

"What's the matter with you, rookie?" Kid pulled me to down to the floor.

"If Griff finds out you were slacking he'll dock your first month's pay." Keeler proceeds to pinch my cheeks and give me a slap.

"I told you we should have just let him miss his turn."

"What turn?" I asked. "Did I miss a turn?"

"Let's go, yannagan, get some clothes on."

A minute later I'm still trying to belt up my trousers as the two of them are dragging me through cars to the caboose. We get to the back of the train to where a kerosene lantern is waiting. It seems that it was my turn to take up the lantern and warn off any trains that might come up on us too fast.

"Al Orth will take over for you in an hour." Keeler lights the wick and hands over the lantern.

"And don't fall asleep!" warns Kid. "There's women and children on this train."

"You can thank us later for saving your hide."

So I'm left swinging that lamp and thinking what a swell pair those little guys are to look after a youngster like me. Of course I rode plenty of trains in the Pacific Coast League and I never could recall passengers being conscripted to take on signal man duty, but this was the South and I figured they did a lot of things different.

The door to the caboose then opened, a conductor stepped out and growled, "Give me that light! Don't you ballplayers got nothing better to do than horse around all night?"

Well, I knew I had taken the goat for a ride. I was blistering and wasted no time marching back through that train to get my hands on those little bastards Keeler and Elberfeld. I didn't get far when I ran into Al Orth.

"I suppose you came to relieve me."

"Of what?"

"Or maybe you were hoping to catch me sleeping on the job."

"I think I smell Willie and the Kid. They told me I should take a look at the blood red moon that was rising. They must have figured you'd get wise and maybe you and me would get into it."

"All I know is I'm going to bust their heads together."

"If I wasn't pitching tomorrow I'd help. They're in 3A and B but be careful. Being short they think it's okay to use any advantage. They've been known to carry brass knuckles, so you best ambush them."

At least there was one decent sort on the ball club. I hunted down sleeper number three and crept up quiet. I could hear some light snoring behind the curtains of the lower berth. I reached in and rudely dragged out the occupant and began to cuff him around.

Too bad the ears I boxed belong to the manager of the ball club. Considering the circumstance, Griff took it better than you might expect. He only called me a stupid son of a bitch for a couple of minutes. Luckily the passengers we waked up began to howl for quiet.

"Get back to bed," he whispered. "You're starting at first base in the afternoon." He crawled into his berth then popped his head out of the curtains. "Do me a favor and turn out to be a ballplayer and not just an idiot."

I slunk back to my berth, having lost any desire to thrash Elberfeld and Keeler, and couldn't sleep the rest of the night. I was nervous about playing my first game the next day and decided I had enough on my mind without concerning myself with revenge. I was going to just forget the entire incident. But as soon as I walked through the dining car in the morning my teammates made train noises as I walked past. *Woo! Woo!*

After having had my chained pulled the night before, I had a little extra incentive that day to do well with the ash and leather. And I came through pretty good. Clocked a pair of nice hits, stole a bag, and provided the club with the best first base play they had seen all spring. I saved my infielders a couple of errors, which won me some pats on the backs, because there's no better way to make friends on a ball club than to bail out a guy on a rotten peg across the square.

And just like that John Anderson was relegated to the outfield to battle with Patsy Doughtery for a job. The boys canned the train noises and started to get chummy with me. The Highlanders had a good shot at taking the pennant, and for the team to succeed I had to contribute, which meant there was no percentage in pestering me.

We finished our series of games in Atlanta, then took the train north to play a final pair of exhibitions in New Jersey before starting the season. For some reason the deeper south you are the slower the trains, the further north the faster, so by the time we approached New York it felt like we were hurtling down the tracks. The passengers that got on were better dressed and talked louder, the landscape grew more crowded with houses and factories, there was a buzz in the air, and my heart started to pump. New York was on the horizon. The big city. The elephant itself.

When we stepped off the train and made our way to the concourse of Grand Central Station I told myself to calm down, I had been to plenty of big towns before. I didn't want to act like a yokel and get the needle from my teammates, but I couldn't help peeking up at the night sky painted on the huge canopy overhead. A second later, I practically bowled over a pair of the natives who weren't shy about recommending I hire a seeing eye dog.

Out on the streets there was even more bustle and jostling, but what really struck me was the overwhelming smell of piss. Horse piss, dog piss, people piss. Mix that with the smoke of coal burning trains and you had one ripe combination that took some getting used to.

The ball club set me up in a boarding house near Hilltop Park that was willing to cater to the less professional classes—theater people and the like. But even before I unpacked my bags I couldn't resist paying a visit to my new place of employment.

Hilltop Park was really just a rickety affair, but to me, never having seen a grandstand that swept from one foul pole to the other, it looked like the Taj Mahal. The park was so thick with seats I couldn't believe that so many people would actually pay to watch us play. Packed to the gills, Hilltop could only accommodate 20,000—but what did I know?

I sat down in a box seat to take it all in. The infield looked as smooth and green as a billiard table. Actually it was one of the worst diamonds in all the majors, with a crop of boulders lurking just under the surface, waiting for just the right moment to poke up and cause you a bad hop. God, I felt so jittery and alive.

A chilly breeze that came shooting in over the huge Bull Durham sign in center field mixed the smell of the sea with the freshly painted stands. I wished I could have slept there overnight but it was time to get back to the boarding house for dinner. I stood up and the slats of the seat stuck to the back of my pants.

Before we opened the league season in Washington we played our final exhibitions across the Hudson River in Jersey City. It was before the game, when I was about to take some practice swings, that Griff brought over three short, fat men, who turned out to be the principal owners of the ball club. They were all dressed like regular swells, so weighed down with jewelry and junk it was a good thing nobody decided to toss them in the river. The one who peddled the most goods was Frank Farrell. He wore English spats, choked the neck of an ivory-handled walking stick and fingered a thick gold chain that rested on his belly and led to a watch the size of a small pie that peeked out of one vest pocket, with a pair of snow white kid gloves hanging out the other. His hands boasted no less than five rings, his lapel a diamond stickpin as thick as your finger. He wore a bowler tipped at an angle on his fleshy head. When he smiled you could see a half-dozen gold crowns. And to top it off was this superior way he had of carrying himself that declared that here before your eyes was the genuine article. Accept no substitute.

Griff introduced me to Farrell and his cronies, Big Jim Devery, the ex–head cop, and Joe Gordon, the front man. Shaking hands with Farrell and Devery was a tug of war, but Gordon was like leading a girl to the dance floor. Farrell and Devery showed their teeth and gave you a blast of their foul breath. Gordon couldn't even look you in the eye.

"Griff tells us you're looking pretty good out there." Farrell leaned with both hands on his walking stick.

I tried to act modest, saying that I wasn't really on my game yet.

"Hell, I never knew a ballplayer to ever say he was. Ain't that right, Griff?"

"I guess so." Griff didn't seem overly comfortable with the likes of Farrell.

"Gamblers never have any luck and ballplayers are never on their game. Gad, that's the truth, eh?"

"In my experience," added Big Jim in a thick brogue, "baseballers generally have inflated notions about how good they really are. Me, I say if you *et* ham for supper then you *et* a ham supper."

"Hey, kid," said Farrell, "You might be interested to learn that your old manager Morley's been kicking ever since you skipped Los Angeles. He said we must have kidnapped you, because you were practically part of his family. Well, if that shit-licking Mick thinks that was using muscle he'd mistake a tea kettle for a steam engine. That's not how we operate this ball club. Strictly legit. Ain't that right, Joe?"

"Yes, of course." Gordon spoke so soft you could hardly make him out.

"Jesus, man, speak up. I could have sworn you were the goddamn president of this business concern. Here's your prized new property from the West, ain't you at least gonna give him the once-over?"

"I'm sure he'll do a fine job."

"Come on, Joe, see how the cat jumps. Feel his muscles. Come on, kid, make it bulge for him."

I make the fattest muscle I can so the president of the team can wrap his doughy fingers over it.

"It ain't your mother's tit, for Christ's sake." Farrell was enjoying himself. "Give it a grip, man!"

Gordon pressed a little harder. "Yes, quiet nice."

"Go take a few swings, Hal," Griff says and I pick up my bat to go.

"Hold on there." Farrell catches me by the shoulder and turns me about so he can grip me on either side and give me a strong whiff of that breath that smelled like a lot of things rotten.

"Whenever I get a new pony," he said, "I like to take a moment with it before I send it out on the track. You know what I mean, Jim?"

"That I do, Frank. The sooner a horse knows his master the better for all concerned."

"There's nothing like the feeling of walking into the stall for the first time and watching that brute shake his mane and rear up. Maybe he even takes a nip at you. But you better believe he won't make that mistake twice."

"You're a goddamn poet, Frank, that's what you are."

Finally Farrell turns me in the direction of the field and pats me on the shoulder. Again I start to go.

"Just a second," he says.

I turn around and he pokes me in the gut with the tip of his walking stick and gives it a twist.

"You're a New York American and don't you forget it."

"Yes, sir."

Now that I was properly branded I was finally allowed to take my cuts.

Chapter 16

It was time to take the train for the season opener with the Washington Nationals. This was before they became known as the Senators and even a couple years before Taft started the business of the President throwing out the first ball of the season.

As it turned out my first championship game in the big show was played in miserable conditions. It rained most of the day and was pretty dark by game time, which was 4:00 to give the federal workers time to get out to the yard. What with the early sunset, overcast sky and the usual smudged-up, grass-stained baseball it was tough to follow a pitch. We jumped on the Nats while there was still some light and the ball was white and round, putting three on the board in the top of the first. Then Chesbro had their hitters chasing the spitter in the dirt all afternoon, scattering five hits, and we came away with a quick four-two win. I had a double for my first major league hit and fielded all my chances. Even though it was a dull affair I had to be pleased with my introduction to the league.

We swept that opening series so easy that I began to wonder if playing in the major leagues was that much different than the Pacific Coast League. Then we moved on to Columbia Park in Philadelphia to play a contending club.

Connie Mack owned and managed the Philadelphia Athletics. Since he refused to wear a uniform he was banned by league rules from stepping onto the field. He had to direct his players from the dugout with a rolled-up program, and if he had a beef with the umpires he had to send out a messenger who always took a lot of abuse since Connie was always stingy when it came to feeding the men in blue between halves of a doubleheader. When he got old enough it was Connie's son, Earl, who had to soldier out to the field to plead the A's case. "You got ten seconds, Earl," the umps would growl. "Jump up and down, wave your arms, give the old man a show, but you tell him that if he sends you out here one more time today the both of you are getting chased. Oh, and be sure to thank him for the brown cheese."

The general public may have thought Connie Mack was some kind of Sunday School teacher because he wore a jacket and tie, but the truth was the guy never had a nickel he wasn't willing to die over. He probably didn't wear a uniform to save on laundry bills. Sure, he fielded some fine ball clubs over the years, but every time he had a championship team he'd sell off the top players to turn a nifty profit. Plenty of years he didn't even go after the pennant, just kept the team respectable for a couple of months for the sake of attendance before cashing in his chips. So Connie even figured out a way to make money by losing.

In 1905, he was still new in town, and to win over the fans from the National League Phillies he was obliged to put a winning team on the field. And he sure had a dandy one waiting for us. After a rainout a large and mean contention of cranks came out to Columbia Park to support their Athletics. Philly rooters have always been known to be brutal on the opposing side but stitch New York on your blouse and they reach back for something extra. They loved their own team—give them credit for that—but even that was a mean kind of love. Screw up a couple of times and even their favorite players would get the raspberry.

And boy did they egg on their side, urging cold-hearted murder even before the first pitch. Eddie Plank took the start and he was one mean bastard on the mound. His first pitch to Keeler was labeled for Willie's ear and sent him spinning, much to the joy of the crowd. This was to be my real introduction to the fashionable set.

The Pacific Coast League was plenty gritty, but in this loop I discovered the game was played at a pace a few notches higher. It was, *Think fast, here's a bomb!* When you weren't opposing the Nats or St. Louis, everybody played quick, smart and obsessed, and if you weren't ready to play just as tough you wound up on your ass nursing a busted lip. And if you weren't ready to back up your play with your fists under the stands after the game, those boys would run you out of the league like a pony hitched to a cart.

Our club was up for the challenge that day and after getting down early we actually battled back to take a six-three lead in the seventh inning. A lot of crowds would be sitting on their hands, waiting for something good to happen, but this one got louder and practically demanded that their team rally, which they did with three runs to knot things up. Finally, in the last of the ninth the A's pushed across the winning run to send home their supporters drunk and singing.

It was one of the most demanding games I had ever played in. I sat so dog-tired in the back of the open carriage that took us back to our hotel that I didn't have the energy to bicker with the Philly fans that tagged along to blister us. There were so many dogs yapping, vegetables and clumps of dirt hurled at us, you'd think we were being carted off to the meet the guillotine.

The next day the crowd was a bit smaller, the two clubs a little on the woozy side, so like a pair of prize fighters we took off this round and played at an easier pace. There was only a modest level of blood and mayhem. Connie hardly had to get off his skinny ass as his boys pasted us pretty good by an eight to one score. We weren't happy about dropping that brace to the Athletics, but were pleased enough to escape that burg of brotherly love and return to friendlier terrain for our home opener.

With the Highlanders coming off that near-miss of the pennant the year before, the club was starting to build a following, eager to see what we had to offer this campaign. The faithful were also curious about this kid wonder at first base that they'd been reading about in the newspapers. You can imagine how I felt.

Here I am—your mail order bride!

Chapter 17

Hilltop Park was fitted out and ready for a new season. Red, white and blue bunting was draped over every railing, stiff and smelling of starch and mothballs. The grass was neatly trimmed. The hawkers wore spanking new ice cream caps and jackets. And before the game we were issued our fresh home whites. God, there's something almost holy about the touch and smell of a baseball uniform that's folded square and never been worn. The flannel is still rough and itchy in a good kind of way. The sharp smell of dye in the lettering reminds you of other spring days and all the hope that goes with the beginning of a new baseball season. This is going to be your year.

It's such a glorious feeling that you want to sit on your milking stool for just one more minute to pound your glove and dream, rather than take the field and have the spell broken. Then this urge begins. It starts with one guy who says something like, "Let's go get 'em today," and it spreads across the room until everyone is beating their gloves like war drums, the manager gives a nod, a whoop goes up and the team gallops onto the field to the cheers of the crowd. You quickly loosen up that flannel, eager to show the home folks what you got in store for them this year.

Then the game begins and you remember what baseball really is. Constant failure. Licking your wounds. Fighting back.

Too bad for the Highlanders the bad weather followed us north for our home opener. Charcoal-colored clouds had been spitting all day, keeping down the gate, and right after the first batter the rain came down in absolute pitchforks, forcing the umpire to call off the proceedings. We grabbed our sweaters and sprinted all the way to the clubhouse in center field. Our virgin whites were soaked through, as heavy as lead, looking dingy and starting to smell like a musty old basement. There went the magic for another year.

Somebody with the ball club screwed up on printing the rain checks so there was nothing to hand out to the patrons who had braved the weather. To make good the club announced that the next day's game would be free to all. Before noon the stands were filled and the streets around Hilltop so jammed that only the coppers on horseback prevented a riot. The ballplayers had a rough enough time getting into the park. Word of us approaching made a wedge in the crowd.

"Here comes Chesbro. Make way for Jack."

"Here comes the new kid at first. The California Kid. Show us what you got today, Chase."

All of us home-side players got cheered and patted as we inched through. I don't know what kind of reception the visiting players got but I doubt it was quite so neighborly.

Hilltop Park didn't seem so big to me now. The bleachers were so packed they looked ready to collapse. Keeping this mob in check were just a half-dozen off duty coppers. They stretched a rope around the outfield, and fans stood ten deep around the entire field. Men even stood on the team benches and were prepared to defend their territory, not that us players were remotely close. We had to sit on the grass twenty feet down the foul lines, praying that no hits came rocketing our way. The spectators, though, didn't seem to mind standing in the direct line of fire. I could smell open bottles of whiskey passing through the crowd and the sports offering odds, so by the time the game got under way the throng was pretty well stewed and made it known that victory was the minimum requirement of the day.

I wasn't sure if our fans were backing us or threatening us, but either way we played with an extra measure of vim and vigor. Give the Nats some credit, they put up a better fight than they did on their home grounds, finally succumbing five runs to three. With an opening win at Hilltop our supporters left the park happy, the pennant race was on and now it was time to see if our club, and yours truly, had the goods for the long haul.

❖

The Highlanders enjoyed a pretty fair April, but come May we started to slide in the standings. During a three-week road trip we could only manage four or five wins, so by the time we returned home in June even our most rosy supporters had to doubt our chances of capturing the American League flag, and fewer of them were willing to make the long trek up to Hilltop to watch us play. That situation didn't sit well with

Frank Farrell, especially after he had been boasting all winter how his boys would be the champs this year for sure.

Our main problem was the pitching that had been so solid the year before. When Orth went out with a split hand nobody seemed capable of taking up the slack. Farrell's answer was for Griff to call on Chesbro every other day, but Happy Jack just wasn't the same mystery to the league as the year before when he marched up the hill every three days, not to mention spot relief duty. The guy had tossed some 450 innings on his way to those forty-one wins in 1904 so it shouldn't have been too much of a surprise that the old soup bone was just plain tired. Being a hurler himself Clark Griffith knew there was only so many throws in an arm, but Farrell wouldn't hear of anybody in his employ giving anything less than the unrealistic. The only thing that mattered to a mug like him was winning now. Today. And what would be the reward for the man who pitched until his wing gave out? If he was lucky, train fare back to the minor leagues.

Farrell almost drove Griff to drink, what with all his sure-fire suggestions and can't-miss prospects he signed. Pitch this kid tomorrow. Bat that guy third. If one of Frank's "finds" didn't pan out right away, he'd cut his losses and sign up another new hotshot that was going to make all the difference to the club's fortunes. We became a revolving door, with players coming through so fast that the regulars didn't even bother to learn the names or pester the newcomers with the old pranks. God, we were so down in the dumps we didn't even have enough energy to torment our fellow man.

The worry was that Farrell's next victim might be Clark Griffith. Rumor had it that Farrell thought Ned Hanlon, the Brooklyn skipper, would do a better job than Griff. That was a rich one. The only thing you could say for Hanlon was that he knew how to manage a second division club because that's where his Trolley Dodgers always wound up.

We went on another long road swing, getting drubbed on every stop when Farrell gets his fill of reading about the bloodshed in the newspapers and catches up with the club in Detroit. To inspire the troops he lays into Griff in front of everyone. It was almost out of sympathy for the guy that we kept right on losing ballgames. Griff wasn't in the market for that kind of pity—he wants to win—so now he really lays into us. He says we're too damn soft. He says we spend too much time piano playing and singing in the hotel lobby and not enough talking about baseball and strategizing how to win. Piano playing makes for soft hands, soft hands make for soft ballplaying; so from that moment forward, he declares, there will be no more piano playing for the New York Americans.

That seemed kind of harsh to us since a lot of baseball players enjoyed harmonizing, often forming barbershop quartets. Most managers preferred it over guzzling beer or plucking those Baseball Daisies and coming down with another case of malaria. There were situations, of course, where music was the cause of friction in the clubhouse. Rival barbershop quartets might develop and ballplayers, being so competitive by nature, would try to outdo each other. Resulting in disharmony if you know what I mean. Generally you had but one piano in the hotel lobby, so you fight over it. Then both groups try to line up vaudeville dates for the off season and bill themselves as *the* official quartet of the ball club. The real problem was when the bad blood spilled onto the field. The tenor from one group would rather roast in Hell than back up the play of the bass of a rival group. Before you know it the team can't turn a simple double play and the manager is wishing his boys were out chasing skirts instead of singing "Down by the Old Mill Stream."

What was really eating Farrell and the reason why he was making life so miserable for Griff, who was making life so miserable for us, was that across the island at Coogan's Bluff the Giants were well on their way to another National League pennant and an appearance in the World Series. After copping the flag the year before, they were expected to play the Boston Americans in what would have been the second World Series. But McGraw and Brush acted like it would be a thoroughly degrading experience to appear on the same field as Boston and cancelled the Series. Then on opening day the next April they raised a huge banner over the Polo Grounds declaring themselves to be World Champions. Now that was the kind of cast iron gall that only an operator like Frank Farrell could truly appreciate. And envy. Public opinion, on the other hand, was dead set against the Giants and it was certain that they would have to take on the American League champs this year, and Farrell would do anything to have his club be the one to give Brush and McGraw their comeuppance. But as early as the Fourth of July, even Farrell had to recognize that his Highlanders would not be the opposing nine and he was burnt to a crisp over it. He was convinced that he did his damnedest to help the club win and that all us greedy, ungrateful ballplayers had let him down. Especially yours truly.

Chapter 18

I got off to a good start my rookie year, but the league has a way of getting wise to you pretty quickly. Pitchers discovered that I was impatient at the plate, that I hated to walk and would swing at anything close. When they stopped throwing strikes I kept on swinging. I swung at balls in the dirt. I swung at balls over my head. I swung at balls so far off the plate I needed a telegraph pole to reach them. And whenever I decided to lay off a pitch—never fail, a straight one would zip down the pipe for a called strike. Next pitch I'm hacking at a ball that almost hits my foot. My brain got so twisted up I lost heart, so by May I was batting but .200 and banished to the back of the order. That's when my teammates tried to help, which generally makes things worse. As I was the new kid, I tried to be polite and give a fair shot to all the hints. Then the newspapers got into the act and suggested I wise up and bat lefty like I really should. But I had batted right-handed all my life, just like my brother John, and had no clue how to hit from the other side. Next my field work began to suffer. I made errors in wholesale lots, mostly throws to napping teammates. That's when a joke made the rounds.

Question: Why do they call the new Highlanders' first baseman Chase?

Answer: That's what his fielders have to do after he throws the ball.

After all the excitement of moving to New York and the grand expectations of opening day, I now felt pretty low. For the first time in my life I had to wonder if I had what it took to play with the big boys. And more than that, I had to wonder if I hadn't wasted enough of my life swatting at balls with a stick. I was living in a grimy city that smelled like piss, getting jeered and joked about, answering to a crook like Frank Farrell.

But Clark Griffith stuck with me.

"It takes time to adjust up here," he said. "I remember when I broke in with the Brownies in ninety-one. I couldn't find the plate with a dog and cane. I figured to be home picking shit with the chickens by Independence Day, but Comiskey was my manager and he hung in with me until I found my feet. Of course, the big son of a bitch traded me to Boston before the year was out."

So as much as Griff tried to reassure me, he left me just as nervous.

Then the newspapers reported that Farrell was talking to John Ganzel again, this time about the possibility of me switching places with him. I'd play first and manage Ganzel's minor league club and he'd get the privilege of crawling back to the Highlanders. Ganzel was unwilling to stomach the humiliation and trust his investment to some youngster, so nothing came of that offer, other than to distract me some more.

I wanted to go home to California. On the street I began to envy young men my age working at real jobs. They could be clerking for a grocer or pushing a broom, but it seemed a hell of a lot more honest and steady than anything I could do with a bat and a glove. Not to mention, no bastard scalded you in the newspaper every time you dropped a jar of pickles.

People kept giving me batting tips but now I didn't pay any mind. I was resigned to my situation: Frank Farrell would throw me overboard soon enough.

I was feeling so glum that I actually found myself attracted to a Salvation Army girl preaching on a street corner. I was attracted to her words, although plenty of fellows had gathered around because she was actually a bit of a looker.

"Are you ready to change?" she cried, giving her tambourine a shiver.

"Yes!" answered her fellow Christian soldiers, armed with tubas and religious tracts.

"Are you tired of your sinful ways?"

"Yes!" She motioned for the crowd to join in but the sinners had other things on their minds than the spiritual.

"Do you wish you were clean?"

"Yes!"

Her eyes that had been circling the crowd now settled on mine.

"Are you ready to admit you've made mistakes in your life?"

"Yes!"

"Do you want to know the cure?"

"Yes!"

And that's when it struck me, something that Jack Chesbro had said a couple days earlier and I had ignored.

"Kid," he said, "Everybody in the yard knows when you've made up your mind to swing at a pitch. You start to wag your tail."

Now I knew what he meant. I'd start to waving the bat behind my ear when I was anxious to swing. The pitchers had picked up on the habit and were sure not to give me anything worth hitting.

"Do you know what you have to do?" The Salvation Army girl pointed straight at me.

"Yes!" I replied and everybody turned to look at me.

"What?" she shouted.

"Hit the goddamn ball!"

And I was saved.

I began to cross up the pitchers, wagging my tail to get them to waste a couple. Now with the count in my favor I began to see some real watermelons to hack at. The hits started to come, my confidence picked up as well and so did the old batting average. Pretty soon I was hitting over .250, the third highest on the club in a year when averages were down across the league. In the field I also improved. I forgot the dicey throws and just held onto the pill to save myself a lot of grief.

Although it wasn't spectacular I had a more than respectable rookie year. For the final couple of months the ball club played a lot better, too, so the season ended with a lot of optimism for both me and the club.

The only thing was, I didn't plan on coming back. Now that I didn't have to return home in shame, I could quit the game on my own terms and get on with the rest of my life.

To smooth my transition to a respectable life, when I got back to San Jose I accepted a chance to make a little extra dough by finishing out the season with the local franchise of the California State League under an assumed name. It was a real shock to the system to play minor league ball again. I had grown accustomed to a fast-thinking brand of ball, so that league didn't know what hurricane hit them. I swatted the apple all over the lot, ran crazy on the bases, and pulled off plays at first base that left the crowd amazed. I turned into a regular gate attraction.

By the end of the California season I was a heavy name in San Jose, feted and feasted by the local sporting crowd. Everybody wanted to hear war stories about the American League and how I fared against the likes of Napoleon Lajoie, Wahoo Sam Crawford, Eddie Plank and Rube Waddell. I demonstrated my batting stroke by hitting napkins with a pool cue. Women gave me a wink and a wiggle. Every poker game in town had an open chair. I never had so many good friends. It was nice to know that when I declared I was quitting the game I wouldn't be lonely.

I had gotten a lot of drinks on the house and treated to dinner, but after a couple of weeks it seemed like I was always getting stuck with the tab. I was making the big league dough, right? Pretty soon I was hard up for cash but didn't want to admit it. Christmas came and this time I didn't splurge on expensive presents for the family. And I guess it was just as well because I didn't feel comfortable going home to face the folks. After I had changed my life, that would be the time to go home.

I started to despise the fast set I was running with. Everybody dressed like swells and acted richer than they had a right to, digging themselves into a hole they could never hope to get out of. They were always scrambling for a buck and taking advantage of the innocent. And now I was stepping into the hole with them. At least I had an escape. If I signed a baseball contract for one more season I'd pull an advance, get out of hock, then wash my hands of that vicious circle. I knew I was an idiot, but what else could I do?

So once again I couldn't quit the game, no matter how much I wanted to.

Chapter 19

I guess I was also a little excited to see how I'd fare in the big show with a season under my belt. And I wasn't the only one. The entire city of New York sensed that something was up with both me and the club. In the infield we replaced Joe Yeager with Frank LaPorte, a little fireplug we called Pot. Little Joe then became the utility player while Wid Conroy got a shot in center field after Dave Fultz announced that he been called away by the Lord to preach full-time. The way some figured it, if Dave had ever learned to hit the curve ball he wouldn't have heard the Lord so clearly. Patsy Dougherty was still with the club, somehow resisting the call to arms in Ireland. He didn't last long, only batting a buck-ninety when Griff shipped him to the Chicago White Sox in exchange for Danny Hoffmann, a guy who had been a top prospect for Philly before getting hit in the eye with a pitch. Moundwise we still had our three big horses: Chesbro, Orth and Hogg. Red Powell was cut loose and Griff decided not to take any more turns pitching himself.

The changes to the ball club were minor but the expectations weren't. A lot of that was because of me. I came to spring training with plenty of confidence in my abilities. Everybody could see it and predicted that I'd tear up the circuit. That talk fired me up even more and I terrorized the minor league clubs we played as we worked our way north.

We opened the 1906 season by whipping Boston four straight games, so by the end of the first week our boosters figured that the league flag was as good as flying over center field. We even started to draw some notice from the rest of the town, which was finally waking up to the fact that the American League was here to stay. New Yorkers respected a club that played a tough brand of ball, and there were plenty of people willing to back a winner in a new league, in spite of all the gas from the Giants about how they were the only *real* big league club in town.

Talk about swell-headed, that entire Giants ballclub thought they were God's own gift. They were the darlings of the Broadway set, the gambling and show biz types that always like to be seen around a hot horse or a hit show. They monopolized all the good seats at the Polo Grounds and after the game loved to blow around with Mugsy McGraw and the star players. But the absolute worst of the lot was Christy Mathewson.

Good old Matty, Big Six, the college boy from Bucknell, pitching in a pinch and all that crap. In his prime the guy could do the job on the mound, I'll give him that, but what really starched us American Leaguers was all the hooey in the papers about him being as pure as rain water. I met him at a party when I was new to town and he gave me the high hat so I knew right then that the guy was a phony. What the papers never told you was how he liked the gaming as much as anybody. If he knew a teammate had an extra buck in his pocket, Matty wouldn't let up until he had the guy cutting cards, rolling the bones or even playing mumbly peg. And once he had the dough in his pocket it generally aged there, because he was the cheapest guy in baseball. He socked away plenty on that fat salary and from those newspaper columns he didn't really write, and those testimonial advertisements for stuff he'd only use if it was given to him for free. And on top of that his Broadway pals would book him to a vaudeville tour in the winter. Nothing too strenuous. He'd start with a few words on what it felt like to buffalo those Philadelphia Athletics the last three games of the World Series: *Well, folks, they were a game bunch, those Athletics, but with Iron Man McGinnity and myself manning the box we felt we had a good chance to take the Mack men even if Rube Waddell hadn't come up lame for their side. We tried to play with pluck and re-solve. Which reminds me of a song. Conductor, if you please…*

The average New Yorker cheered for the Giants but he also loved the game in general, and at Hilltop Park at least he knew he didn't have to be George M. Cohan to get a decent seat.

They stopped calling us the Invaders, and we began to become known as the New York Yankees.

Then we lost seven out of eight.

We would have been happy to be called the Invaders over what the fans started to call us. By the first of May we had fallen so far off the pace that the cranks were ready to murder us they loved us so much.

"To hell with them all!" Griff had us gathered in the clubhouse after another rotten loss. "You play for me. We play for each other. We'll make some ball clubs in this league squirm before the year is out."

The trouble was that Frank Farrell figured we played for him. By this point he had dropped all the malarkey about Joe Gordon being president of the club and took open control, which only meant more meddling and gumming up of the works. Just in time we began to win ballgames, and I mean in bunches. Luckily Farrell took all the credit and stayed out of the picture long enough for Griff to instill a fiery spirit in the team. We became real scrappers, the bugs picked up on our attitude and began coming out to Hilltop in bigger and bigger numbers. That rotting firetrap became a real rollicking joint.

Unlike the rest of the team I started off hot swinging the bat and stayed that way, piling up the bingles and a few long pokes as well. And once I got on the bases I was stealing like a sinner, always ready to jump on any mistake to nab an extra bag. In the field was where I really began to turn some heads. I played all over the lot in a style nobody had ever seen before.

It was actually at the Polo Grounds watching the Giants that I found the key to playing first base. We had an off day and I went to see the Boston Nationals take on the Giants so I'd get a chance to see the great Fred Tenney play the bag for the visitors. After Comiskey, Tenney was considered the best ever to handle first base, and since I was being touted as the next Fred Tenney I wanted to see what he had to offer. We didn't have the best of instruction in those days, so to pick up a trick was pretty exciting. What I saw Tenney do was to straddle the bag and wait to see if the peg from his infielder was true or not. Only then would he shift his feet to touch the bag. I had been taught—like everybody else—to rush over, plant my foot and wait for the ball. There was no problem if the toss was true, but if it was off line I had to make an awkward hop to reposition myself, and since you generally had to use both hands with that pot holder of a mitt we used, it was easy to get pulled off the base or drop the ball.

I took that hint from Tenney and refined it some. I played way off the base, near the mound on one pitch, in short right field the next. I told my fielders not to wait for me to get to the bag, just heave the apple over. Soon I perfected the knack of taking throws on the dead run and kicking the bag with either foot as I slipped by. What Tenney did in straddling first base I did at speed. High throws, balls in the dirt—I snagged them all. People stopped called me the next Fred Tenney. Fred who? Now I was *the* Fancy Dan of all Fancy Dans. I was catching fly balls in right field and foul pops behind the plate. I could field a sacrifice bunt down the third base line and nail the lead runner. One time I tagged a guy out at the plate on a suicide squeeze and still had time to wheel and nail the batter at first. I was chucking the ball all over the damn yard, my teammates started to stay awake, and I was picking off runners like July flies.

Word spread around the league that Hal Chase had gotten as brash as green paint, especially when it came to crashing in on the bunt. Napoleon Lajoie, "The Frenchman," told the Cleveland newspapers that I had better not try any of that cheeky stuff on his ball club. Larry was the brightest star in the American League and had everybody shining his boots and wanting to be his pal. He'd cram the ball down your throat at second base and guys would get up smiling because he was smiling. *Oh that Larry!* He even had the goddamn umpires in his pocket. If a pitch was close and he didn't offer at it you could bet your granny's life it wouldn't be called a strike. *Larry knew the strike zone for God's sake!* Well, the way I figured it, the Frenchman was good enough without getting all the breaks, and I said so, too.

So when Lajoie and his Cleveland club came to Hilltop everybody was buzzing over the showdown between the star and the upstart. The grandstands were packed for the first game of the series to see the fireworks, and the fans didn't have long to wait. Barely five minutes into the game Lajoie came to the plate in a bunt situation. Even though he was a top man knocking in the runs, everybody was expected to lay down the ball for the sake of the club. If there was one exception to the rule it was Larry but I had a suspicion he would want to test me with a bunt. Before he stepped in the box he glared at me. I blew him a little kiss.

Our pitcher takes a stretch, peers over at first, and just like the base runner I read his move and break for the plate to field the sacrifice. Lajoie begins to square around but at the last moment he pulls back the bat and smashes the ball right at my head. I didn't have time to do anything but throw up the mitt, the ball slammed into my palm, stinging like hell, but somehow it stuck. Then I turned to chase the runner back to first. Well, the Frenchman never got out of the box. He just dropped his head and walked back to the bench. The crowd didn't react right away, the play happened so quick, but once they took it all in they cheered like mad and tossed their hats into the air. My teammates then started to give Larry the business. He looked at me, smiled, touched his cap in salute, and spit some tobacco juice. Hell, he really was a hard guy not to like.

That's when I finally got a nickname that stuck. No more of that California Kid stuff. Now I was known as Prince Hal. The Prince. I was the best player on the team and became royalty, with all my comings and goings duly noted in the daily press. And considering how New York supported seven morning papers and six in the evening, plenty of ink was slopped around on my account.

I fed off all the attention and kept getting better and better. After I ended one game by digging out a wild throw with my bare hand for the force out at first, the Hilltop supporters could take it no longer and rushed the field to haul me onto their shoulders. I was carried around the bases in triumph. At first I was a little scared. They could have easily ripped me apart in their worship. And that's really what it was. Worship. Hail the conquering hero! Long live the Prince! When I relaxed and enjoyed the ride it felt great. More than that, it felt *right*. It felt like I was born to ride men's shoulders.

Then another feeling came over me. A scary one. I looked at all these people below me, cheering themselves hoarse over a ballplayer, and I began to despise them for degrading themselves by raising me up so high.

When the mob finished taking me around the bases and dropped me on home plate they returned to normal. I trotted off to the clubhouse in center. But I don't think I was ever the same after that. For two minutes I wasn't a ballplayer anymore. I wasn't even human.

Chapter 20

During a long homestand in May we won eleven games in a row to get ourselves back into the pennant race. For the next two months we traded off on first place with Philadelphia while Cleveland lay no more than a game or two back. Other than the usual tailenders, Washington and St. Louis, the one club we weren't worried about was the Chicago White Sox, the "Hitless Wonders" of Fielder Jones. Maybe that outfit didn't push across too many runs, but they got great pitching from Altrock, White and Big Ed Walsh, played tight defense, and exhibited a hell of a lot of pluck. In May they weren't even a .500 ball club, but come July they hit their stride and rose to fourth place in the standings. Then in August in a stretch of ten days they sprinted past everyone on their way to winning nineteen games in a row. With that run Philly dropped out of the chase and Cleveland struggled to hang within five or six of the lead. As for the Highlanders, we dropped six games to the Sox in two weeks and were lucky to stay in contact.

During a crazy three weeks it seemed like nobody could win but the White Sox and the tailenders. We played hard but there was always something that would crop up to cost us a ball game. During a season you always run into dry spells, but Frank Farrell didn't see it that way. Late in August after we've dropped three more to Chicago, Griff calls a team meeting. He's got a report from some private dick that Farrell hired to tag after us. You could tell that Griff was ashamed he had to read it to us, and we were absolutely steaming, not that there was anything too racy in the report. Mostly it was guys breaking curfew to slip out of the hotel for a couple of beers. Player A paid a visit to a house of assignation. Player B was spotted crawling out of some apartment window at three in the a.m.

"There you have it, boys." Griff returned the report to its envelope.

"The owner of this ball club wants me to inform you that any man who'd rather fool around than win the pennant can ask for his release."

We tried to laugh it off, calling each other Player A and B, but our feelings were stung. Maybe we were involved in some off-field antics, but once we put on that Highlander uniform there wasn't a player on the club who didn't give everything he had to win a game. We certainly didn't deserve the insult of being followed around like that.

Some clubs would have folded right then. Instead we rallied and made a run at those stinking White Sox. We won the next four games, dropped one, then peeled off fourteen straight victories. Talk about an exciting pennant race. It was like the Highlanders and the Sox were strapped together in a knife fight. Despite being crippled with injuries, both teams refused to lose ballgames. Our biggest problem was the schedule. Our last twenty-five games were all on the road. An entire month of living out of a grip, riding trains and eating in hotel dining rooms was enough to sap a healthy side.

A final series of four games with the Sox late in September figured to be the key to the championship. The first two games went our way and we took over the league lead. Then they pasted us seven to one to edge back in front. The final game became crucial, since either we would pull ahead by half a game or fall back to where we started the series, one-and-a-half out. Happy Jack came through with one of his best outings of the year and we outscrapped Chicago in a one to nothing, necktie affair.

That Sox ball club looked absolutely spent when we left town, and we figured to waltz our way to the flag. Maybe that long road swing finally caught up to us, because it turned out that we were the ones to fall apart while Chicago found the courage to bounce back. We got swept three in Detroit, split four in Cleveland, then dropped two out of three in Philly, all the while the White Sox kept winning. Taking a final brace from Boston didn't matter; we lost the pennant by three full games.

Coming so close yet falling short was tough to take after the grind of a long season. We fought hard, overcame a peck of injuries, a tough schedule and a rotten owner to get a taste of the lead near the end, only to see it slip away so quick. We lost to a fine team in those Sox, which they proved in the World Series by the way they handled the Cubs that had racked up 116 wins over in the National League. Still, we couldn't help but feel that we were really the better club that year.

I finished the year batting .326, third highest in the league, to establish myself as the finest first sacker in the game. At the age of twenty-five I found myself a star of the national game. My teammates depended on me, the fans adored me, the newspapermen courted me, and the competition in the American League feared me. Now I was indeed the cock of the walk in the big town—along with swellheaded Christy Mathewson.

Maybe I had experienced all the personal glory a man could. I knew I had made a promise to my brother, but I was just a boy then, and didn't know any better. Now I could look at things straight on. John urged me not to waste my life on baseball, yet look at me. I was making it big. People knew my name. Think of all the good things I could accomplish in life because people paid attention when the Prince spoke. How was that a wasted life? In fact, the more I thought about it, the clearer it was what my brother really meant: Use baseball for a greater cause. I was destined for big things and by quitting the game I would be forsaking my call. So I had to keep on playing, right?

This time when I went home to winter in San Jose I had no intention of quitting the game and looked forward to receiving next year's contract. I had been making $2,500 a year, which was better than most, but I expected quite a jump in pay after the year I posted. And it was important that I have more money. The influence of reputation is one thing, but think of all the good I could accomplish in the world with that extra dough.

I had good reason to expect a hike in salary because of a conversation Farrell and me had near the end of the season. He told me what an honor it was to have such a fine young man such as myself on the payroll. He actually had a tear in his eye when he said, "You'll see my true appreciation when you receive your new contract in the off season."

I wasn't going to take advantage of the man. I would be happy to join the ranks of Lajoie in the American League and Honus Wagner in the National League making five grand per. Sure, I was worth a lot more than that, considering how many paying customers came out to watch me at Hilltop and all the other yards in the league. Because I would be just a third-year player I was content to wait my turn for the really big money.

When that contract finally arrived in the post I was shocked to see that it called for only $2,750. Was that how that lousy crook Farrell showed his appreciation—with a whopping two-hundred-and-fifty buck rise in salary? I pictured Farrell sitting in his office, his spats hiked up on the desk, smoking a Havana, and dreaming about all the suckers in the world he was going to bilk. Well, I wasn't one of them. It would take nothing less than five big ones to get the Prince back to town.

I returned that contract with a note suggesting that Farrell hire a new girl to do his typing since she didn't know how to do numbers properly.

He wrote back to assure me that Alice was a wonder with the typewriter and that he was looking forward to a new baseball season and please find enclosed another copy of my contract calling for twenty-seven-fifty. I replied that unless Alice figured out how to type 5's, as in $5,500, I wouldn't be able to figure out how to sign my name. A week later another contract arrives with a note explaining that the best Alice can manage is a single 3, as in $3,000. Then I confide how I know plenty of girls in Manhattan who could type any number you asked, and certainly $5,500 was one of the easier sums to master. I offered to refer Farrell to some names but he says no thanks, Alice will do just fine, and returns the contract that calls for $3,000.

Dear Frank,

Thought you might like to know, since you always struck me as the curious kind, that the girls they got working in the California State League office are real crackerjacks when it comes to typing 4, 5 and even 6.

Your pal,
Hal

Dear Harold,

Am delighted to hear of efficient help on coast, but our girls here in the east are plenty smart and always looking to improve their game. Take for instance Alice who has just learned to type $3,500. Afraid that's the best she can do. We all reach our limits.

Wishing you all the best,
Frank Farrell
Club President

Dear Frank,

I really hope you're getting something on the side because if that girl of yours can't peck out $5,500 it's going to cost you the best ballplayer in the American League. By the way the weather in San Jose is swell. It's a great place to play ball.

Regards,
Hal Chase
Ballplayer

Dear Mr. Chase,

Please be advised that the last offer of $3,500 stands and is final. Expect you either to report to Hot Springs, Arkansas during the first week in March or read in the newspapers of your retirement from the game. In any event we *wish you the best of luck in whatever field outside of professional baseball you may decide to pursue.*

Cordially,
Frank Farrell
Club President

Chapter 21

I tore up Farrell's final offer and returned the pieces to him without a note. Now the only way we talked was through the newspapers. I told some local writers that I had signed a deal with the San Jose club that would make me part-owner and that as far as I was concerned Organized Baseball could call the California State League an outlaw outfit until they popped an artery because fans out west knew good ball and would support it.

When spring camp opened Farrell put out stories on how inflated my head got near the end of the last season, and even Griff declared that no ballplayer was indispensable to the Highlanders. Though Farrell acted like he didn't care if I ever rejoined the team, pretty soon another copy of that $3,500 contract arrived. After I sent it back again, the newspapers began touting the prospects of George Moriarty, a youngster that was all the talk for the Highlanders in Hot Springs. He was a sure fire cinch to be the club's next star first baseman. Well, George was a nice guy and turned into a decent utility player when he joined the club late the year before, but it was an absolute joke to suggest he could replace the Prince. I told the California papers that Frank Farrell was kidding himself if he thought such carnival tricks were going to lure me back to the American League. Besides, I said, I was set to make plenty of dough with the San Jose club and wasn't so sure he could come close to matching their offer.

The truth was that the best San Jose could do was $3,000. By now the Highlanders broke camp and were working their way north, and it didn't look like Farrell was about to budge. When the club was about to leave Atlanta for New York to start the season, and I was ready to give up and take the money on the table, a letter from Griff arrived. He said that if I joined the team he thought we'd have a grand shot at winning the flag, and although he stayed out of salary squabbles, he felt confident that if I came down from my number Farrell would be willing to meet me at $4,000, which represented a hefty jump in salary for a player with only two years under his belt.

At the bottom as a P.S. he wrote, *Don't forget what happened to John Ganzel.*

When Farrell telegraphed the new offer I took the olive branch, and soon I was on a train heading east. I caught up to the team two days before we opened the season in Washington. Moriarty moved over to third base, the Prince was back where he belonged and all was right with the world. The way we sized up the league, Chicago had been lucky the year before and by not adding any more sock to their lineup weren't likely to repeat as champs. Philly still looked tough, as did Cleveland, but we felt the Highlanders deserved the nod since we boasted two of the top batters in Keeler and myself, and two of the top moundsmen in Orth and Chesbro. We also added a decent third starter in Slow Joe Doyle, one of the biggest stallers in the game but a guy who knew how to win.

We got off to a fair start and after a month-long road trip returned home in June as a .500 ball club. Now we figured to hit our stride, string some wins together and make our bid for the lead. Only trouble was that string kept getting cut. We'd win a couple, lose a couple, and soon found ourselves bogged down in the middle of the pack. We weren't a bad nine; we just weren't as good as we thought we'd be. A lot of smoke and not enough bang. Chesbro lost as many games as he won, a lot of that due to injuries, but it was becoming obvious that he wasn't the big horse he once was. Orth lost his touch, and even though Slow Joe held steady it wasn't enough. At the plate, for the first time in his career Wee Willie Keeler wasn't hitting .300, dipping all the way to the .230's.

I played solid in the field and was still the best hitter on the club, despite a slow start due to rust. I'd sneak the average over .300 but I could never keep it there for very long. After landing the big contract, of course, I was supposed to bat .400 and make the team a winner no matter how hammy my supporting cast. Farrell and the fans acted like the holdout was the cause of the club's problems, that our pitchers would have thrown better and our batters would have hit better if I hadn't been so greedy.

The only saving grace was that across the island the Giants were suffering through a rotten year, too. Both sides preferred not to antagonize the other and for once didn't throw down the challenge of a seven game city series at the end of the campaign. Usually it was the team faring worse in the standings with nothing to lose that goaded the other. The Highlanders started it in 1904, only to have Brush laugh it off when he asked, "Who are these people?" A couple seasons later when it was the Giants out of the race and the Highlanders the only New York club in contention Brush declared that the public *demanded* a city series. Now it was Farrell's turn. "I heard something was going on at the Polo Grounds," he said. "I didn't know it was baseball. I figured it was polo."

Now in 1907 neither club could see much advantage in playing the other. The Giants won more games but fared a lot worse in the standings because the race was tighter in the American League where the Detroit Tigers made the kind of move that the Highlanders expected to, and instead of me it was their young star, Ty Cobb, who appeared destined to accept the torch from Lajoie as the league's best player.

Cobb's rise seemed to tarnish my image, and don't think Farrell failed to point that out. The guy liked to sit in his box behind first base and ride me and the ball club worse than any heckler that the Giants ever sent out during the early days at Hilltop. He was rough enough on me, but he was absolutely brutal on Chesbro, who had tossed too many innings for the club for too long. That sort of service was completely lost on a gorilla like Farrell.

"Je-sus Christ, Chesbro," he'd roar. "Why don't you just serve it up with a ladle?"

Jack would be trying to work out of a jam, his infielders yapping it up to give him support, and he has to hear the goddamn owner of the team slam him in front of the hometown crowd. Soon everybody in the yard is giving the hee-haw to a guy who's working with nothing but a spitter, a two-cent fastball and a shoulder turning purple it's so ripped up inside.

Still, the one who took the most abuse from Farrell was Clark Griffith, who had to field all his stupid suggestions. After almost every home game Griff would get blistered, then handed a bunch of screwy notes that he was supposed to decipher and follow like Scripture in order to revive the fortunes of the team. Hell, if it wasn't for Griff we would have finished lower in the league than we did.

The only player on the Highlanders that Farrell didn't ride was Kid Elberfeld. He always had a soft spot for Kid's fiery disposition, and the fact that the guy was having one of his better years at the plate didn't hurt either. Farrell even liked it when Kid got in Dutch with the umps, often paying a fine out of his own pocket.

It was a thoroughly rotten summer on the field, and I began to doubt my decision to keep playing baseball. It would have been easy to throw in the towel, but I decided that the important thing to remember was all the good I could accomplish by being a big name ballplayer. And the only way I could do that was to get the old batting average over .300 and show Ty Cobb who had the real goods in the league.

To get in some extra work, not to mention a couple extra bucks for my trouble, I played in New Jersey with a semi-pro team on Sundays, when we were still banned from playing in Manhattan. If you used another name everybody looked the other way. After a while it wasn't the extra work or the dough that brought me out to New Jersey. It was a girl.

For the first time in my life, you see, I fell in love.

Chapter 22

U nless a ballplayer was a complete ape he could find a woman hang- ing around the hotel or some nearby watering hole willing to show him a good time. Most of the boys were easy marks for a Baseball Daisy. He could be one of the smartest guys to ever put on the flannel but just to keep some Sadie happy he'd wind up in hock to his ball club, always borrowing on next month's salary. And if he hadn't salted away a nest egg by the time the team had gotten all the use out of him and waived him out of the league, you can bet that girl wasn't going to follow a washup to Oshkosh, Wisconsin. She'd latch onto another arm—before she was washed up herself and some ballplayer waived her out of the league.

I got more than my share of feminine attention, but I always figured I was too smart to let any girl get her claws in me. Then I met Nellie Heffernan. She was just a simple girl from New Jersey and as far as I was concerned she had it all over those Baseball Daisies. She was honest. She was real. She was the kind of girl my brother John would have approved, not the painted up, sharp-tongue type I was usually partial to.

I knew Nellie's brother from a regular poker game I played in. One Sunday afternoon between a doubleheader of semi-pro ball in New Jer- sey he introduced us. She was all dressed in white and I remembered her twisting this frilly parasol. When I said I was pleased to meet her, she flushed and looked away. Nellie was just an Irish Catholic schoolgirl, barely seventeen years of age, and just like that, without having to try, she had me hooked. Compared to the smart crowd I'd been running with in Man- hattan that thought the civilized world ended on the banks of the Hudson, she struck me as refreshing.

After playing ball one Sunday I asked Nellie to go for a carriage ride. I was so sappy over the girl I was glad the horse knew where we were going because I sure didn't. She had copper hair that lapped up the sun and green eyes that could have been stolen from the center of a marble. I wasn't usually shy but it took all my nerve just to press my leg against hers. She didn't seem to mind. Or notice. She was as innocent as an unlicked lamb. Probably the only men she had ever kissed were her dad and uncles. And I wanted her to stay that way. You know, *pure*. Unspoiled by this rotten world.

We began to keep company as much as I could manage. To Nellie I wasn't a baseball star, I wasn't Prince Hal, I was just her caller, her beau, and that was plenty enough for me. At the end of the night I knew the most I could expect was a sanitary peck on the cheek, and even that was a thrill. Yes sir, I was bitten by the bug, but good.

There were plenty of times during that miserable baseball season that only the thought of seeing Nellie pulled me through. And it wasn't just the customers in the stands and the fathead owner I had to contend with. My teammates took to resenting me, in particular Kid Elberfeld, who still remembered me as a dumb-ass rookie swinging a lantern at the back of a train.

After awhile, I have to admit, I started to get a little lusty. I had been used to some regular action with Daisies that only put up resistance for show. With Nellie I was lucky to get an extra hug and even then she made me feel like I was *naughty*. I wondered what my pals would say if they could see how I wilted when the girl scolded me.

Other than going to church Nellie had never been out socially, so as a treat I suggested we hop the ferry into Manhattan.

"You don't have to do that for me," she said.

"I want to."

"It's too expensive."

"Not when you travel with the Prince."

It took some convincing before she let me take her to some of the smart places in the city. The men could care less that Nellie wasn't too sophisticated. That she was a looker was all that registered with them. It was the women who slipped me the disappointed looks, when they weren't busy pitying the poor thing.

"No, Dearie, the 'e' ain't pronounced. It's French."

It's not like these dames were Mrs. Astor or anything, but you wouldn't know it the way they lorded over Nellie, treating her like a speck in the soup. And when they left the party they made sure to whisper loud enough for her to hear, "Don't stay a stranger, Prince."

Nellie took her lumps and declared she found all my friends to be *elegant*.

But I didn't want her picking up all those fake airs. I liked her just the way she was and decided I would only see her in New Jersey. No more dates across the Hudson. I was surprised that she was disappointed.

"Not for myself," she said. "It's just I know how much you like your friends in Manhattan. I wouldn't want you to give that up for me."

"You don't belong there, Nellie."

"I'm sorry if I embarrass you."

"Of course, you don't!" And I spent the rest of the evening reassuring my poor girl.

Well, maybe I was a little touchy about how she didn't fit in. When I wasn't seeing her in Jersey I still liked to rotate on my own. The old crowd accused me of getting religion. Some of them were convinced it was their duty to drive me back into the fold. I tried my best to prove I was the same old wisecracking Prince. I guess they sort of cowed me, and I figured that if they ever learned what meager return I got on all the dough I shelled out on that little package they'd have a sweet old laugh on me.

That's when I started to take a few more liberties with Nellie, much to her dismay.

"Harold, please act like a gentleman."

"I'm no gentlemen. I'm a baseballer," I said. "Didn't your mother ever warn you about my sort?"

"She did. She thinks you're different."

"And where'd she get that notion?"

"From me?"

"And where'd you get it?"

"From *you*."

"Ah, Nellie," I moaned. "I'm trying to be good. You have no idea how hard I try. It's just that I care for you so much."

"And I'm fond of you too. I have to go in now." Then she turns to offer me her cheek.

So I take the ferry back to Manhattan, feeling as randy as ever, hearing in my head my friends cackling with laughter.

I begin to seek out some of the old Daisies, figuring it would ease the pressure, but all it does is give me even more of a red comb for Nellie. She gets more upset with my *mashing*, and I start to take out my frustrations on the other girls.

"Hey, not so rough!" some Daisy would say.

"Why'd you think I invited you here? To sew for me?"

It wasn't like I was a complete heel. I'd usually toss a couple bucks on the bed and tell them to buy a new hat.

I begin to lead something of a double life depending on which side of the Hudson I'm on. One night I'm drunk and roaming the streets of the city like a regular crusher, and the next I'm in Jersey sitting in a porch swing as Nellie's mom serves us lemonade and her father's shadow keeps watch on the window shade. Nellie just chirps away, about what I had no idea, and I'm so worked up I can hardly sit still.

It's only August and that baseball season feels like a nightmare that won't end. Every day the club finds a way to lose; there's nothing I do now that will please the owner, fans and newspapers; my teammates are jealous; and at night I'm being led around by the nose by this slip of a girl. Is it any wonder that I got rougher with those Daisies? I began to cuff them around a little, not as hard as a lot of guys, but hard enough to notice.

"Hey, why'd you do that?"

"Who says I need a reason?"

"I ain't one of your cheap creme puffs. If I get smacked around I want a reason."

"I went oh for four today. Is that good enough?"

"You had a double and a walk. I heard you talking *wid* Mike."

"Who said you could listen in?" And this time I really give her a smack, since she deserved it.

Early in the season I would forget about baseball by thinking about Nellie; now the ballfield became a place to forget about her. But one day when I wasn't even thinking about it, I started to write her name in the dirt around first base with the toe of my spikes.

"Hey, Chase," called Elberfeld from his shortstop position. "Get your fucking head up."

"Yeah, and why don't you get your rotten throws up?"

That was enough to get a hothead like Kid to charge across the field. Lucky for him a big guy like Chesbro was pitching and stepped in the way. Griff wasn't too pleased and pulled me aside later.

"I know this has been a tough stretch, Hal. Just remember you're a professional and give it all you got. That's good enough for me."

"Sure, Griff. Thanks," I said. But what I was thinking was, *Mind your own business you old washup.*

Chapter 23

One evening, just before the ball club was to make our last western swing, Nellie's folks attended a parish supper and left us alone. They would have made us go along, only I had to leave early.

"Harold, I've been meaning to ask you something."

"What's that?"

We were rocking on the porch swing and I'm practically wrestling with myself I'm so het-up. Already I've dropped my hand on her knee only to have Nellie peel it off without so much as missing a word of whatever it was she was prattling on about. I figured it was time to give it another try.

"You don't have to tell me if you don't want to. Harold!" She slapped the back of my hand, gives me a disapproving look, then gets up to fetch a pitcher of lemonade.

I follow her inside and take up the settee in the front parlor where we have our drinks and her little Scotch terrier, Coco, naps at her feet.

"What I was saying—well, I was just wondering."

"What?" I lay my hand on her knee again and this time she doesn't buck me off.

"You don't have to tell me if you don't want to."

"Tell you what?"

She bites her lip and looks down at Coco. "How much money do you make playing baseball?"

I was too surprised to say anything at first.

"I'm just curious. I suppose I could have asked my brother. They must pay you rather well."

"You're just curious?"

"A little."

"Well, I'm a curious sort myself."

I reach under the hem of her dress, throw her back onto the settee and run my arm clear up her petticoat. I'm in an instant rage. Nellie is terrified and begins to squeal. I cover her mouth with my free hand and begin to work her with the other. Coco, the little rat, wakes up, starts to bark and snap at my ankles. All I can think about is how this little bitch has made a fool out of me, and nobody, especially no goddamn girl, even if she is the slickest Daisy a ballplayer ever met, can make a fool out of the Prince. I try to keep her quiet, shake off that dog, hike up her dress and fumble with my belt.

That's when the grandfather clock struck the hour to scare the hell out of me. I look over at it and am startled to catch a glimpse of a man's face. I let go of her before I realize it's just my own reflection in the hallway mirror. But the spell was over. I hitched up my trousers while Nellie, heaving with tears, clutched Coco to her face. The runt kept barking at me.

"Come on, Nellie," I said. It's not like I finished or anything. "You know you shouldn't have asked me that question."

She just looked up at me with a face so full of horror that it threw me for a second. Maybe she really was just curious. Maybe she didn't know any better.

I pulled at my hair, unable to think. I turned and caught another look in the hallway mirror that almost floored me. It was just a momentary thing but I thought I saw my big brother John. Only, it wasn't the way I remembered him. He was no longer a young man, he had wrinkles about his eyes, and he was dressed like some kind of cheap whorehouse piano player. No jacket, just a flashy vest, with garters on his sleeves. A real sport. A bad egg. A boy gone wrong. It was just a flash thing, because I realized quick enough that it was my own reflection again and this was how I dressed now that I was the big shot ballplayer. Now that I was the Prince.

What had this girl done to me? I was seeing nightmares with my eyes wide open. I reached for my roll and began to peel off some bills when I caught myself. What was I going to do, toss Nellie a couple bucks and tell her to buy a new hat? I just hustled the hell out of there, leaving Nellie to cry and Coco to snarl and snap at my shadow.

❖

I was still pretty shook up when the ball club arrived in Detroit for a four-game set. The grandstands were crammed full of cranks in love with their young Tigers. Hughie Jennings really had his side cooking and they wasted no time going after us. In the first inning Cobb knocked in a pair of runs with a bingle. Standing on first he's so fired up you could almost see steam rolling out of his nose.

Because I'm feeling out of sorts, I have this urge to talk to somebody, to *share* something with a fellow human being. Even if it was with someone as disagreeable as Ty Cobb.

"Nice hit, Ty." I took up my position to hold him on.

"Fuck you, Chase." Cobb's attention was fixed on Chesbro, who's wetting one up on the mound, stalling for time and looking to find a way out of the early jam.

"Really, I mean it," I said. "That was a sweet hit."

"I mean it, too. Fuck you, Chase."

"You're not a very happy person, are you, Ty." I had no idea why that came out, and the sincere way that I said it must have caught Cobb by surprise. He dropped his guard and looked up and over at me. For an instant we weren't two big league ballplayers, a couple of dogs scrapping over a bone, we were just a couple of young men who didn't have a goddamn clue how we dropped in the middle of this world or what it all amounted to in the end.

He was just a confused southern hick playing ball up north, scared to death that somebody might see through all his tough talk and bold ways and maybe hurt his feelings.

We both got snapped back to reality when Chesbro, unaware we were having this moment over at first base and desperate to get out of the inning, spun and fired the pill to me. I was as surprised as Cobb, but I was facing the play, my instincts took over, I snatched the ball and dropped the tag on the guy as he tried to scramble back.

"Okay, asshole," he sneered. "You're in my book."

"Oh yeah, I'm shaking, Reb. I'm shaking like a leaf."

That play broke me out of the mulligrubs over Nellie. What was the big deal, anyway? I decided I should be willing to meet her halfway. I'd forgive her for pulling that chorus girl stunt asking about my money, and she'd give me a pass on the rough stuff. I figured I'd just act like nothing ever happened, she'd take the hint, and we'd forget all about it.

So on the Sunday the ball club returned from the road I went out to Jersey City to pay my girl a visit. I found her rocking on the porch swing with Coco asleep on her lap. She was looking awful glum.

I pushed open the gate. "So who stole your jump rope, kid?"

She barely looked up at me, offering not even the promise of a smile.

I walked up the porch steps and leaned against a post. Coco, the rotten bowzer, woke up and began to growl.

"I guess you heard I raised my batting average twelve ticks. Not bad for the road, huh?"

"I'm sure I could care less how you fare with your baseball playing." She tucked Coco under her arm and marched to the screen door. I stepped in her way. "Kindly allow me to pass, Mr. Chase."

"Come on. Can't we sit down and talk things over?"

"I don't believe there is anything between us to talk about."

It had only been three weeks since I saw the girl but it seemed like I forgot how really beautiful she was. I was smitten all over again. I was willing to say anything, do anything, *be* anything just to have things back the way they were.

"Oh, Nellie," I sighed, "Please don't hate me. Because if you do I'll turn so sour on life I'm afraid what will become of me."

The words came from my heart and she must have felt it.

"I don't hate you. I want to hit you. I want to hurt you. But I don't hate you."

"Good, because I think ... I think I love you, Nellie. I mean it. I love you more than anything. More than baseball itself."

"It's a sin to lie."

"It's no lie. I love you. And I never said that to a girl before."

"You mean you never *meant* it before. I'm not that silly."

"I know I've been bad. But I want to be good, more than you could ever know."

Coco's yapping left no doubt what he thought of my sincerity.

"Go if you have to. I understand," I said.

I stepped aside to give Nellie a chance to go inside the house and give me the brush-off. She took a step, opened the screen door, paused a moment, then dropped Coco on the floor and locked him inside.

She looked at me and said, "Lord help us both."

Chapter 24

Somehow it just got taken for granted that Nellie and I were engaged to be married. I came over to her house for dinner one night and her mom cries at the sight of me and her dad is pumping my hand like I'm a slot machine. Even my old pal her brother is there to slap my shoulder black and blue. Not even so much as a "So we hear you two are getting serious." Her folks didn't even seem to mind that I hadn't asked for permission. Nellie gave me a shy little smile to ask me to forgive her, but it was all right with me. I wanted to marry the girl more than anything in the world.

Her folks sent a notice to the papers and naturally the New York dailies found out about it and went nuts. Since there was no pennant race to yammer about, the sports writers couldn't resist playing the society page angle. Seeing how Prince Hal was getting married it had to be covered as a royal wedding, not that there wasn't a lot of baseball speculation on how marriage might affect my play. The general opinion was that it would do me some good, that it might actually be just the tonic to settle down a wild colt like myself.

With Nellie at my side I figured I could get my life back on track and contribute to making the world a better place. Just becoming a devoted husband, and maybe a father, would go a long way toward that end.

And then I started to run around again. I couldn't expect Nellie to satisfy my needs until our wedding night, so it seemed like the thoughtful thing to do was to turn to a Daisy for relief. I don't even remember the gal's name. I don't know if I ever knew it. She gave me a headache, I remember that much.

"Honey, you're a caution!" The Daisy must have said that once a minute. When I reached my limit I told her to can it. She thought I was kidding and I boiled over.

"Don't you understand plain English, you slich?"

"Hey! Nobody talks to me like that."

All in a huff she threw off the bedclothes and began to gather her things. Her back was pimpled. Her underthings were yellow. Everything about her began to make me sick. Her chirpy voice. Her peroxide hair. The fruity perfume she swam in. I couldn't wait for her to dress and clear out. But the more disgusted I got the more excited I got. I grabbed her by the waist and wrestled her back on the bed. She cussed and slapped at me, kicked her chunky legs, but she wasn't much of a match for a fine conditioned ballplayer. I pinned her down and started to grind away. I had her by the throat and choked her while I went at it. She soon went limp and gave up the fight. When I had finished I was panting so hard it was like I had just finished circling the bases on an inside-the-park home run. I collapsed in a heap beside her body.

She opened her eyes. "Honey, you are a caution."

Near the end of that rotten baseball season I began to get cold feet over marrying Nellie. I was confused and counting the days until the end of the season, just trying to mind my own business, when one day I'm in the clubhouse reading a newspaper and Kid Elberfeld comments, "Maybe the team would be better off if you stopped reading about yourself so much."

"I was only trying to find mention of you, Kid. I hope you're still with the club."

"I actually play for the club and not myself. It just finishes me the way you get away with all your tricks."

"Maybe you should sign on as manager."

"If I did I'd fine you so much you wouldn't be able to afford a shit sandwich."

"I'd shoot myself before I'd play ball for a hunk of cheese like you."

By now we're going at it jaw to jaw and our teammates have to step it. Kid swears he'll meet me anywhere at any time, the usual hot talk that occurs on most every losing ball club. Generally it's a matter of letting off steam and in a day or two, after a win, you laugh about it over a beer. But not this time. Not with Kid and me.

The club managed to finish out the season without any murders or suicides being committed, we even won the final four, which made parting for the winter a lot easier to take. Most of the boys had their trunks packed and tickets purchased days in advance, eager to get out of town. I was one of them. Nellie expected me to stay to plan our wedding, and here I was running away.

Again I finished out the West Coast season by tearing up that California State League. That was nothing new so why lose a button, right? So long as I was treating I had plenty of friends. I holed up in San Jose for the winter, passing the time with cards, pool and general tom-catting around. I didn't even give Nellie a thought.

It was just after Christmas, when I was shooting pool and having some beer and toast for breakfast, that someone drew my attention to a notice in a week-old New York newspaper.

Nellie Heffernan has finally received permission from her parents to take the train west to meet her fiancé, Hal Chase of the New York Highlanders, in San Jose to be married without delay.

Chapter 25

I never knew the New York newspapers to go out of their way to tell the truth, but they generally got some facts straight and I had to figure that Nellie was on her way to nab me, likely escorted by some well-armed relations. I thought about beating it for the hills, but let's face it I wasn't the kind cut out for the woods. What was I going to do, cook for myself? And the desire to run didn't last long. In a way it was a relief that she was coming after me. I knew I was going to have to deal with her sooner or later, and as I looked around the pool hall at my so-called buddies, all of them bleary-eyed from drink at ten in the morning, I realized how miserable I was with this crowd. How could I keep allowing people to drag me off of the straight and narrow? Thank God, I thought, that Nellie was coming to save me.

I wired her brother to learn what train she was taking, and I was waiting for her at the station, dressed to the nines and cradling a bunch of flowers. When I caught sight of her my heart practically stopped dead. Even though she was dressed on the prim side for the long train ride and her hair was pinned up to make her look older and more seasoned, there was no hiding her looks. Not expecting me to meet her, she looked past me for a porter to help with her bags. Then she recognized me.

I took off my hat and walked towards her. I had never felt so in love and ashamed in my life—at least since the last time we went through this business. This time I couldn't pretend that nothing had happened, that I had an innocent explanation for everything.

"I—I—I'm sorry." Her eyes were so fierce I had to look down. "You shouldn't forgive me, Nellie. I don't know why I have to act so wicked."

I stood like that, head bowed, for I don't know how long before she said, "There, there," and drew my head to her shoulder.

Then she whispered, "You know what I could really use? A drink."
And the way she said it I knew she didn't mean lemonade.

So I picked up a bottle and took her back to the room I booked. While
I poured the drinks she laid a suitcase on the bed, opened it and removed
a small revolver.

"Were you afraid of running into the James Gang?" I said.

Then she pointed it in my face.

"Don't be fooling with firearms."

"Maybe I came to shoot you."

"That thing would be lucky to cut through a vest coat."

"I'm aiming at your head, not your wallet."

"How could you even think of shooting such a handsome head?"

"Actually," she said, lowering the gun and tossing it in the suitcase,
"I was going to shoot you in the eye."

"Any particular one?"

"Your batting eye." She began to undo her bodice. "I'm not as stupid
as you think."

All of a sudden my schoolgirl is stepping out of her dress.

"You're full of surprises today, Nellie."

"Shut up." She took me by the hand and pulled me down on the bed,
something I had dreamt of for months and now I felt queer about.

"Can't we just talk a little?"

"What's there to talk about?"

Maybe I had corrupted a sweet, young girl, but who stays innocent
forever? Not girls that looked like her. And it's not like she could keep up
the tough act for very long. The next day she was back to being Nellie again,
all giggles and curls—but maybe that was just an act now, too. On New
Year's Day, 1908, Nellie Heffernan became Mrs. Hal Chase. It was just a
small ceremony with a couple of pals to serve as witnesses and a preacher
we hired for a couple of bucks. He couldn't resist saying a few words, all
of them directed at me.

"When you take your wedding vows, it's nothing to sneeze at," he
said. "You're asking for the very curtain of Heaven to open up to let your
words be heard."

He had me going, so that when I said I'd take Nellie as my wife I was
never more serious in my life about giving my word—at least not since
my brother died. I felt good about myself and happy enough, but it was
only later, when we went out to supper to celebrate, that it really hit me.
I began to feel lightheaded, I got chicken skin, then this tingling sensation that began deep in my bones, came to the surface and danced on the

ends of my hair. I had to shudder it was so electric. Maybe that preacher had been right.

It's not like I started to hear voices or see angels or anything like that. It was just this prickly feeling. And when I thought about something and it was on the mark, I'd begin to tingle and I knew the Lord was giving me the thumbs up. *Now's your chance to change, young man. You have a helpmate. You have a reason to mend your ways.*

"What are you smiling about?" Nellie asked.

I guess I was smiling like a kid. She was too, so I figured she must be going through the same thing. And she should have, being a lot more religious than me. Was this what they meant by wedded bliss? This joy was mine and the only thing that was in the way that I could see was baseball. I mean, if I finally gave up the game would this be my reward?

The feeling stuck with me for the next day. When we went out for a walk in the evening to watch the sun set I swear it was the most beautiful thing I had ever seen. Everything was beautiful. How could I have been so blind?

"Don't you want to just stay here forever?" I said.

"I hope the sun never goes down."

"Let's stay here, Sweetie."

"All night?"

"No, let's settle here. I'll find a job. I'll find something more suited to me than playing baseball. I don't know what but with you by my side and God's help—"

"Give up baseball?"

"I'm ready to. Yeah, I am."

"And live here?"

"Isn't it beautiful country?"

"And what about me?" She was angry all of a sudden and I didn't know why. "I didn't wait all my life to escape Jersey City just to waste away in the middle of nowhere. I want to live in Manhattan. I want to do things. But no, you always have to think about yourself."

The setting sun was replaced by her tears. I felt terrible and wanted to comfort her. By the time I was through I promised her everything, an apartment in Manhattan, the works. That meant, of course, I'd have to keep playing for the Highlanders so we could afford the kind of life and meet the kind of people she desired.

And there went my bliss. The feeling was gone. And there went my chance to change. Somewhere over the left field fence.

Chapter 26

That year I decided not to hold out for more dough. When Farrell mailed me a contract calling for the same salary, I signed and sent it right back. After my last season I knew I was in no position to haggle and was lucky Farrell didn't try to give me a cut.

When I reported to spring training I sent Nellie to New York to set up house. I was glum about putting on that uniform again. At camp they saw my moping around as just more of the Prince's swell-headed attitude, like I felt I was too good to get in shape like the rest of the club. I didn't try to change anybody's opinions. Whatever they wanted to think was fine with me.

Considering how poorly the club had fared, the smart money expected Farrell to clean house, at least dump the manager. But for once the guy held his fire and gave Griff another chance, and he passed on the vote of confidence to us players. One thing you had to give to Griff was that he stuck with his boys. Maybe too long. Being an old pitcher he should have seen that Chesbro and Orth were spent, yet here he was declaring to the newspapers that the pair was still the best around. And just to prove his point he didn't look to acquire any arms to replace them. He said he was pleased with the batting order, too.

So we were pretty much the same ball club that proved a disappointment the year before, and a lot of people had to wonder why Griff stayed pat. When we opened the season of 1908 and jumped off to a tremendous start, the same people declared Griff a genius. The defending American League Champion Tigers lingered at the gate as we won the first fifteen out of twenty games. The schedule was in our favor; still, we were knocking the stuffing out of the ball, running the bases like fiends and scoring a ton of runs. That helped to cover over the fact that our pitching staff was already springing some leaks. Griff was worried enough to finally start beating the bushes for some live arms.

Our supporters were high on our chances, not just because of the fast start, but because they felt we finally had the missing piece to the puzzle—a good luck charm. My wife. Everyone was captivated by the pretty girl who had roped in the Prince, and since the team was winning it didn't take much imagination to link her to it, especially since she attended every game and sat in the same seat. One day she took sick and stayed home—we got clobbered and that cinched it. Nobody felt right about starting a game unless Nellie was comfortable in her lucky seat.

Most clubs had charms or mascots. The year before we had Johnny, a one-armed bat boy who had crippled himself by jumping off the back of a moving train, which was a popular trick with the city kids. The way ballplayers saw it, when something horrible happened to a person they deserved a payback. It was the law of averages at work. Maybe by taking on an unfortunate mascot some of the good breaks might rub off. So teams accumulated more than their share of mangled kids and nut cases. At least our charm was pleasant to look at.

Nellie held up her end of the bargain. It was when we hit the road for a long stretch in June that things went sour. First Wid Conroy sprains an ankle, next Elberfeld takes a deep spiking, Lucky Glade—one of our new pitchers—comes down with a mystery ailment, Keeler tears something in his wrist, Kleinow gets suspended for spitting at an umpire, and Hogg is benched because he still hasn't gotten into condition and looks like a pregnant seal. And just when the dark cloud looks like it might be about to lift, Niles is overcome by the heat in Cleveland and almost dies on us. Lucky Glade then returned to the hill only to decide not to cover first base on a ground ball because of the heat; it costs us a ball game and him a twenty buck fine. Rather than pay up, he went home to Iowa, never to pitch in the fast company again.

We started June in first place. By the fifteenth of the month we had dropped to sixth. Actually, all of the eastern clubs were having trouble in the West, a fact which did little to console Frank Farrell. He hopped a train to join the club and lend fuel to the fire.

The way the season was shaping up it was making the previous campaign seem somewhat pleasant. There's nothing worse than to play in a town like New York when you're practically crowned champs in May only to watch the nails pop out in June. The best we could hope for when we got home were empty stands or maybe a newspaper strike.

We stopped playing like a team and started to act like a bunch of guys looking for cover. Maybe I didn't have the best of attitudes, but the worst of the "me-first" ballplayers on the club was Kid Elberfeld. Sure, Ganley from Washington tore up Kid's shin in an absolute bush league take-out slide at second and you have to allow a guy a chance to heal up, but it seemed like the more the team lost the worse was Kid's limp. After a while he was hobbling around like a peg-leg pirate. The least he could do was encourage his teammates from the bench, yet he seemed to enjoy watching us screw up. The way I figured it, Kid had become the crippled mascot on our bench, our very own bad luck charm.

So Farrell finally catches up to the club in St. Louis. He and Griff generally got along, mostly because Griff had been around the game long enough to never forget who signed the checks. That's when Hogg got into the act and went directly to Farrell to complain about Griff not giving him a fair chance to pitch. He just knew he could carry the team on his shoulders if given the chance. Griff tried to explain that Hogg was still in no condition to face major league hitters, but Farrell ordered him to unsuspend Wild Bill and start him against the Browns on the very next afternoon.

Well, Hogg got slaughtered. The Brownies, who never hit much, decided to make up for lost ground all in one afternoon. They belted the ball all over the lot on Bill. He was so tired from backing up bases and dodging bullets through the box that it looked like the slob might do Niles one better and actually succumb from heat and exhaustion. Just when he looked ready to collapse, Griff walked out to the mound and us infielders gathered around.

Wild Bill was panting and watering the hill with his sweat.

"Well, are you satisfied?" Griff asked him.

"I'd be doing okay if I could only get some support in the field."

That was enough for Griff to leave him in to absorb a few more runs. Griff walked out again.

"Well?"

This time Bill answered, "You're the boss."

"Take a shower." Griff took the ball and patted him on the rump. "You stink."

After the game it was Farrell's turn to lay into Hogg for lying to him about his chances.

"Re-suspend the worthless bastard!" Farrell decided to air his gripe in front of the entire club.

"I'll suspend a man for not getting into condition or for disobeying orders," Griff said, "but not for poor play when he gave an effort."

"You call that an effort?"

"He tried his best. He was game. He should have never been run out there."

"He threw the ball like a goddamn washer woman."

"He threw as well as I told you he would."

"Are you talking back to me, Griff?"

"I'm simply stating the facts, Mr. Farrell."

Farrell stormed out of the clubhouse, passing through a pack of newspapermen. That's when the rumors really began to heat up that Clark Griffith's days of running the New York Highlanders were numbered.

Chapter 27

The word going around was that Farrell was looking to replace Clark Griffith with a player off the team. Since I was the best the Highlanders had, I figured I should claim the prize. Here was my chance at management. And *respectability*. Maybe it wasn't banking or manufacture, but it was still management and that makes a difference in this world. Look at the Giants' Mugsy McGraw, blowing around town with all the big names in New York. Those sort of connections could really increase the prospects of an ambitious man. In America you could parlay opportunity into anything you desired. If the breaks went your way, even the White House could be your address. In any case, there was a lot of good a man could accomplish once he gained respectability.

When we arrived in Philadelphia for the final series in a long road trip Farrell seemed content to at least wait until we returned home before making a change. Then we dropped a tough one after battling back to take a lead in the eighth, only to watch the A's nip us at the wire. In the evening Tom Davis, our club secretary, spread the news that Griff had just checked out of the hotel and that Mr. Farrell was calling us together in one of the meeting rooms.

I showed up to find Farrell already passing out cigars. The boys were laughing, acting like there was something to celebrate, like it was all Griff's fault we had tumbled in the standings, and now that we were rid of the guy we could finally set sail. They were all sucking up to the fat blowhard, accepting his smokes and stashing them away for later.

Everybody's standing around, puffing away like the mills of Youngstown, Ohio, when Farrell says it's time to get down to business.

"You all pretty much know the score," he said. "Clark Griffith is no longer associated with the ball club, owing to poor health. He asked to be relieved of his duties so he could return home to Montana for a well-deserved respite. It was with considerable regret that I finally gave in to his importunities."

The boys puffed and mumbled among themselves how there had really been no choice in the matter.

"Nobody tried harder to win or took losing tougher than Griff. He will be sorely missed, but we must carry on. I'm sure he would have wanted it that way."

Farrell took a long, serious look at his cigar, allowing a moment of silence for Griff, then threw back the flap of his coat, stuck a thumb in a vest pocket and struck a pose like he was Howard Taft.

"The way I look at this baseball season, we're only in the middle of the back stretch and there's plenty of track to go. You boys know of my involvement in the race game. I've owned my share of winners and, I admit, to my share of dogs, too."

Farrell gave a wink to let the boys know they could chuckle at his expense.

"And if there's one thing I've learned at the plant it's that no matter how choice the horse flesh, if you don't have the right jockey in the saddle you ain't got crowbait. Take Roseben, for instance, the finest mount in my stable. At first I gave the ride to Johnny Wise. Don't get me wrong, Johnny is one of the busiest little monkeys in the game, but no matter how hard he tried he couldn't bring home the goods with Roseben. I gave Tim Morris a shot and all of a sudden I'm spending as much time in the winner's circle as the crapper. You see what I'm getting at, boys?"

"Yeah," says Keeler. "Our new skipper is Tim Morris."

Everyone starts to laugh, only Farrell doesn't get the joke, so they quickly gag on their cigars.

"What I'm saying is that Griff came close but he never took the bunting and I decided it was time for a change—because his health wouldn't permit, that is. I think I know the kind of man we need in the saddle. Someone who already knows the personnel. As a matter of fact he's standing in this room right now."

Farrell turns to deliver his words straight at me.

"As a spectator I've always admired the way he plays the game, not just for his skill but for the ginger he brings to the field. I have complete confidence that he's the man to bring the Highlanders through the pack to take the glory at the wire. Of course I refer to Kid Elberfeld."

The guys are starting to slap Kid on the back and pump his mitt even before Farrell has said his name. It's like I'm the only one surprised. Make that, *shocked*. Everybody on the club must have known that Kid was being named manager over me. Hell, the only reason for this floor show was to break the news to the Prince in front of everyone so he wouldn't throw a cat fit. And the way the boys were yukking it up and looking at me sideways, I knew they were happy to see me knocked down a peg or two.

I couldn't believe that Farrell would tap that fucking squirt over anyone, not just me. Kid was scrappy, I always gave him that, but he wasn't much smarter than the foul pole and never could manage his temper. He had antagonized every umpire in the league for so long we were certain to never get a break from that quarter. And anybody with a doughnut for a brain should have been able to see through that bum leg routine. Kid had been selling out the club for weeks and now he gets rewarded for it.

After accepting all of the congratulations, Kid Elberfeld takes the floor with a cigar jammed in the corner of his mouth. Even though he's dressed for the occasion he still looked like a punk pickpocket.

"When Mr. Farrell informed me that Griff was unable to continue his duties and asked me to take over the ball club, I'd be a liar if I said I thought I was the best man for the job. I ain't."

That got everybody to crying, "No, no, that's not true!"

"I told him I was just one of the boys and that I might be too easy on you, but he asked me to think it over and maybe confide in some of yous. Well, it was your encouragement that made all the difference and I agreed to give it my best shot."

A rousing cheer went up. *Hip! Hip!*

Then Kid looks me square in the eye. "I want to make a pledge to you guys. I'll stand shoulder to shoulder with you during the rough times, but in return I expect everyone, and I mean *everyone*, to give his all in every inning of every game, no matter what the score, to make the Highlanders a winning side. There will be no special cases on my ballclub."

With that the biggest cheer of the night went up. Then Farrell announced he was springing for drinks at the hotel bar. No nickel beers around the corner tonight.

I downed a quick one to be polite, then left to give the boys plenty of time to cluck about me behind my back. The idiots had no clue what they were getting with Kid Elberfeld. But I knew. And I wouldn't forget the Judas act they pulled on me. They were in my book. Every last one of them. They were in my book.

Chapter 28

The first day under Kid's command the boys came out to the ballpark with the kind of spunk they hadn't shown for weeks. That's the way it generally is in baseball—change managers and you get a quick kick in the pants. The energy might last a while, maybe even a couple of weeks, but a ball club will soon find its level. On this particular afternoon the Highlanders battled Philly for the full nine and into extra innings before the game had to be called on account of darkness. A no-decision. And that was our sprint for glory with Kid Elberfeld in the stirrups. We finished up the road trip by losing to the A's three to nothing, returned home and kept right on losing. We might win on occasion, then drop them in bunches. Six. Seven. Eleven losses in a row. There was no use spurring that plug. By the middle of July we settled to last place and watched as the rest of the league disappeared around the turn. Farrell stayed clear of the park, so at least we didn't have to put up with him. The newspapers reported that he was spending more time at the racetrack, where at least if his animals refused to cooperate he could have them shot.

Our loyal supporters weren't so loyal now, and the newspapers suggested Farrell give the team back to Baltimore. Even Nellie stopped coming out, because the handful of people who did attend the games were plenty brutal in their comments. I said I didn't mind that she stayed home, but the truth is I felt she should have been there to support me. Hell, I had been ready to quit baseball, so it was really for her sake I had to suffer the scorn of an entire city.

Life in the dugout was miserable. As a player Kid Elberfeld had taken losing as well as you could expect, but now that he was the manager he took everything personal, like the players intended to make him look bad. And don't think that the power of being in charge didn't go straight to his empty little head. He wasn't content to just tell you where you went wrong on the field, all of a sudden he became an expert on *everything*. He corrects the boys on their table manners, advises on how much to tip, suggests what to wear on any occasion, and teaches how to invest your money like he does. Whatever the subject Kid would straighten you out, and not exactly with world diplomacy. If there was a way to make a player feel lower than a snake's chin, Kid would find it. A pitcher might make a mistake and Kid would march out to the mound to give a public demonstration on the proper way to hold on a runner, as every mug in the park is howling at the poor guy who has to stand there and take it.

Instead of trusting us to call our own plays like veterans were used to, Kid started to signal everything from the bench. We got so distracted trying to read his signs that were are all mixed in with his ticks caused by the stress of being in charge that we screwed up even more. His strategy was pretty loopy, anyway. When it backfired, which was more often than not, it was never his fault. No sir! *You* missed the sign. *You* didn't execute. So *you* take the blame. Just to completely cover his ass Kid began to give more than one sign on the same play, so you weren't sure if he wanted you to bunt the man over or swing away. If you called time to ask which one he wanted, he'd chew you out and still leave you just as ignorant. Finally you picked your poison, knowing that if you came through he would grab all the credit, and if you failed he'd fine your ass for not paying attention.

Kid went on a fining binge, showing a true genius in that direction. At first he stuck to the usual crimes. Not running out a grounder cost you. Showing up late for morning practice cost you. Then he steered into uncharted territory. He fined players for making errors in the field and for not hitting in the pinch. Pretty soon it cost you if you didn't come up with the outstanding play when the club needed it. The boys got so nervous about botching a play they tried to avoid the ball. That's when Kid turned an eye to our off-the-field conduct, fining us for using the butter knife by mistake or coming to dinner with a wrinkled shirt.

It didn't take long before Kid hadn't a friend on the club. All the players that had supported his selection now longed for the return of Clark Griffith. When Kid walked into a room the place turned as quiet as church, since the general conversation was how much everybody hated his guts. Even his oldest pals, Keeler and Chesbro, stopped talking to him.

Naturally, Kid and me had a special relationship. I was the one guy he didn't fine or tell how to dress. If he didn't recognize that I was the star player, Farrell did, and I figured part of the deal was that Kid had to find a way to get along with me. And there wasn't much he could say about my game, since a couple of days into his reign I turned an ankle and took to the bench to heal up. I was soon ready to go but I kept begging out of the lineup, limping around the clubhouse like a Civil War veteran.

"How's the ankle?" he'd ask me every day.

"About the same. How's the shin?"

He hadn't returned to the lineup yet himself. After telling everybody how to play the game and fining his old pals into the poor house, Kid knew damn well that once he kicked a ball everyone would have a swell laugh at his expense.

"Maybe you should see a doctor," he said.

"And who's going to pay the bill, the ballclub? That's a laugh."

"Well, give it a couple more days."

I'd give it a couple more days and still say my ankle wasn't getting any better. Finally Kid declared that his shin wasn't coming around and that he's all in for the year. That ended the stalemate. The next day I took the field again, but mostly because I was bored watching from the bench.

One afternoon at Hilltop someone sitting in Farrell's personal box calls me over.

"Remember me?" he says. "Fat Jack Delaney. I'm the guy that rescued you from Clucktown. Just thought I'd take in the funeral."

"It's a great place to catch a nap. We won't wake you."

"I thought we might also discuss a little business."

"How's that?"

"The smart boys think you're laying down on Elberfeld. They think you wouldn't be overly upset if the club doesn't win another game this season."

"Is that why Frank sent you, to find out?"

"Farrell can choke on a chicken bone for all I care."

"So why do you care?"

"Think about this, Prince. A body who lays down on a selective basis can stand to make a tidy sum."

I had nothing more to say. I turned and marched straight back to first base. I knew what Jack was asking.

That afternoon I played as hard as I did all season. I dove all over the lot, bore down on every at-bat, and cheered on my teammates like I hadn't done for two years. Even though we still lost six to three and I ended the game with a fly out to center, I could at least feel good about my effort.

I was trotting out to the clubhouse when Kid caught up to me. His shin seemed to have undergone a miraculous recovery.

"Nice game, Chase," he says in this real snide voice. "Real nice effort."

"What are you getting at?"

"Just that you're the cute one."

"Aw, go douse your head in kerosene."

"That'll cost you ten, mister."

"Make it twenty so I can call you a little asshole."

"You must think I'm blind as a post."

"No, just dumb as one."

"I saw who you were chatting up before the game."

"Are you looking to get punched?"

"Try it and Ban Johnson will fix your ass for me."

I was burned up pretty good. I busted my tail for a last place team only to get fined and have my honesty questioned.

The next day I asked around for Fat Jack and got the address to a pool hall in the Bronx where he conducted business.

I found Jack by himself, hunched over a table running a rack. He knocks a long shot, a banker, and I field the cue ball before it has a chance to hit the rail.

He looks up and smiles. "I thought I recognized those sure hands."

Chapter 29

There was a general feeling in America that somewhere along the way we had lost the trail. For years people had been abandoning the farms and small towns for the lure of the big cities and all its evils: the graft and kickbacks of crooked politicians, the white slave traders, the dope rings, the filthy, crowded tenements. The only god that America really served was the Almighty Buck. Some people, like Billy Sunday, were bent on reviving the land. They didn't have enough clout yet to take on John Barleycorn but they had enough to prohibit something. Like horse racing. And so one morning we wake up to discover that the New York state legislature had decided to close the tracks.

Farrell and his Tammany Hall pals fought back, but the upstate politicians had the votes, and in the summer of 1908 the racetracks were chained and padlocked. What this meant was that in the middle of a baseball season there was a bunch of gamblers like Fat Jack Delaney looking for action to replace the ponies, because they weren't about to transfer their operations to Baltimore or Louisville.

Of course, there had always been betting on baseball. Ban Johnson was no dope, and after the track closings he ordered the owners to police their yards. The owners were no dopes, either, and didn't want to antagonize some of their best paying customers. Particular sections of the grandstands were known thieves' markets where operators conducted business, although side betting between friends and strangers took place all over the park. So to make things look good the cops made a show of escorting a few of the derbied boys out one gate, only to let them come back in another. That's how baseball nipped another problem in the bud.

They had to know that some party would try to get a player to rig the outcome of a game. It was common enough with horse races and prize fights, and around World Series time there was never a shortage of rumors about a fix in the works. The club owners realized that a major gambling scandal could kill the game, since it had almost happened once before. Thirty years earlier four Louisville Grays were caught fixing games and to restore public confidence had to be banned from professional baseball for life. Now the owners made a few ejections, the thieves markets keep on thriving, and everybody pretended that fixing a baseball game was as impossible as splitting the atom.

The one I blame the most is Ban Johnson, an old newspaper man, for selling the public a bill of goods on "clean baseball." He made it like a religion and a birthright for every American. According to the Gospel of Clean Baseball the game had come down to us as pure, and it was the duty of those exceptional club owners who were entrusted with steward-ship to make sure it remained that way.

The truth is that all they ever cared about was *profitable* baseball. When Ban Johnson challenged the National League he used clean base-ball as a wedge. He saw that the game had a less-than-savory reputation and that if you could get women and professional men out to the ballpark you'd stand to make a hell of a lot more money. He blasted the National League for clinging to "quarter ball." That was the price of admission that permitted you to suck down booze at the mahogany bar in right field and place your bets with the bookies. Johnson's new league eliminated the open-air saloons and charged fifty cents, a price the better classes were willing to pay in order to help drive out the riffraff.

So how did the Nationals answer the challenge? They tried to fix games themselves, not for the gambling but to control costs and maintain their profits. The idea was called Syndicate Ball. It was going to put the game on a solid business basis just like the coal, steel and the railroad industries. All the owners would pool their assets and in return receive shares of stock in the syndicate. The players would just be workers, divided up among the clubs, paid on a scale and transferred across the league depending on need and the whim of the board of directors. Pretty soon you start moving players around to make sure you have exciting pennant races. And what comes after that? One team wins and another team loses as part of a master plan. You're fixing games.

Old man Spaulding himself, the founder of the National League, had to come out of retirement to squelch that syndicate plan, but not before there was a civil war among the Nationals that allowed the Ameri-can League to gain an equal footing. Although Spaulding hated Ban John-son they agreed on one thing: baseball was good. Too bad most of the country still considered the game about as wholesome as a carnival peep show.

It was when the leagues signed the National Agreement that they really played up the clean baseball angle. But now, a few years later, the gamblers were moving from the racetracks to the ball parks, like rats changing ships. Other than some token arrests, how did the stewards of baseball reply to the threat? By telling the suckers a fairy tale.

After years of painstaking research a commission set up by the great Spaulding himself on behalf of Organized Baseball announced their scientific conclusion about the true origins of the national pastime. The game of baseball was invented in the village of Cooperstown in upstate New York in 1833. The scientific evidence for this was a letter from an old coot named Graves who claimed he was present on the day a young man named Abner Doubleday unveiled his plans for a new way of life. Baseball.

When I heard the news I wondered who the owners thought they were fooling. Whoever heard of this whistle stop, let alone the inventor? I figured that story would get laughed out of every news room, pool hall and tavern in the country, and for the most part it did, but for some reason a lot of people liked the idea. Even though it was an outright whopper, the gulls fell for it, loved it and were soon willing to defend it. I guess people just wanted to believe that baseball sprang from the virgin country, created in one day by one man, who happened to be a war hero. And any bastard preaching evolution ought to be strung up.

I guess you had to admire Johnson and his mob the way they gave the suckers what they wanted. A Currier & Ives lithograph. Baseball in the country, a place where a lot less people now lived but wished they still did. Nobody would actually want to move back to the country, since that wouldn't be progress. It was just a nice daydream and it helped distract folks from taking notice of the drunken brawls in the ball parks, the umpire beatings, the assignations with whores. They forgot their pastor's condemnation of the game from the pulpit. They forgot that decent hotels refused to rent to ballplayers. And they forgot completely about those four Louisville Grays. Baseball was good. Baseball was clean. Baseball could never be corrupted. And the best way to keep it that way was to pretend it had always been that way.

Chapter 30

F at Jack Delaney showed me to a back room where they kept a store of pretzels and pig knuckles. We both knew why I came, so I cut to the heart of the matter.

"What about those Louisville Grays?"

"They sent telegrams. The saps should have been drummed out of the game for being so stupid. You conduct business in cash with nothing in writing that might come back to haunt you."

"That's it?"

"Pick your spots and don't get greedy," Jack said. "All gaming boils down to sticking to a system and managing your bankroll. Let the suckers and the dopes bet on hope and a prayer."

"Who would even put money on the Highlanders to lose?"

"Boston on the next homestand is a nice target," Delaney said. "Offer the right odds and there'll be a few patsies who still want to believe Chesbro has an arm instead of a suitcase handle."

"Have you gotten to anybody else on the club?"

"You *are* the club."

"What about the pitcher? He's got the ball half the game. He's the one to change the outcome."

"But ain't you always been the exception, Prince? You see plenty of action at first base. If anyone can figure a way to lose a game and not look like a busher, it's you."

So I'm looking at the merchandise in the storeroom, not knowing what to do.

"It's just a game," Jack said. "Nobody's gonna get killed. So what if the team loses a hundred times this year instead of ninety-nine."

"I'll have to think about it."

"Goddamn, if you don't turn out to be the serious one. We could have some fun together. I bet I could even teach you some tricks, little brother."

"Forget it," I said. "I've thought about it enough. I can't do it."

"Oh, Prince, you disappoint me."

"And don't ever bother me again."

◆

The Highlanders took to the road, and if I thought we had already endured the worst stretch of a season that any club could suffer I was dead wrong. We lost thirteen out of fourteen. As soon as we showed up at the yard we were beat. We had no gumption, a situation Kid Elberfeld didn't help any with his constant yapping, fining, scapegoating and general discouragement.

We had a new pitcher going for us against Chicago one day, John Warhop. Just as he was about to take the field Kid calls out, "Chief, see if you can keep from getting killed before the third inning."

With that kind of backing from the skipper is it any wonder the other side jumps on the guy for a quick four spot? And that's just the beginning of the carnage. Only when the White Sox are tired from running the bases does Kid come out to fetch the boy.

"Real nice job, Chief. I knew I could count on you."

"Just lay off, okay?" Warhop looks ready to cry.

"What the fuck did you say?" Kid sticks his mug in the pitcher's face. He's fixing for a fight—a fight he knows he can't lose.

"Nothing."

"Yeah, well that will cost you twenty."

"For what?"

"*Nothing.*"

"That's not fair."

"Make it twenty-five," Kid says. "Now *that* ain't fair."

So after the game Warhop is having his arm rubbed down and grousing to our trainer, Mike Martin. In addition to packing all the equipment, running errands and safekeeping our watches and wallets, Mike would provide a sympathetic ear when needed.

Kid walks by just in time to hear Mike tell Warhop to keep his chin up. And Kid just goes off. He accused Mike of being a turncoat and trying to undermine his authority on the club, and just like that he fires the guy.

I watched this business, not saying anything, waiting for Kid to finally look my way.

"Don't nobody in this room forget who's in charge," he said, then brushed past me and out the door.

That was it. Something had to be done to get rid of Kid Elberfeld. If I had to play to lose, so be it. Only losing could rid you of a rotten manager. And if I had an opportunity to take up with the likes of Jack Delaney to get a little dough for my trouble, why not? The way I saw it, the dough wasn't what was important. What I was really after was much bigger. Justice.

❖

After staying away from the ballpark for weeks, Nellie decides to attend the game I agreed to toss. I tried to talk her out of it.

"You're meeting someone there, aren't you?" she says.

"What are you talking about?"

"You're meeting some girl."

"Where'd you get that brain wave?" Now I was really waxed, since I had actually been completely faithful to Nellie. The only times I fooled around was on the road.

Finally she stayed home. Too bad I couldn't talk everyone else out of coming to the game. Fat Jack was sitting in Farrell's box again, not that I was about to pay him a visit or even look in his direction. I was edgy enough and had no idea how I was going to drop this game to Boston.

As I pondered the question of how, the lead-off man stings the first pitch and the ball scoots through my legs for an error.

"Nice play," Kid yells from the bench. "Very *pro*-fessional."

The Red Sox bunt the man to second, he steals third, then walks home on a sac fly, so in the matter of two minutes we're down a run and there's no question who's to blame. Even though it's a small crowd, in a way there's nothing worse. You can hear every mug cussing you out. With a big gate at least it becomes one huge howl.

I could even make out Delaney's voice: "My granny could field better than that!" Compared to what else was being said, Jack came off as one of my bigger supporters.

During our first ups I thought it would be a good idea to redeem myself a little. Later on I could try to find a better way to tank the game. I came up to the plate with men on first and third and looked to hit a sacrifice fly to get back the run I was responsible for. I didn't want to ignite a rally, just get things back to level. I get my pitch, try to loft the ball, only I jerk my head, and ground a sharp one to shortstop for a quick double play. We're out of the inning and now the bugs are really giving me the business.

"What would we ever do without you, Prince," grumbles Kid Elberfeld.

Generally I'd bark right back at him. This time I just bite my lip and try to bear down to make a better showing of myself. In the top of the second I make a nice play to slap down a drive slicing towards the right field corner. Too bad Chesbro is late covering the bag, which throws off the timing. The ball winds up behind the plate and the batter trots down to second where he would have been if I hadn't fielded his liner.

Kid throws his cap and kicks it. "Can't *anybody* on this goddamn ball club make a play?"

Jack knows he's to blame for this one, so he takes offense. "Why don't you just button your lip, you little shit?"

"Why don't you just shut up and throw the ball, you fat ox?"

So Chesbro throws the ball. Right at Kid's head. Elberfeld storms the mound with murder in his eyes and everybody has to rush to keep them out of striking range as they jaw at one another.

The umpire is Tim Hurst, a tough old salt who over the years had more than his share of run-ins with Kid. He takes the slow route to the mob scene between the mound and the dugout. He pulls a pocket watch and says, "If this field ain't cleared in exactly thirty seconds the ball game will be awarded to Boston by default."

Kid now forgets all about Chesbro in favor of his natural enemy. "You no good robber, you won't be happy until this team is fifty games in last place." Everybody steps aside to let Kid belly up to the ump.

"Twenty seconds," is all Hurst has to say.

"Since when is a conference with my pitcher, grounds for a forfeit, you mutton head?"

"Fifteen seconds."

"I swear I won't rest until you're digging ditches—"

"Ten seconds."

"—or doing *something* more suited to your stinking rotten, abilities."

"Five seconds."

"Go on and do it, you son of a—aw, the hell with it." Kid turns to slap Chesbro on the rump. "Go after 'em, Happy." Then he trots back to the bench.

Suffering a forfeit wouldn't have mattered much, since we went down that day as easy as honey on a spoon. The ball club didn't really need me to help them lose that one. By the time it was over I didn't look any worse than most on our side. What a sorry day it was. I felt rotten about myself and I couldn't see how I was any closer to ridding the team of Kid Elberfeld or gaining justice for Mike Martin.

All I had was some pieces of silver for my efforts, and now I didn't want them.

Chapter 31

When I got home I wasn't in too chipper a mood. I needed a little comfort right then, but Nellie wouldn't even look up from the magazine she was skimming, putting on a pout because I wouldn't let her come to the game. I just let her stew. A few minutes later I could hear her sobbing.

"Got a cold or something?"

"As if you care."

"I married you, didn't I?"

"You're not married to me. You're married to baseball."

If that didn't take the cake. Not six months earlier I was ready to walk away from the game and lead the quiet life, only to have her drag me back to this stinking hell. "What do you expect," I said, "I met you second."

"Maybe you could grow up a little."

"What? And rob you of the chance to reform me?"

"Plenty of men change once they get married."

"Is that what it says in that *literature* of yours?"

"You should read some. It wouldn't hurt any."

"I got my fill of reading in college. I don't need this right now, Nellie. We dropped a tough one today. I got a lot on my mind."

"Well, so do I."

"Like what?"

"Like having your baby," she says.

There it was, your typical ambush. She can't just tell me straight out. No, she has to make sure I feel like a lout. She's having *my* baby and I don't even care.

"So what, you want a pillow or a medal?"

"I don't want a baby. Not yet!"

"You're acting like it's my fault."

"It is."

"No more than yours."

I took a powder and went out in search of a drink. I hadn't planned on looking up Delaney even though I was supposed to catch up with him at his place. I had decided to wash my hands of the guy, then Nellie has to pull a fast one.

Delaney was waiting for me in the back room, and before I said a word he was holding out a wad of greenbacks. I should have stuffed them down his throat. Then I thought, what difference does it make? If I didn't take the money it would only end up with Delaney or some other crook who'd put it to bad use. The right thing to do was to keep it out of their pockets. So I put it in mine.

"Everybody on your side looked like they'd never seen the elephant before," Jack said. "It's tough enough to get any action on the team. And Jesus, Prince, you looked like a rabbit begging to be shot and tossed in the stew."

"I guess I'm not cut out for this business."

"You just take things too seriously."

"It doesn't matter. Nobody wants to bet on the Highlanders anyway."

"We could do all right on some side bets. It'll be fun. Listen to Jack. You got to let down your bars. Enjoy life for what it is."

"I have plenty of fun."

"A guy like you should have more. You should be grabbing it with both hands."

Delaney kept feeding me the blarney until I agreed to give the side bets a try. He made it seem like we were only doing it as a prank. I don't know, I think I went along because I was in the mood to do something stupid.

❖

No matter how rotten the home side was playing there was always side bets to be had at the park. A dime says Keeler gets a single. Double or nothing says Chase takes off for second on the next pitch. You could get down a bet on almost anything, and by the end of the afternoon, if you got a live one going, you could realize a tidy sum. At least, that's what Jack said.

Delaney and me worked out some hand signals and I tried my best. The problem was I couldn't be looking at Delaney every few seconds and not tip things off. Not to mention, for us to make any real dough I had to screw up quite a few times in an afternoon. For all that anxiety and grief I wound up with twenty bucks for my trouble.

"That's a pretty good day, Hal," Delaney said when we met up later.

"That's it for me. No more."

"You're acting serious again."

"Why should I look like a muffer for loose change?"

"True enough. I'll come up with something bigger."

"No thanks."

I walked out on the guy, went to a bar and blew that twenty. I didn't want it contaminating my pocket. The thing with a crook like Delaney is you have to make a clean break. Once they get a hook in you they won't let go. And I had enough trouble with Kid Elberfeld pulling his Napoleon Bonaparte act and Nellie moaning over motherhood.

Then I got accused in one of the newspapers of laying down on the club. The notice said that Kid Elberfeld had tried his best to instill some ginger in the team but it was tough to succeed when the star player refused to give his best effort. It was hoped that marriage would have had a good effect on young Mr. Chase but the results were so far gravely disappointing. Perhaps if the Highlander's swell-headed first baseman were forced to earn his daily bread like everybody else, he might better appreciate the chance the game of baseball was affording him—*unless he had other business that was more important than winning ball games.*

I had to figure that everybody was wise to my doings with Delaney. Hell, I wouldn't have been shocked to find out that Jack himself had tipped off the papers just to get me back in line. I didn't know what to do—so I panicked.

I hustled back to the apartment and packed a couple bags to skip town for California.

"What about the baby?" Nellie asked.

"What about it?"

"You can't leave me. That's not how a husband is supposed to act."

"I'm not leaving you. I'm just leaving."

"But the season isn't over. What about the team?"

"They can lose without me."

"Hal, what are you running away from?"

"Nothing! I got things to do."

"What things?"

"Things!" I crammed the last shirt in a suitcase and snapped it shut. "Listen, you're not due for another six months. I'll be back way before then."

"Will you? You don't even know anymore when you're lying or not."

"Think whatever you want to think, Nellie. I'm leaving and you can't stop me."

I did. And she couldn't.

Chapter 32

For abandoning my ball club I was banned from playing in Organized Baseball for the rest of my life. I finished out the season with the Stockton club of the outlaw California State League and I figured that was it. I had wasted enough of my life hitting a ball with a stick, and I didn't even enjoy playing the game any more. The bastards had seen to that.

I decided to go home again for Christmas. This time my brothers-in-law couldn't resist asking questions about the big leagues. They hadn't heard yet that I was barred from the game and I didn't bother to tell them. As soon as the conversation turned to baseball my Mom found a reason to leave the room. My old man wasn't even home for Christmas Day to give me the business, but I changed the subject on my own. The last thing I wanted to talk about was baseball.

I followed Mom into the kitchen where she was fixing some dessert. She had begun to look elderly. Maybe no one else noticed, since they saw her regular, but I could tell she was getting on. And it was more than the lack of any color in her hair or that the wrinkles that had turned to creases were now turning into folds—it was the lack of fire in her belly. The kitchen curtains were on the shabby side, the same ones I remembered from the last Christmas I was home. She had always been one to change the curtains to cheer the place up.

"I don't even know your wife's name," she said. She didn't sound disappointed so much as tired.

"Nellie. Nellie's her name."

"Have you thought about having a family?"

"As a matter of fact, Ma, we're anticipating."

"Weren't you going to bother to tell me?"

"I am. I did. I mean that's why I came in here."

"How far along is she?"

"Six or seven months."

"And you left her in New York by herself?"

"She has her folks. She's okay."

"And she didn't mind you leaving her like that?"

"I didn't murder the girl! I needed a break from New York. She understands."

"No need to get worked up, Hal."

"Who's worked up?"

I went back to the living room and sat in a chair off by myself. Then something caught my eye, a deep gash in the side table, and I remembered how my old man raised that ivory-handled hunting knife I got him for Christmas and took a hunk out of that table. Now here I was sitting in the same chair. A stranger in the middle of his own family. Mom acted like the old man was dead. Is that how she acted about me when I was away?

The next day I went looking for my father. Nobody had mentioned him on Christmas, let alone dropped a clue on his whereabouts. I walked down to the saw mill that had seen some better days, too, now that the old man left the running of it to one of his hands. A man there told me I'd likely find him in a small cabin a couple miles into some woods.

Well, it turned out to be small enough but it required an act of generosity to call that lopsided shack a cabin. It was more like a shed, a crazy-quilt affair tacked together out of soap boxes and crates, with grease paper over the windows and a mismatched door salvaged from a town house.

I called out as I approached, not wanting to be mistaken for a trespasser. I didn't get a reply so I stepped up to the door and gave it a rap. No answer. I peaked in a window but the grease paper made everything look muddy. I could make out a table and a chair, and finally in a corner I thought I could see a body laid out on a mattress.

I pushed open the door.

"Dad?"

And there he was, the old man laying on a bare mattress, staring at the ceiling, holding a bottle of unlabeled booze on his chest. It was home-made poison the locals called Clear Kill.

"Hey there!" I tried to sound cheery, even though the place stunk of rotting food, dirty clothes, and scattered jars of stale piss.

He didn't even turn to look my way. I knew he wasn't dead because that bottle bobbed up and down on his chest.

"Damn, I'm tuckered out." I sat down in his only chair. "Jesus but I forgot how hilly the country is around here. I got so used to walking on sidewalks and riding on subway trains my legs just aren't up to regulation. Call me citified if you want."

But he wasn't calling me anything.

"So how've you been?"

Not even a grunt.

"Besides going deaf."

Slowly he turned his head to look at me. God, he was wretched. He had the yellow eyes of an alki-stiff, gray stubble all over his neck and jaw, and about as much weight on him as an ax handle.

"What do you want?"

"It's Christmas."

"So?"

"So merry Christmas."

He drank to that, spilling some of the Clear Kill down his neck.

"You know," I said, "You were right about the East."

"I don't recall saying anything about it."

"Everything's rotten. And it's all heading this way. Just like the polio that killed John. He's lucky he died when he did."

"He died too young."

"I know, if only he had lived longer he would have changed the world for the better."

"Maybe he would have."

"No. If he had lived longer it would have been the world that changed him."

"Do you know what killed your brother?"

"The bug."

"No," he says. "I did."

"Don't be loopy."

"It was God's punishment for my ambitions."

"There is no God. There's nothing *but* ambitions."

"Just the same," he said, "He's still punishing me."

How do you answer that kind of thinking? I left him to drink himself to death and never saw the man again.

Before going back to my rooms in San Jose I had one more visit to pay. I stopped by John's grave. This time there were no flowers. The finish to the stone had worn off enough that I couldn't see my reflection no more. He was just another stiff in the ground. Maybe no one even remembered what a sweet ballplayer he had been on the town team. Hell, there wasn't even a town team any more. And the Mayo brothers had quit playing semi-pro. They were all probably getting fat now and raising kids, putting away a dime a month to pay for a marker of their own someday. Everything had turned professional and the only Chase boy folks talked about was me. I played in the majors. I was making the big dough. *Grow up to be like him.*

I got back to San Jose to find a letter from Frank Farrell. He wished me a merry Christmas and a prosperous New Year, hopefully with the New York Highlanders. He wrote that if I wanted to come back to the team he thought he could square things with the league about my lifetime ban. I should have known that sort of thing was only reserved for pikers like John Ganzel, not the true stars of the game—at least not until the day my game fell off. Farrell wrote that I might also be interested to know that Kid Elberfeld was now ancient history. George Stallings, who had once run the Detroit Tigers, was hired on to run the club. So what did I say to a nice raise in salary and a fresh start?

I began to laugh like a nut case. No matter how hard I tried I couldn't get rid of baseball. Organized Ball damned me for eternity, and eternity lasted but three months. So why not? I wrote back to let Farrell know I was his boy, then wired Nellie that I was taking the train back to New York.

Generally on those long cross-country train rides I would kill the time in a poker game. This trip I was out of sorts and just kept to myself, but it was more than a rotten mood. I began to feel feverish, and by the time we reached New York I barely had enough strength to step off the train.

Nellie's brother had been sent to fetch me and a good thing, since I dropped at his feet like I'd been shot. He got me home and they called in a doctor, who didn't take long to reach a verdict.

I had the smallpox.

Chapter 33

When I was a kid just the mention of smallpox would make your stomach squirm. Due to modern medicine most of the victims pulled through, but we still couldn't get out of our heads the picture of ghost villages and entire Indian tribes wiped out by the pestilence. And even if you survived, the smallpox would leave its mark on you: a large moon crater scar, a deep gouge of skin.

Since it took so long for me to see the doctor, I came close enough to dying, and if I wasn't so fit maybe I would have. I never fell into a coma but I did drift into this dreamy state where I couldn't tell when I was awake or sleeping.

I felt something soft and cool on my forehead. Then I smelled roses. I opened my eyes to see it was my brother John mopping my brow with a damp cloth.

"You shouldn't be here," I said. "I'm contagious."

"It's not like I'm tired or anything."

"I'm sorry, John."

"What for?"

"You're dead."

"I'm not the one who's dead," he answered.

That's when I woke up for real. I sat up in bed. It was daylight out but the curtains were drawn and it took a minute for my eyes to adjust and my brain to clear. I realized I was looking at myself in the bureau mirror and slowly I began to make out my features. Slashing down my cheeks and across my nose was a patch of pocked skin where the smallpox pimples had burst open.

I lost my breath for a second.

I knew that every day for the rest of my life I would have to look at that ravaged face in the mirror. I fell back onto the pillow to cry. Only I couldn't. The horror I felt was replaced by anger. I sat up again to take a deep, long look at my new face. I was determined to stare in the mirror until it stopped making me sick. If I looked like a monster, those were the breaks. Slowly I began to smile, if you could call it that. It was more like a thin and twisted curl of the lips. Hell, that's not a scar, I thought, that's character.

For a change I missed spring training for a reason other than holding out. I was reinstated to the league with no trouble, but I was just too weak from the pox to play. In the meantime Nellie gave birth to a little girl we named Mary. She went nuts over the baby and wanted me to share in the joy. She'd force me to hold the little thing and I'd hand Mary right back.

"Doesn't Daddy love his little girl?"

"I'm afraid I'll hurt her with these big mitts of mine."

It wasn't until the beginning of May that I felt strong enough to work out with the Highlanders. I was happy enough to get out of the house and play some ball, but I couldn't shake this foul mood I was in. It was like I was looking for someone to blame for the smallpox. I dared people to stare at my scarred face. I dared the newspapermen to ask me about laying down on the club. But because of my illness I was given a pass. When I made it out to the yard my teammates, some I hadn't met before, were glad to see me. All the old scrapes were forgotten. Kid Elberfeld was blamed for everything, leaving me with a clean sheet. And I was still angry.

Actually there weren't many of the old players back. George Stallings wasted no time in doing things his way. The guy had been an odd choice for Farrell, especially since Ban Johnson had blackballed Stallings from the league for meddling, after he tried to buy the Tigers when he was managing the club and Johnson was trying to land a deal in other quarters. Farrell pretended he didn't know anything about the controversy, since it happened before he bought the New York team. He convinced Johnson to at least let him honor the two-year contract he signed.

George Stallings was a Southerner who, away from the ball field, acted like a plantation owner; but put a baseball uniform on the guy's back and he turned into a foul-mouthed roughneck. He had been in the game long enough to know that being gentle wasn't the way to get results. The first tough call was to drop Chesbro, even though our supporters still had a soft spot for the big guy. After that it was a lot easier to dump the others.

Stallings and I had a let's-get-acquainted chat. He said he was counting on me to provide some backbone for the team of youngsters he had
assembled. He knew what I was capable of, and the first base job was waiting for me as soon as I felt up to it. The way I figured it, I didn't need him
to give me back my job. Prince Hal was still a gate attraction and Farrell
would throw Stallings back on the scrap heap if he was stupid enough not
to start me.

When the newspapers announced that I was finally strong enough to
play, you better believe that town was excited. At home plate before my
first at bat, I was presented with a silver-plated loving cup. I had to smile.
A loving cup for me! The fans rose to their feet to cheer the Prince. To
welcome him back. All is forgiven! Even my teammates and the clucks on
the other side stood to applaud.

To oblige them I raised the cup over my head and presented it from
one foul pole to the other.

Look at all the goddamn cattle, I thought. *Look at them all.*

Chapter 34

Every little thing about George Stallings began to curl my guts. For one thing he was a nit-picker. The guy was always pulling off lint from his street clothes, picking at things that nobody else could see or care about. At the dining table he'd brush away invisible crumbs. And when we rode an elevator he'd lick the tip of his finger to polish out some smudge on the brass plating that only he could see. On the field he was just as crazy. He was always picking up after the boys who liked to eat peanuts and toss the shells in the dugout. It took a while before I noticed that the bench was always spanking clean when we came in for our ups. The next time I took up my position in the field I looked in to see the old maniac picking up the place in a major hurry, like he was expecting company.

Stallings was also absolutely goofy with superstitions. He had a lucky trunk, one of those huge old steamer trunks that stood five feet high. What he needed for the road could fit in a couple of grips, so there was no reason to make our trainer, Doc Barton, haul that trunk all over the American League. The one time when Doc left it behind in New York, Stallings cussed him out so long and hard he traumatized a whole train platform of women and kids.

One inning, as we're about to hit, Stallings spies a peanut shell that somehow he missed picking up between innings. Of course we can't start to hit before he's picked it up or who knows what disaster will happen to us? He hustles over, but the first pitch is already on its way. He freezes. Bent over, his fingers not quite reaching the shell, he looks up to see the batter crack the ball for a single. Now Stallings is convinced that he can't move or he'll jinx the rally, so he stays doubled over. Hit follows hit and we run through the entire order before making an out, by which time Stallings' back has locked up. Doc Barton had to walk him to the clubhouse all twisted up. It took fifteen minutes for him to finally disappear behind the center field fence and we could get on with the game.

The rest of the club got a kick out of the incident. And the way they looked at it, the skipper had taken one for the club. Hey, we batted around so he must have been doing something right—right? Personally I thought he was a goddamn fool who had no business running a soda fountain, let alone a major league baseball team.

I think he was eager to get on my good side, because Stallings soon named me captain. I was the first captain of the New York Yankees, which was what we were being called more and more. But I wasn't fooled. Stallings knew he occupied my rightful position, and making me captain was just admitting the truth that I should be running the club. The guy was tossing me a bone and I was supposed to wag my tail for joy.

The newspapers said that Stallings named me captain hoping that the responsibility would encourage me to play harder when my health allowed, but I was already starting to find my game. I was determined to show everybody I could still knock it around. I didn't need any more incentive than that. Too bad the rest of the club was comprised of so many mutts or we might have made a serious run at the pennant. We were a lot better off than the year before; the fans could see some hope for the future and began to visit Hilltop again, even though the place was starting to rot and fall apart. That was the year Pittsburgh opened Forbes Field and set off a wave of concrete and steel ballparks. Everyone, including Farrell, wanted one of these baseball palaces. What that meant to me was that a gate attraction like Prince Hal would have more sway than ever.

The entire season was full of change for the game. The league added a second umpire to the field to eliminate a lot of the cheating that went on behind the back of the one. Even the old carriage ride to the ballpark was history, now that all the cities were required to provide a visiting clubhouse—not that most of them were anything more than a few hooks and a rusty spigot. Baseball was seeing itself as a business and should be run as one. To me it was all just a sad state of affairs. But the pox had left me too weak to waste much energy on complaining. I needed every ounce to play the game and keep from getting knocked on my ass by my enemies around the league. Twenty umps on the field wouldn't be enough to protect me. Mostly I kept to myself, played the game then went home to rest. If some people wanted to think because I was quiet I had turned over a new leaf that was their problem.

Nellie was just like the rest of them. Because I wasn't out carousing with my pals she thought it was on account of having the baby. Motherhood was working wonders in her so she figured fatherhood should do the same for me. Her and her folks would go cuckoo over the kid, declaring every sound and move to be rare and *precious*, but all I saw was an anchor that kept an able-bodied guy at home and even there you couldn't do what you wanted. Don't smoke that cigar, it'll bother the baby. Don't make that noise, it'll bother the baby. Don't do anything, it'll bother the baby.

One of the Sunday afternoons when Nellie's folks would come to visit, Nellie gets this idea that they should go out for an ice cream cone and leave me to watch little Mary by myself. I guess the plan was to encourage Daddy to get closer to his little girl. All I wanted to do was sleep, exhausted as I was after a long week of playing ball, and I was just happy to get rid of them. Besides, the baby was fast asleep.

She stayed that way for maybe two minutes.

I tried everything to quiet her down and let me nap. I dangled house keys in front of her, wound up her favorite music box, surrounded her with stuffed animals. But she kept crying until I reached my limit and I finally gave that bassinet a good kick. Now it was like a fire alarm had gone off she's wailing so loud.

"All right, all right," I said. "*Daddy'll* pick you up."

So I held her to my shoulder and gave her a few pats on the back and pretty soon she stopped crying. Nothing to it. I could feel her little heart beating. I carried her over to the window to see if Nellie and her folks were on their way back. I stuck my head out but there was no sign of them. The baby made one of those happy gurgling sounds, so I figured she was ready to lie back, only when I tried she started to fuss again. Not too loud. Just a warning shot. I looked at her and I didn't see my daughter, Daddy's little heartthrob, I saw this clinging, bloodsucking reptile. I took it over to the window to get a better look. *This is my flesh*, I thought, as I held her by the open window. *This is my blood. I was put on this earth to bring forth more of my flesh and blood so when it comes their turn they can bring forth more flesh and blood until we choked the goddamn earth.*

"We're home!" Nellie cried.

"Caught in the act!" her Mom said.

"Where's my Kodak?" added her Dad.

Then they see that I'm holding Mary out the window, four stories above the street, and she was wailing like mad.

Nellie rushed over to relieve me of the baby, a look of shock in her eyes.

"I wanted to see if you were coming," I said.

Her father tried to laugh it off by saying, "Typical. I pulled some dumb stunts myself the first time."

Pretty soon they convinced themselves that I was quite the silly goose as a father. But I'd get the knack of it. And what stories they'd have to tell Mary when she grew up!

◈

After a game one day I'm on my way home when somebody steps out of a doorway pointing something at me. It's Fat Jack Delaney holding out a dollar Havana, smiling like a ward heeler out to get my vote.

"I heard you had a baby, Prince. So I brought you a cigar."

"The father's the one who gives out the smokes, Jack, or didn't you get the word?"

"All right, then we're celebrating my good fortune. Go on, take it."

So I accept and as he lights it for me I check out his clothes that look a cut richer than the ones I remembered.

"So you rob a tailor, Jack?"

"No. I just tapped the secret of prosperity."

"Yeah, how's that?"

"I had an experience. I got involved in some small potato affair and my partner figured I was skimming a little off the top."

"Which you were."

"Which I was. And he sent a couple of fellows to play with me in the alley. Left me there to count my teeth and do some thinking."

"That's an item."

"I got caught because I wanted to get caught. I wanted to get punished. You catch my drift? Deep down I was just too honest for my own damn good. I realized I was a crook and the sooner I admitted it to myself the happier I'd be."

"So you're a crook?"

"That and then some, my boy."

"And now you've let yourself prosper in the world. Is that what I'm to think, Jack?"

"I'll let the results speak for themselves."

"So why did you decide to share your testimonial with me?"

"You know how it is. Once you get the good word, you want to share it."

"And you weren't about to ask me to dump any ball games?"

"I got plenty of action to handle already," he said. Then he took a long draw on that stogie and gave me an even longer look. "So do you know who you are, Prince?"

"Why don't you bottle it for later."

"If you let yourself go, I mean really let yourself go, there's no telling what you're capable of."

"I'll keep it in mind." I tossed the cigar even though it was sweet and I had hardly tapped it. "And if you bother me again, Jack, you won't have no teeth left to count."

I was pretty scalded all evening over Jack. The nerve of that two-bit mug to lump me in with his sort. Every little thing that Nellie or the baby did annoyed the hair off me. And of course when I went to bed the baby had to cry and squeal every five minutes.

"Honey, would you check on her?" Nellie said about the tenth time.

I don't know if I did or not. I kept drifting in and out of sleep. Finally I conked out, only to have Nellie shake me awake. She was hysterical and frantic as hell. I couldn't understand at first what she was trying to say. Then she showed me, and I knew that something terrible had happened.

Our little baby girl was dead in her cradle.

Chapter 35

A s if it was some kind of consolation, the doctor told us that babies sometimes die for no reason at all. The poor little thing could have smothered on its own pillow, who could tell? He put down "crib death" on the certificate.

"But the main thing," he said, "is not to blame yourselves. You're both young. You'll have more children."

That fact didn't help console Nellie or her folks too much. The only reason her parents didn't go over the edge was they had to keep her from going absolutely nuts.

The ball club gave me a couple of days off to sort through my feelings. Not that I had any. I was just numb. When I rejoined the team I was just happy to get away from all the gloom at home. But I had to put up with everyone's sympathy.

Stallings pulled me aside for a private word.

"It's times like these," he said, "that reminds you baseball is just a game."

As if I hadn't heard that one before.

The season winds down and while the last thing anybody wants to consider is next season, it's all I can think about. By then I figure to have my strength back, and I could get a little payback around the league, not to mention in my own clubhouse.

So the equipment is packed and stored away, the gates at Hilltop Park are chained up, and the players were boarding trains bound in all directions. Most of them went back to their hometowns where they had jobs for the offseason. Some of the thrifty ones might even own a store. The big dream for a lot of the boys was to open a hardware store, since screws and nails don't tend to spoil. Only the best players made enough dough to take it easy, maybe do a vaudeville turn, or just keep in condition with the Indian clubs at the Y. I didn't have to work—probably would have benefited from the exercise, but I was too busy with other pursuits.

A couple weeks away from the field and I started to finally catch up and feel strong again. I began to run around town like a sailor on shore leave, charging after every skirt that flapped in the breeze. I had been cooped up so long I guess I couldn't help myself. The funny thing was how having my face disfigured with the smallpox seemed to make me more attractive to women. I looked risky or something.

I left plenty of clues at home of what I was up to. Lipstick on a hand-kerchief. Phone exchanges on slips of paper. Nellie had to be wise, but she didn't say anything.

Sooner or later I figured she'd start in, and one day after another night of running around and losing the race with the bloodshot sun, she rousted me out of bed.

"I know what you've been up to."

"Congratulations. Now how about a cup of coffee?"

"I don't care what you do anymore."

"That's smart."

"All I want is another baby."

"Don't go loopy on me again."

"I want another baby."

"And I want a pot of oil. Is there anything on the burner?"

"I said I want a baby!" she screams.

"So who's stopping you? I'm not the only pump in town."

I threw on some clothes and got out of that joint to get some air. I must have walked all the way down to the Battery and back. Having a kid had been a mistake in the first place and now Nellie wanted to throw good money after bad. Well, the way I figured it, that was her concern. I didn't plan on looking backwards no more. If she wanted to strike a deal—give me a baby and you can do what you want—I was willing to take her up on the offer.

When I got home Nellie was already in bed in the dark, even though it was only nine o'clock. I pulled the chain on the overhead light.

"You're drunk." She shielded her eyes.

"I'm here." I began to undress. "You still want that deal?"

"Just get it over with," she said.

"Don't worry, I will."

And I did.

By spring training Nellie was pretty far along with the new baby. I did what I wanted and she didn't complain so we actually got on pretty well. The ball club was getting ready to make camp and this year I decided it was time to hold out for more dough. Farrell and me had danced this number before, and since both knew how the other stood we actually came to terms a little earlier than I expected. I joined the team two full weeks before the season opened.

Stallings tinkered some more with the lineup, sacrificing some hitting to bolster the pitching staff, and it looked like a decent enough mix. The Yankees were fast out of the gate and by June were on top of the standings. Back to the yard came our front-running fans. At the head of the parade was Frank Farrell, who never could resist the limelight, assuring everyone that this year he would bring the city of New York an American League pennant. He also couldn't resist taking a few jabs at the Giants, who had to contend with a Cubs team that was running away in the National League. Brush was the one that year to float the idea of the Yankees and Giants playing a city series at the end of the season. Farrell was the one to dismiss it, telling the newspapers that, unlike some ball clubs he could name, his Yankees had other plans for early October than to square off against a bunch of second-raters.

As for me, I was feeling fit again. I was really soaking the ball, stealing bases and fielding the best in either league. The ball club fed off of my play, we won games, and Stallings looked like a genius—which was the last thing I wanted to see. But I figured it was a long season, every ball club cools off and has to face a reckoning, and when that day came and that club had an owner as panicky as Frank Farrell, I knew the worm would turn.

Things flared up even sooner than I expected. One day a writer asked me why the Yanks were playing so well and without malice in my heart I told him that it was all a matter of chemistry. The way it got repeated to Stallings, though, it sounded like his star player was looking to hog all the credit for the team's success. Stallings blew a fuse, declaring that *somebody* had a hell of a lot of nerve considering how *somebody* had held out most of the spring and wasn't even around to mix any chemistry.

That was enough for me. I had made an innocent remark, but his was a personal attack. So I let up on my play just to show him, just to show everyone that the real spark of the club was the one and only Prince Hal. And we lost games, you bet we did. The papers noted how I seemed to have lost interest in playing, an item that might have riled me in the past. This time I just shrugged it off.

I wasn't too surprised that the flies should come around. On the street one morning I look up to see Fat Jack Delaney approaching me.

"Prince, I'm surprised to see you out and about so early in the day."

"Yeah, what a coincidence."

"Sorry to hear about your little girl."

"Things happen."

"You have to carry on as best you can."

"So I saw you in the back of the church for the service. I was surprised how hard you took it, Jack."

"I should have said something to your wife. I'm sorry."

"That's all right. I could see you had gone all soft."

"It does make you think."

"It doesn't pay to think too deep," I said. "So I guess the suckers have come out of hibernation now that the Yankees are winning some games."

"That's true enough, Prince. But I can pass on this one. Considering."

"Oh, it's all up to me?"

"Entirely."

"You're goddamn right it is. It's my reputation at stake. You know how many little kids look up to me? What would they think if they thought I wasn't playing on the square? Well, I'll tell you, Jack. They'd love me even more for being a big swindler. All that matters to boys today is how big you are. Not how good."

"Kids have always been like that, I suppose."

"No, things have gotten worse in the world. Maybe people need to be taught a lesson."

"And you plan on teaching them one, Prince?"

"If not me ... who?"

Chapter 36

I decided that the first game of the upcoming St. Louis series would be choice pickings. The Brownies that season were pioneering new ways to lose ball games, even for them. They were a number of games behind the Senators, who were stinking up the league in their own right. There would be plenty of money willing to back the Yankees no matter what the odds. This time, though, I didn't come down with a case of the nerves. I bided my time.

Neither side threatened to score until St. Louis managed to get two men on with only one away, then Schweitzer hit a drive down the left field line that looked like sure trouble when Bert Daniels raced over for our side and made a great backhand stab of the ball. That looked to kill the Browns' rally, which I knew might be the only one they'd manage that day. Their next man dribbled one to Roach, a kid playing short. He made a clean throw to first, only I short-legged it, arriving at the bag a fraction too late and allowed the throw to sail into the stands. Both runners scored. I just stood there and glared over at Roach, like I couldn't believe what a bonehead throw the kid just made.

St. Louis built a four to nothing lead before the Yankees started to chip away, scoring one in the fifth and posing another threat in the sixth. I stepped to the plate with Wolter on first. Too bad the pitcher didn't know I was looking to hit a double play grounder, because he threw four wide ones and I had no choice but to trot down to first with the walk. LaPorte is up next and he promptly pokes a single to right to cut the lead in half, and when the outfielder kicks the ball I'm obliged to take third. Our next batter pops up for the first out, which brings to the plate School-boy Knight, the leading hitter on our club. After he gets down in the count by two strikes, I signal for LaPorte to take off on the double steal. Knight obliges by striking out, the Browns' catcher fakes the peg to second, and I come running home, acting surprised to be tagged out. That double play killed our chances and the Yanks dropped a tough one to the last-place team in the league.

I may have looked unfortunate on that botched double steal, but I didn't look crooked. And it was sweet to watch Stallings suffer on the bench.

Our next target was a weekend Detroit series at home. The Tigers were looking to nab their fourth straight pennant, and after screwing up three straight World Series they were still a hungry ball club. I played it on the level the first game, and it turned into a real batting bee that the Yankees took eleven to eight. That got the suckers eager to lay down their dough with Delaney for the second game. Because the Tigers bounced back strong I didn't even need to help them any.

Now I figured was a ripe time for the Yankees to go into a little losing spell and for Jack to parlay our winnings into a nice little kitty. The dopes who lost on Saturday's game were eager to win back their dough on Monday. Once again the Tigers needed no help from me to paste the home side eight to one.

For the last game of the series, Jack's pigeons are doubling up to break even, and I'm hoping the Tigers take care of business and I don't have to step in. But this one turned into a real duel as neither team could score. The later it went, the more skittish the players, who didn't want to make a mistake that might cost their side the game. I stayed calm and waited for the perfect chance to lose yet dodge the blame. By the eighth we're still scoreless and now I can't worry about the art of the thing—I have to butcher a play just to get the job done or we lose all our dough.

The Tigers got a hit out of Davey Jones then tried to bunt him over. The ball is punched right back to our pitcher who is all set to cut down Jones at second, when seemingly out of nowhere the Prince flashes in, scoops up the ball, and takes a long look at second before tossing to first base for the sure out.

The pitcher is annoyed that I got in the way.

"Go for the ball if you want it so bad," I say.

On the bench Stallings is pacing and cussing like a camel driver.

Cobb is the next batter and he lines a single to center to score the only run of the game and send a sorry bunch of gamblers off to hock the family plate.

Nobody on the Yankees is in a very good mood the next morning when we catch a train to begin a three-week swing of the league. Stallings expects us to act like we're escorting Lincoln's body back to Springfield. So when I start to whistle a sprite little tune I picked up at the theater, he snaps like an overwound watch. Half the team grabs him, half grabs me, as he's spitting and fuming and giving me a good piece of his mind.

"You warped son of a bitch, I ought to take a whip to your rotten hide!"

There was no reason to hold me back. I stayed as cool as lemon sherbert. "Hey, Skip, we lost a couple games. Do you want us to blow our brains out?"

"I'm wise to your little ways." A train pulling into the station drowned him out. He was turning purple and bucking so hard that he ripped the seams in his jacket. "If it was up to me," he shouts, "I'd ship you off to some fucking silo league. Maybe the owner of this club can't see shit through the trees, but as long as I'm manager you play to win. Let me go, boys, I've had my say."

Only, they don't let him go. They let go of me. Like they expect the Prince to back down and say he's sorry. I straighten my coat, reach inside my jacket and pull out a deck of cards.

"Thank God none of them got bent," I said, and stepped onto the train.

The club had fallen off the pace set by Philadelphia, and Farrell after all of his big talk about a pennant was getting jumpy. Just to make things worse I began to sow some little seeds of discontent. One night I bought Charlie Hemphill a beer and disclosed that our young utility player, Bert Daniels, was angling for his center field job. The kid had been on a recent hot streak and I said I heard him boasting about nabbing a batting crown if only he could land a regular berth. Charlie was called Eagle Eye but that season he was seeing the ball no better than a mole, batting .230, and was a little insecure about his place on the team.

Then I paid young Bert a visit to let him know how I thought it was a rotten shame how some people couldn't let others just be themselves and how there was no call to mimic personal habits. With a little effort Bert was able to pry out of me that old Eagle Eye was giving him the business behind his back by making fun of the way he sucked his teeth when he talked.

"The guy's having a rough year at the plate," I said, "So naturally he's afraid."

"Of what, Prince?"

"Why, of you, Bert. Didn't you know? Heck, everybody on the club thinks you deserve a regular position. It's just too bad that so-called manager of ours will wait until hell freezes over for one of his favorites to come around."

Before long, those two guys are looking for half an excuse to take a pop at one another. In Cleveland, Bert comes off the bench to deliver a pinch-hit double and score a big run for us. Charlie hadn't gotten a loud foul all afternoon, so he was in no mood to see the youngster succeed.

"Jesus!" declared Bert. "I really knocked the blood out of that one." You could always count on a ballplayer to go fishing for somebody on the bench to ask him how he laid into a ball.

"Jesus!" mimics Charlie.

"Maybe you'd be better off imitating the way I hit," says Bert, "instead of the way I talk, *busher.*"

"Oh yeah, *busher?* Well, I've been in this league for ten years and I'll still be here when you're back home delivering ice for a living."

"Not if you keep swinging like a rusty gate."

"And if you think you got the goods to do the job every day you're just pissing in the wind."

"Oh yeah? You can just suck my teeth."

Charlie didn't seem to know what to make of that last one, but it must have sounded like fighting words to him, because he went for Bert's throat. The two of them are rolling around on the dugout floor; Stallings grabs the bucket of oatmeal water we keep for drinking and douses the both of them to break it up.

Naturally all the younger players sided with Bert and the veterans with Charlie, so by the time we left Cleveland we were a divided ball club. And if that wasn't bad enough when the Yankees boarded the train for Detroit their star player, Prince Hal, wasn't with them.

Word had it, he was headed back to New York to inform the owner, regretfully of course, how bad his ball club was falling apart.

Chapter 37

Frank Farrell said, "George Stallings couldn't manage a pea patch." I was chatting with Frank in his Fifth Avenue offices, smoking his tobacco and drinking his spirits. He sat hunched forward at his desk, looking quite concerned.

"He lucked out last year and the boys were game for the first half of this season," I said. "But now the man's got everybody pulling in different directions. Did you read in the papers about the fight in Cleveland?"

"What was that all about?"

"Just Stallings having a little of his southern fun. Tie the tail of two cats together and watch them fight over a clothes line."

"They're a uncivilized lot down South."

"The club deserves better. You deserve better, Frank. All this talent you assembled, there's got to be the right man out there to harness it for you."

"What about yourself, Hal? Have you ever given any thought to managing?"

"I have enough on my plate as captain trying to keep harmony."

"But if I got rid of the disruption you could take on the strategic end of things."

"I guess you're right."

"And there'd be more money in it."

"It's not about money," I said. "It's about the ball club."

"Of course Stallings has a binding contract that runs through November." I could see Frank already starting to have second thoughts. "I have to keep my word, naturally."

"That would be the honorable thing." *And the cheapest.*

"So why don't you just go back to the team and sit tight? Next season we can give you a shot with the reins. How's that sound to you, Hal?"

"What's he going to say about me leaving the team like this?"

"There's always a reason to be found."

"My wife is going to have another baby soon."

"There you go. You were worried about her and went home. What can anyone say about that? Especially after what you went through last year."

I lowered my eyes.

"Sorry, Hal. I shouldn't have brought that up."

Before I rejoined the team Farrell telephones Stallings with my excuse, which left him with no choice but to swallow the situation and stick me back in the line-up. Bert and Charlie were still feuding and the club seemed in as much turmoil as before I left. We got swept by Detroit and were lucky to take one out of four with St. Louis. Before the Chicago series Stallings tried to rally the troops for one more push to the top. The boys responded and we took three out of five from the White Sox before returning home, where the team rewards him with a great homestand.

I avoided Jack Delaney the entire time. I was on my way to running the New York Yankees and didn't want to be beholden to some cake and coffee gambler. When Prince Hal took charge the next year, everything was going to be on the up and up. Then I'd show the bastards they had me all wrong.

With the team winning again, Farrell was suddenly too busy to meet with me when I wanted to talk over some ideas for next year's team. Maybe the guy was thinking about welching on our deal. Maybe he had even pulled a fast one, tricking me back into uniform.

That's when I decided to pay Jack Delaney a visit. You'd think that after a month of being left out in the cold, he'd be a little happier to see me.

"You treat me like I'm one of your girlfriends," he says.

"I've been busy, Jack. My wife's having another little one. You know, the blessed expense."

"You sure it ain't the blessed excuse?"

"I got a proposition that should make you happy. We're still business partners, right?"

"Are we?"

"I don't see nobody else in the boat."

"I hear you think you're going to manage the Yankees."

"I *am*," I said. "And when I do, the paydays will be over, partner. Any funny stuff on my watch and I'll be wise to it."

"It takes a thief, they say."

"So do you want to get in a little more action before the curtain? Are you in or are you out, Jack?"

The guy was starting to look old and weary. No more of that blarney about solving the riddle of life. "I'm in, Prince," he said. "You know I'm in."

The Yankees were set to face Walter Johnson. Delaney said he knew of some ham and eggers who refused to believe the kid was as good a pitcher as he was showing. They thought they had him pegged since his rookie year, didn't like to go back on their opinions, and could be goaded into betting against him to prove it. When Johnson first came up to the big show, he was just a long-armed rube wearing his grandfather's suit that was four inches too short. A clunkhead his teammates named Barney. He had plenty of heat on his ball but it wasn't until the 1910 season that he really showed. If you had to face the guy you knew it, but it took the smart alecks a little longer to get the word.

Well, on this particular afternoon Barney looked pretty confident warming up, tossing from the side in a buggy whip motion that fooled batters into thinking he only possessed average stuff. Step into the box and you discovered he threw a rocket with a hop on it. Just to disconcert you even more his catcher would whistle as the ball came in. I knew that if my side had a prayer of getting to him it would have to be early before the guy settled in.

So Bert Daniels leads off for the Yanks with an easy roller to Killifer at second who lets the ball squirt between his legs for an error. Wolter then bunts Bert over to second, which brings me to the plate. I don't want to strike out and look bad, so I work the count to two balls and no strikes, and guess that Barney'll come down the heart and I'd have a chance to lay some wood on the pitch. Sure enough, I top an easy one to McBride at short, a perfect grounder to keep the runner pinned on second. The only problem is the busher heaves the ball into the stands, Bert scores, and I'm awarded second base whether I like it or not.

Barney is upset now and cussing to himself on the mound. At least it was his version of cussing. "Goodness gracious sakes alive!" he grumbled.

Schoolboy Knight steps up to the plate, plays it smart, working the count to his favor like I did, and gets a pitch he can handle. He dumps a short one into left. As soon as it plunks off his bat I know it's going to fall in and I can score easy. Instead, I act confused, get hung up between bases and have no choice but to settle on third base.

Now Barney is really blistering himself. "Great Scott animal crackers!"

The only out he has is the sacrifice bunt and he looks lost in the woods. I call for the old double steal move. Schoolboy takes off for second, I make sure to leave too early, the catcher fakes the peg to second then waits for me to waltz home to make the second out of the inning.

That break was all Barney needed to get out of the inning. He powders three straight past LaPorte and we can't touch him the rest of the day. His team pecks away until they manage to post a couple of runs to take the win.

Stallings is burned all afternoon about us letting Johnson off the hook in the first inning. And hadn't he seen that botched double steal play somewhere before?

Chapter 38

In morning practice Stallings had us work so long on the double steal that everybody was ready to kill the Prince.

Afterwards when we're done for the morning, Schoolboy Knight steps up to me. "Butchering that goddamn play cost us two ball games in one month."

"I put on the hit and run yesterday," I said. "Too bad the batter had his head up his ass."

LaPorte began to fire back, then stopped to consider if maybe he had missed the sign.

"I got the steal sign, too," Schoolboy said. "And if it was the hit and run, where the hell were you going? Home to grandma's house?"

I just gave him a smile. "Who am I to argue with the leading hitter on the club. I hear you're going to replace Ty Cobb on all the Coca-Cola advertisements."

That drew a chuckle from some of the boys, but Knight wasn't about to back down. The only reason he was called Schoolboy was because Connie Mack plucked him straight off his high school team in 1905. Since then he had grown into a real strapper, standing six-three.

"Maybe we should settle things right now." He began to ball up his fists. He was standing up for a buddy so he probably thought he had justice on his side. From my experience that meant he'd likely get the crap kicked out of him.

But before anything could start, Stallings arrived and stepped between us. "Save it for the league, boys. Save it for the league."

We took the train to Boston. We were only a game behind the Red Sox for second place and Stallings was keen on taking that spot. But the team was pulling in different directions again and we lost the series. On the long train ride to St. Louis the younger players are holed up with me in one car and the older ones with Schoolboy in the next.

"Don't count on General George leading this army next spring," I told the boys.

"So who'll take over?" asks Bert Daniels.

"I'm not at liberty to say."

"It's you, Prince, ain't it?"

"I've said all I can. That's all you'll get out of me."

By the time we reach the Mississippi River they're all convinced that Stallings has a loose screw and is heading for the dust bin anyway. Now when he flashes a sign to one of the younger players who weren't allowed to call plays on their own, they look over to me to see what I think. I flash the opposite sign. By sheer luck the plays work out in our favor and we win a couple of games, so Stallings doesn't say anything.

Then we move on to Chicago and blow a game when Wolter on first ignores Stallings' hit and run sign, stays put and the game ends on a double play ball. Wolter knows he's in trouble and doesn't waste time dashing for the clubhouse. Stallings ran the guy down like he was a wounded buck and gave him an earful in the middle of the outfield grass.

"I guess I missed the sign," Harry says.

"That's a lie, you wall-eyed little shit. You looked down to Chase for his opinion."

"So what if he did?" I said, butting in. "It's a free country, last I heard."

"There you are. I thought I smelled something burning." Stallings forgot all about Wolters. He forgot all about keeping a lid on things. "You're suspended, big shot. You hear that?"

"Try telling that to the owner of the ball club."

"Maybe I'll just tell the league instead. They'll be interested to know what you've been up to."

Since the league kept its office in Chicago he didn't have far to go. Too bad he had a bigger enemy than me in Ban Johnson.

I was quick to get on the horn to New York.

"Does he have a southern fried brain?" Farrell said.

"He goes over the deep end sometimes. I don't think he means any real harm."

"Don't stick up for him, Hal. I don't need him stirring up trouble with the league."

I thought that Ban Johnson might throw Stallings out of his office on his ear. Instead he tells the newspapers that the New York manager had leveled some serious charges against player Chase that would require careful consideration. While Johnson deliberated, Farrell recalled Stallings to New York for some conferrals, leaving the traveling secretary, Tom Davis, in charge of the club. The only thing Tom could manage was a checkbook and since I was the captain he deferred to me on running the team in the field.

The Yankees are a complete mess now, and we go out to lose an ugly one against the White Sox. The next day I call for a meeting and tell everyone it's time to put away harsh feelings and start to play as a team again.

"Who says you're the manager?" asks Schoolboy.

"I say so."

"Is it true, Tom?"

"Well, ah," stammers Davis, "I believe that technically I'm in charge."

"Belly up to the real world," I said. "Farrell and me cut a deal when I jumped ship that time in Cleveland."

"And I thought you went home on account of the wife," said Schoolboy. "You mean you had us all worried over nothing?"

"You really want something to worry about? There's going to be some changes made next year, and I suggest that anybody serious about making their living in this profession had better prove something to me in the last three weeks of the season."

That was enough to motivate the most of them. Schoolboy, though, must have thought that being the leading hitter gave him an edge. Even if the Yanks dumped him he'd have no trouble finding work in the big show.

We took the field against the White Sox and went after them pretty good until late in the game when the Sox filled the bases with two outs. Choulnard hits an easy grounder to Schoolboy at short. He fields it clean and has plenty of time to get the final out to any base he wanted. Instead, he just holds the ball. I'm ready to take the throw at first and he just looks over at me and smiles as the tying run crosses the plate. The next batter drives in a couple more runs and that's the old ball game.

I didn't go haywire. If Schoolboy thought that the Prince was going to lose his grip and take a poke at him, he didn't know who he was messing with.

By now the New York newspapers made it sound like I had pulled a real fast one to take over the club. Farrell reaffirmed that Tom Davis was the man in charge, as he boarded a train for Chicago to get to the bottom of the situation.

While Farrell steamed west, Ban Johnson, after staying mum the last couple of days, called in the writers and cut the feet out from under Stallings. He announced that after a thorough investigation, all the charges made against Hal Chase were proved to be utterly false. So that when Farrell stepped off the train in Chicago there was nothing he could do but offer up George Stallings' head on a silver plater. And name me the new "boy manager" of the New York Yankees.

Chapter 39

When Farrell and Brush announced that the two New York baseball teams would finally square off in an October city series, everybody forgot about the flap between Stallings and Prince Hal. My first at bat when we got home the game had to be stopped so four men could carry in a couple of huge horseshoe bouquets of flowers to congratulate me on my promotion. All the players gathered around to pose for a group picture as the grandstands cheered.

I smiled. I waved to the cattle.

Now that we had a common enemy in Mugsy McGraw and his puffed-up Giants to look forward to playing, the team rallied together, forgot our differences, and went on a tear. We won the last nine out of eleven, including three straight in Detroit, to nip the Tigers for second place.

The day before the city series was set to begin, I was buying a newspaper in a candy store when who do I run into but Fat Jack.

"Congratulations," Delaney said.

"On what?"

"On making manager of the ball club."

"I should have known it wouldn't take you long to bring up baseball."

"What do people generally talk to you about?" he says. "World events?"

"There's no business on the city series, Jack."

"I know, Prince. There a new sheriff in town."

"So clear out. And don't run into me by accident no more."

I was sort of proud of myself for giving the brush to that cheap crook. Sure I had to break some eggs to get where I wanted, but now that was all going to change. I could start making a difference in the world. I could do good. The first thing, though, was to take care of those Giants because, let's face it, being the nicest guy in the world don't mean a thing if you're not a winner.

My club had suffered a rash of injuries to close out the year, so before the first game of the city series I stood on a milking stool to rally the troops.

"I don't give a good goddamn how shorthanded we are," I said. "I wouldn't have it any other way. You know why? Because the longer the odds the sweeter the victory, boys. The fewer the heroes, the bigger the share of glory. Maybe those Giants got us outnumbered; maybe they got the advantage of the home field; but I say, so what? I say this battle's ours for the taking. I say that someday there'll be plenty of ballplayers sitting on their butts somewhere who'll reckon their careers were pretty damn cheap because they didn't play for the Yankees when they creamed those swell-headed Giants. So what do you say, are you with me, boys?"

They shouted their heads off, grabbed their mitts and ran onto the field—then dropped the series in six games.

◈

During the off-season Nellie had her baby, a boy she wanted to name Hal Junior. As far as I was concerned she could call the kid anything she wanted. Like that was supposed to make me more of a family man? I didn't even want to go near the boy. He just looked so fragile. Like an egg shell. I didn't remember Mary being like that, but I had been so weak from the smallpox there was a lot of things I couldn't remember.

During the off-season the rulers of baseball were up to their rotten tricks again. For 1911 they introduced the cork-centered baseball. Maybe it wasn't packed with as much dynamite as later on when Ruth, Gehrig and Foxx were swatting them out of the park in record numbers, but it changed the game enough.

For one thing you couldn't bunt the new ball with as much touch. And in the field you weren't sure how hard to charge in. If the Frenchman had been hitting one of those cork balls when he faked the bunt on me, he'd have ripped my head off. Take one of those new sizzlers in the palm of a pancake glove and you'd feel the sting down to the roots of your teeth. And just like the infielders are pushed back, the outfielders have to drop a lot deeper. You don't dare the batter to smack one over your head because that's exactly what the guy would do, even if he was only a hundred-pound shortstop. With most of the fences still four to five hundred feet from the plate, the last thing you wanted was for that hot ball to scoot past you. So what you got was a lot of dump hits, fewer runners thrown out on the bases and, in general, a lot less exciting brand of ball.

Not knowing yet that the odds didn't favor the bunt play as much, we kept playing station-to-station ball for a time. But why give up an out to plate one run at a time when you can take your chances and maybe bundle three or four together? So why bother stealing a base when you can trot home behind one that lands in the outfield seats? All the tricks and angles that players used to dope out in the hotel lobby or on those long train rides just weren't worth the effort anymore. A cheap homer now counted more than brain work and sound team play, so of course the players fell into bad habits and grew lazy. Too bad the goddamn fans loved it.

A lot of guys felt the same way I did about the wrong direction the game was going, but all they wanted to do was bellyache. Nobody wanted to accept responsibility. There was nothing you could do about it, they said. But I had to wonder if I was as ruthless as the next guy, if I couldn't gain control of one of those baseball clubs and make a difference. Look at Charlie Comiskey. Look at Connie Mack. They were just players and they took over franchises. Why not the Prince? Somebody had to look after the game. Any fool could see how the bastard owners were killing it. They loved to act like guardians of baseball, especially when it helped to keep down salaries, but all they really cared about was the loot. Only a few months earlier they were still making the players go into the stands to tangle over foul balls. This year they figure, "Why sweat twenty cents?" when a lot more people would come out to the yard to watch the batters launch rockets? Besides, now you wanted to change balls every few pitches to make sure the batter got a crisp one, white and tight to whale away at. I could see the way things were going. Next you prohibit the trick pitches: the spitball, the nickball, the smudgeball. And if the fielders feel like they're under the gun, then just give them bigger and fatter gloves. Pad up the catcher. Stick an army helmet on the batter.

The owners said they were just improving the game. But I knew better. They were ruining it. Just to make a buck.

Chapter 40

I discovered the next season it's tough to be a cracker jack baseball manager when you got a lot of lunkheads in your line-up. You have to make sure your players don't hit the sauce too much, the greenhorns don't eat themselves out of the league, and that none of those road trip Sadies spring a trap on your starting pitcher. And do you think any of your players appreciate your efforts? But that's just a way of life for the man in charge, whether it's the alfalfa leagues or the big show.

I also had to put up with my share of simple jealousy. I may have been the new manager of the team but I was still the Prince, the big star making the big dough, and the boys expected me to keep on proving it. I showed I still had it, despite all the extra responsibilities. I batted .315 with a lame arm and two bum ankles. There were times I could hardly walk, yet I found a way to run. I showed them. Too bad the players quit on me. We won as many as we lost, but never made a serious run at the pennant, because as early as May the boys decided we didn't have a real shot of winning. And besides, why make the Prince look good?

I knew they were all knocking on me as soon as I got out of range, especially the players that were left over from when George Stallings ran the club. I started to trade them away, telling Farrell that I needed my kind of players before the Yankees could show their true colors.

There was one player that I had no intention of moving and that was Schoolboy Knight. Sure he had been our leading batter the year before and Farrell was partial to him, but I would have still begged to keep him on the team.

From the first day of spring he came in with this smug attitude, like because he had one good year at the plate I couldn't touch him. He also began trying to live up to his name, Schoolboy, by dressing like a college man. He bragged how he had begun to take some night classes and even brought books with him on the road. While everybody else was playing cards, Schoolboy would have his nose stuck in a book. I told him that when he graduated college we could compare our degrees. Sometimes I brought along a book myself and we sat across the aisle from one another on the train reading, neither one of us willing to be the first one to put down his book.

This season Schoolboy got off to a slow start with the willow and began to lose confidence in his swing. I continued to pencil him in the four hole, making sure he knew how much the club depended on him. And how did he repay my confidence? He kept slumping. But I kept running him out there and telling him how much we all needed him. By mid-season he dropped the baseball star attitude. He stopped bringing books on the train and I figured maybe he was giving up the bookworm act, too. Then one day I discovered that Schoolboy had a dirty secret.

I caught the guy squinting at a sign and in a flash I knew the situation. Schoolboy Knight had gone nearsighted, and for a ballplayer that's like losing a leg. Maybe if you were employed in a bank you could wear spectacles to work, but not on a baseball field. Even if you got caught wearing them away from the game, the other players in the league would ride you so hard you'd be out of the bigs in no time. Ballplayers prided themselves on being tough, and tough men don't have bad eyes. At least they don't wear glasses. More than a few in the big leagues were walking around half blind and ready with all kinds of excuses to explain why they weren't able to hit the old apple the way they used to.

So I began to ask Schoolboy for the time off a clock or to read a distant billboard, anything that would make him scramble. By September when I strode into the clubhouse he'd slink away to a corner like a dog that's been kicked too many times. That's when I said I had to think about the club and shipped him off to Washington where his batting average continued to drop for a couple more years. By the time he turned twenty-eight Schoolboy Knight was out of the big time.

All in all I thought I did pretty good as a manager. A dry spell near the end dropped us into the second division but we still finished at .500. If I got rid of the dead wood and brought in the right personnel, I figured to be showing Connie Mack and Mugsy McGraw a few tricks before I was done.

I went in to see Farrell over the winter with a list of players I thought we might be able to get. Only, he had other plans.

"You had a great year hitting. Don't get me wrong, Hal," he said.

"But have you ever thought what you could do with that lively ball if you didn't have the extra responsibilities of being manager?"

"I admit there were a lot of distractions, but next year I look to smack a few more long balls."

"I still think you'd be better off with less worries if you didn't have to manage the team and play at the same time. It's not efficient."

"Well, I'm willing to think about it, Frank."

"The thing is, I got somebody else in mind. Harry Wolverton. He played over in the National League for years. And he's been doing a hell of a job managing Williamsport in the Tri-State League."

"That's not quite the same as managing in the bigs."

"You never managed anywhere, Hal."

"Well, now I got the experience. If you give me a chance to bring in my kind of players I'll get you that pennant."

"The thing is, Hal, I already signed a contract with Wolverton. I just didn't want you to talk me out of it. Hell, you got a convincing way about yourself."

"Maybe you want to dump me altogether."

"You're still the best damn ballplayer in the American League. I wouldn't trade you for Ty Cobb and Sam Crawford put together."

"I would."

"Yeah, well Detroit ain't about to make the offer." Farrell looked away for a second then came back with this soft look on his face. "You're just too young. When your playing days are over, you can be the manager for the Yankees for the next thirty years."

So what chance did I have? If Farrell thought that the new blood would have better luck than me—well, we'd see about that.

Chapter 41

It didn't take long for Harry Wolverton to get acquainted. He held court with the newspaper writers that followed the team, wearing a floppy sombrero and smoking an enormous cigar and offering what the scribes called his "nit-witticisms." Those writers were a hard-boiled lot and made it clear that what might pass for colorful behavior in the Tri-State League wouldn't cut it in the big town. They made Wolverton out to be a first-class blockhead, which didn't help the new manager gain respect from his new team.

Harry wanted to be regarded as a good egg by his players, a guy who was fair and upfront. But that always got lost because he'd say something dopey. It was all little stuff. He had been away from the big leagues for a number of years and forgot how expensive it was to travel the loop, so he spent more time complaining about prices than he did talking about baseball. Cabs, tips, shoeshines—all of it obsessed the man.

"Holy mackerel," he'd say. "How can they charge that much for a glass of milk and still be able too look themselves in the mirror in the morning?"

Harry was very keen on mirrors—and people looking into them, especially in the morning. If the team came up short in a close game but fought hard, he'd march around the clubhouse, clapping his hands and saying, "At least we can look ourselves in the mirror, boys. We can look ourselves in the mirror in the morning." But if we didn't make a good showing, he'd shake his head and mutter, "I don't know how any of you guys can stand to look at yourselves in the mirror in the morning."

One day I asked Harry for some advice on buying a mirror for my wife. A few of the other players listened in.

"Let me understand you." Harry was wearing nothing but his sombrero and rubber-soled sandals. For some reason he liked to show off his tubby little body. "What does your wife plan on doing with this mirror?"

"Just looking at herself in the morning."

"Are you thinking of full-length or just hand-held?"

"Gosh, I don't know, Skip."

"It's important. Ask the wife."

"But it's supposed to be a surprise, Harry."

"Then you just have to be sneaky."

The next day I tell him that the wife is partial to oval mirrors.

"That's a shape. What you want to know is does she want to hang it on the wall or does she want to hold it in her hand."

"Gee, I didn't realize the subject was so deep."

"Hal, I can't help you unless I got the facts."

The next day I tell him that my wife needs a new hand mirror.

"Well, I wouldn't pay too much for it," he says. By now the entire ball club is in on the joke and gathered around. A couple of the boys are pretending to cough. Some have to step outside.

"Now you could go to your fancy department stores like Stewarts, but I say you can get the same kind of quality at a much cheaper price by going to your Woolworths or better yet—"

One of the boys starts to run for the door but can't make it before starting to laugh, which sets off the entire clubhouse. Now everyone is doubled-over howling at the manager.

Harry is furious and when things start to quiet down he says, "Maybe you fellows should spend more time thinking about baseball than horsing around. If I played on a last-place club I don't know how I'd ever have the nerve to look myself in the—"

The boys were ready to explode again.

"Aw, forget it, you bunch of lazy slugs."

Wolverton was right about us being a last-place club. We got off to a rotten start, never improved much, and made a comfortable nest at the bottom of the standings, content to wait out the long summer. Not able to earn our respect, he could never kick us in the ass to at least make a decent showing. We were just a "joy club," playing out the schedule, riding the rails, boozing it up, playing cards, and picking the Daisies. Of course, if we went up against a contending club and we had something against their players, we might get up our dander and try to trip them. The other side always figured to sweep us, so they might get tight around the collar, and we could prove a problem. But for the most part if you got us down a couple runs we'd fold up like the evening newspaper. Sometimes a contender might take up a little collection for a joy club to encourage them to play harder against another team fighting for the pennant. The understanding, of course, was that you'd also go easy on the team paying you off. And that's what it was. A payoff. A fix. A tailender could toss games to the highest bidder and not even a team that got beat out for the championship would raise a fuss, because nobody's hands were clean. Ban Johnson and the owners looked the other way, too. Anything that didn't make the game seem saintly they didn't want to see at all.

All I really cared about was maintaining my batting average. And making sure Harry Wolverton won a lot less games than I did as manager. If Farrell thought the Prince had done such a poor job with the reins, what did he think now?

Since we were losing anyway, I didn't see any reason why I shouldn't take advantage of the situation to gather the odd buck, so I decided to look up Fat Jack Delaney.

"Well, it's been a long time, Prince." We were back in his favorite pool hall, in the storeroom with the pigs knuckles and pretzels and jars of hard-boiled eggs.

"I thought you might be looking to do some business again."

"And I thought you went the straight and narrow."

"I haven't changed, Jack. Everybody else has."

For one thing he sure looked different. He had lost a good bit of weight and he didn't look the better for it. His face looked pasty. Loose skin hung around his jowls. And he seemed down in the dumps. His voice was on the wheezy side.

"Hey, didn't we have some fun together?" I said.

"Did we?"

"We could have some more."

"Nobody gives a fig about that club of yours. Ten years in New York and not a single pennant. The Giants own this town."

"There's always a sucker. You taught me that one, Jack."

"For small potatoes, sure. How I'm sick to death of the small potatoes. If I made just one big killing in my life I'd feel I had at least accomplished something. I'm still in the same goddamn pool hall I used to sweep up as a kid."

"Are you under the weather or what?"

"You want to have some fun, Prince? Make some friends on the contending clubs. Hopefully pitchers. Hopefully at World Series time."

"What are you saying, I should convince a guy to toss ball games when he has a chance to win a championship?"

"What's a championship?"

"A share in the World Series gate, that's what."

"You'll never stop thinking like a baseball player, will ya?"

"I know that flag is why we play the game."

"The game!" he said. "You think clubbing the ball and running around in circles and taking two-bits at the gate is the *game*."

"That pretty much covers it."

"The game plays you."

"You got the syph or something, Jack? Maybe you should see a doctor before it eats away your entire brain."

"And baseball is just a little part of a bigger game. The world itself, you dumbshit baseball player. The world."

I just left him in the back room talking to himself. A few weeks later I heard that Jack was dead. His insides had all been eaten away by worms or something. He smelled so rotten at the end that even the priest giving him the last rites couldn't stand to be in the same room with the guy.

Chapter 42

I spent another winter burning up the town. I barely ate two meals a week at home or said ten words altogether to Nellie. But she never said a word, just tended to our baby. She was all patience and understanding. If she wanted to enjoy being miserable, as far as I was concerned that was her business.

One night I went out to dinner with a pal. Afterwards we stop at a joint where we spot a pair of lookers that looked like they were having a pretty crummy time. Their dates had drunk too much too fast and were slumped in their chairs. I gave the girls the eye and they gave it right back. Since I knew the owner of the place, about thirty seconds later that table was clear of the dishes and the deadwood.

The one I favored was named Anna. I slid my chair up against hers. She backed off to light a cigarette. I waited until she had taken a puff before I picked the nail right out of her lips and flicked it on the floor.

"Haven't you heard," I said. "Those are bad for you?"

"Who made you my doctor?"

"You could do a lot worse. At least I got warm hands."

"Just what Manhattan needs, another caveman."

"There ain't but one of me."

"That's a relief."

I put my hand on her knee and she throws it off in a flash. "If I wanted to waste my time on a masher I'd telephone Hal Chase."

"What if I said that's who I am?"

"I'd tell you to go home, Honey, because the way you were going this spring you'd be lucky to hit a rug on a clothes line."

When people started to recognize me and come up like they always do, you should have seen her attitude change. A couple drinks later and she's sitting on my lap to keep off the competition, and telling me her life story. Anna said she grew up in the Bronx. Her father was a dentist who did pretty well for his family but could never give her what she really wanted in life.

"And what's that?" I asked.

"Class," she said. She was kind of drunk now and in a feeling sorry for herself mood. All her life she had read the society pages in the newspapers, knew all the comings and goings of the Astors and the Vanderbilts, and dreamed of one day being a part of it all. She wanted to be listed in the Social Register. Not one of those upstarts with new money trying to horn in, *the cash register*, but the real thing. She knew that the odds were stacked against a Jewish girl from her neighborhood marrying into that crowd, so she lowered her sights to that Broadway-sporting crowd where a pretty girl with a Bronx accent didn't need a pedigree, just an arm to hang on as she went through the door. Of course that also happened to be the crowd the Prince moved in.

Anna was a golddigger who made no bones about it and that was refreshing enough for me. We became a steady thing and I took her to all those places she heard were posh and popular that without her I would have found kind of tiresome. I kept amused by telling her who was who, who hated who, who was catting around on who. She took it all in and asked questions. She was keeping her own kind of book because to her this was the fast company and she was looking for every edge. Compared to her, Nellie was just a sandlot player.

❖

As for the Yankees, the Harry Wolverton days were already forgotten. After managing a major league team to 100 losses he wouldn't be looking himself in the mirror in the morning or managing another team in any league for quite some time. To draw some attention in the newspapers Farrell thought he pulled a smart one when he hired as his new manager big Frank Chance. He was the longtime arsenic of the Giants who had played first base and managed the Cubs to a pair of World Championships. For that the Chicago writers dubbed him the Peerless Leader, but the players called him Husk, short for Husky, because he was really big. And dumb. When it came to baseball, he was smart enough, especially by skipping out on his aging club to snap up the Yankee offer.

Chance demanded a free hand in running the team, and Farrell was always accommodating when it came to promises. So right away the guy decides that the real problem with the Yankees was a lack of discipline. To keep us concentrated on baseball and out of range of those Southern whores, Husk packed us off to an island in the Bahamas for spring training, which he ran like army boot camp. You can bet the boys didn't take long to resent him for that. A ball diamond had to be laid out and Husk made sure it was located a few miles from the hotel, so we had to ride bicycles to get there. The infield was so damn sandy that it felt like you were running on the beach, which is probably where the stuff came from. The players would cramp up, but Husk forced us to work through the pain then bicycle home. Several players developed leg injuries, which really slowed our progress. And because there was no opposition on the island to play against we pretty much spent our time playing catch, taking infield and getting pissed off at the new manager.

Husk took an immediate dislike to me. He figured he had been around the block a few times and had the Prince pegged as a tunnel maker, the kind of guy that would get everybody grumbling against the manager. But Husk saw to that himself, with all his annoying habits and sandpaper personality. A lot of it stemmed from a beaning incident that left him deaf in one ear and a little loony.

Frank Chance had always been known to crowd the plate. Nasty pitchers—and only the nasty survived in the bigs—would come in high and hard at him, to see if that wouldn't loosen up his toes. But even after getting hit in the head a couple of times, Husk held his ground. Then a Cincinnati hurler named Jack Harper nailed him good, sending the big guy to the hospital where they actually performed the last rites. Chance recovered but along the way lost the hearing in one ear, not to mention a screw or two. As soon as he got the chance he traded for Jack Harper, then let him rot on the bench. He offered him a contract for a huge cut in pay and there was nothing Harper could do if he wanted to continue in Organized Baseball but sign and hope Chance would let him go. Eventually the guy gave up and quit the game.

Frank didn't lose his hearing right away. It came on gradual so it affected his voice in a queer kind of way. Nobody felt like risking injury to enlighten the big lug, so he developed this pip-squeak wail that would really grate on your nerves, especially when he was cussing you out—which was constant, because the guy also suffered from nagging headaches that always kept him out of sorts.

We got constant reminders about how the Cubs always did everything right and we were a bunch of muffs who couldn't ever hope to compare to the likes of Tinker-to-Evers-to-Chance. Of course it's not like those Cubs never made a bonehead play, and we knew all his talk about them playing like a family was so much blue moonshine. Everybody knew that Tinker hadn't shared two words in ten years with Evers and about the only thing they'd agree on was how much they'd like to murder the Peerless Leader over at first base.

When the season opened everyone on the Yankees hated the new manager and were just trying to make the best of another bad situation. Usually when every club is tied for first place you start off with a rosier attitude than that. You had to wonder how long we'd hang in there. Not very long, if I had anything to say about it. Chance figured me to be a tunnel maker on the team, so I planned on being accommodating. It was the least I could do.

Chapter 43

It didn't take much talent to imitate that quirky voice of Frank Chance. Pretty soon I developed a regular vaudeville routine to entertain my teammates.

"Take Three Finger Brown," I'd screech, "Now there's a pitcher. I think some of you boys for the sake of the Cubs—I mean the *club*—should maybe have a farming accident like he had. It might improve your curve ball."

Before long everybody was pulling the stunt of mimicking the manager, with the exception of Jeff Sweeney, a catcher Husk had brought over from the Cubs. Then I came up with a new trick. I discovered that if you stood on his deaf side, and talked just low enough you could mouth any kind of horseshit and he'd pretend to understand every word.

"Taylor's got a hop on the ball today, Skip," I might start off innocently enough.

"Hmm-hmm."

"I said, Husk, that you're as ugly as a monkey's ass."

And the guy would just bob his head like he was mulling it over or something.

"Mind if I fart in your face?"

The boys always got a kick out of that one. Except for Jeff Sweeney, of course.

You didn't need a crystal ball to know that the Yankees hadn't improved much. We were still a pretty rotten ball club. Not having the greatest collection of talent in the league to start with and no respect for the manager, we were just a bunch of guys pretending to be a team. We were well on our way to becoming another joy club.

On the homefront I was growing more fed up with Nellie. I left her a million clues about Anna and me, but she refused to take the bait. She just minded the baby and suffered in silence. I knew what she was up to. She'd make me feel so bad that I'd finally give in and come back to the fold. Well, I was tired of having people pull that number on me.

One day she's giving the baby a bath, singing to him. I look at her standing in front of the window with the sun pouring through to catch her hair and make it sparkle and I remembered when I fell in love with the girl and how crazy I was about her. Her voice sounded so pleasant, the way she sang and cooed at the baby, that I couldn't stand it.

"Can the little birdy act, will ya?" I said.

"Little Hal likes it."

"Well, it's bothering me!"

"I was singing to the baby. I wasn't bothering you."

"What's with this bee in your bonnet?"

"I don't know what you're talking about."

"Oh, yes you do. So why don't you just say it instead of putting on this happy motherhood act. A decent husband would stay home at night. A decent husband would play with his own son. A decent husband, my ass!"

The baby started to cry.

"I hope you're happy," she said.

"Yeah, blame me."

"Well, he wasn't crying before you started in."

"You want me to help?" As I stepped forward she quickly pulled the baby out of the water and clutched him dripping wet to her breast.

"What's that all about?" I grabbed her by the wrists. "Are you afraid of me now?"

"No, Hal, please."

I start to pry the baby away from her.

"How do you think this makes me feel to have you treat me like this?"

"I'm sorry, Hal. I'm sorry. It's all my fault."

"Give me my son."

She lets go rather than see him hurt. I didn't really want to hold the baby. Now that I had him I didn't know what to do. And the way Nellie looked just killed me.

I handed back the baby.

"Leave me." I was so shook up all of a sudden I could hardly speak.

"Take the baby and go home to your parents. Please, Nellie. Please, listen to me. Please, save my son."

Hell, it was what she needed to hear.

I stayed away for a couple days, giving her plenty of time, and sure enough when I came back, Nellie had cleared out with the baby. I figured the divorce papers would be on their way soon enough.

I caught up to Anna and told her that my wife had run off and pretty soon I'd be a free man.

"So you want to get married?" I said.

"Ain't that kind of sudden?"

"Do you or don't you?"

"I need to think about it."

"Come off it. As Mrs. Hal Chase you could conquer the known world. At least what you know of it."

"You don't have to be so mean."

"I'm asking you to marry me, kid. How's that being mean?"

"Believe it or not," she said, "I never been asked before. Can't I take some time?"

"What's there to think about?"

"Maybe I just want to ... I don't know."

"Play hard to get?"

"That's not it at all."

"The offer's on the table. I'm a man of my word. You know me, Anna, I won't come back a second time."

"Okay, all right," she said. "Yeah, sure, I guess I'll marry you. I'm not doing anything better."

Chapter 44

I didn't have trouble finding like-thinking men to replace Fat Jack Delaney, not that there was much business to be done. Delaney had been right about the lack of interest in the Yankees. We were turning into the St. Louis Browns of New York City, the poor American League cousin of the Giants. After we dropped the first ten home games in a row there were no bets to be had on the Yankees, and what work we got in I did sloppy. I dropped throws. I struck out on balls over my head. I didn't care if anyone suspected what I was up to or not.

I kept making fun of Frank Chance and talking into his deaf ear. After it stopped being funny and I got bored with the trick, that's when Jeff Sweeney decided he could take it no longer and ratted to Husk. I was taking a shower when I heard the big guy's whining voice, "Chase, you son of a bitch, come out here."

So I step out, naked as a jay, and start to towel myself off. "Got a problem, Husk?"

"You're the one who's got the problem. With me."

I cocked my head to one side, pretending to have trouble hearing him.

"You heard me good, you goddamn twisted bastard."

"Must have got water in my ear."

"I'm wise to your little games."

I noticed Sweeney standing behind Frank, as if the big guy needed some back-up. "Did he go and tattle on me?"

"Get up your dukes, Chase."

"I'm naked, Husk."

"Get dressed so I can beat the living shit out of you."

"Can't you take a little ribbing?"

"You can play all the tricks you want on me, but I should take a horse whip to you for what you're doing to this proud game."

There it was, another guy getting all high and mighty about the game of baseball. He couldn't wait for me to get dressed, he marched straight to Frank Farrell to demand that either I left the club or he would, but not before making some accusations against me to a few writers. Considering the club's awful record and that I'm no longer the young phenom in the league, Farrell didn't need much convincing to unload my contract. The trouble was with Chance going to the newspapers. They weren't going to print his charges, that wouldn't be good for the game, but word got around the league quick enough, and clubs weren't willing to trade good value for bad. Finally it was Charlie Comiskey, always looking for a bargain, who made an offer that probably even he didn't think Chance would accept, but Husk was angry enough to snap it up.

I got traded to the Chicago White Sox for a mediocre shortstop named Zeider, who could barely walk because of a case of bunions, and a first sacker named Babe Burton who wasn't exactly a three-alarm fire. The wise guys said that I got traded for a bunion and an onion. And don't think Farrell thought it was funny. Frank Chance's days with the Yankees were numbered, too.

I was tired of New York, anyway. A change in scenery might actually help me to get my game back to the top shelf. The one who was bothered the most by the trade was Anna. She thought she had just married a real prize in the big city and a few weeks later I'm telling her to skip the plans for storming New York and to start packing for the plains.

"What's in Chicago?" she cried.

"Plenty of cattle and lots of wind. You'll want a heavy coat."

"What am I supposed to do in Chicago?"

"Be my wife."

"Like that'll keep me busy."

"I thought you told the justice you'd marry me for better or for worse."

"He didn't say nothing about Chicago."

❖

They called Charlie Comiskey the "Old Roman" because the older he got the more he resembled a schoolbook picture of one of those ancient Roman senators. But people who thought he looked noble never had to negotiate a contract with the old skinflint. He made it seem that offering you a contract for your baseball services was a pure act of charity. But when he landed the Prince for a bunion and an onion, he made the mistake of letting the pleasure of cheating the Yankees get the best of him. He bragged to the newspapers how with Hal Chase added to the line-up the White Sox were now odds-on favorites to cop the American League pennant. Normally he'd poor-mouth a player's abilities to get more leverage when it came time to sign a contract. But he was also in a tough spot because he needed to spur interest in his White Sox, which hadn't accomplished much since the glory days of Fielder Jones and his Hitless Wonders. And don't think all of this was lost on me. I'd remember come winter.

The change of scenery actually did give me a lift. Putting up good numbers was my way of getting revenge on Chance and Farrell and the rest of my enemies. I led the team in batting and added the punch to the order that Comiskey was looking for, but in the end we were no match for the Philadelphia A's. In fact we were no match for most of the league and finished the year in fifth place.

Unlike Connie Mack, Comiskey really did want to field a winning side. He just didn't want to pay for it. He had the best pitching in the American League, but rather than spend money to improve the hitting, he was always hoping to get by with the bare minimum at the plate. It worked once with Fielder Jones, why not again? Even when he drafted good players from the minors or traded for them, Charlie would gouge them over pennies and make everyone so sour they weren't eager to produce for him. The result was that the Sox were always a few cards short of a winning hand.

In a couple of years he'd finally get the lucky draw—only he'd find a new way to screw it all up.

Chapter 45

After the season, I met with Comiskey to negotiate my new contract. His office at the ballpark was just a drafty rat hole that he shared with his little weasel of a secretary, Harry Grabiner. All the players hated Harry, since he witnessed you crawling before the owner to plead for a modest raise, or beg not to be given a cut. And compared to Harry with all his numbers that proved that in spite of what the world thought you really had a rotten season, the Old Roman seemed like the old softie.

Comiskey admitted to me up-front that I had been a wonderful addition to the Sox.

"You made some fine plays in the field, Hal. And yet ..." He paused to warm up by blowing into his hands.

Across the way Harry was working at his desk with a muffler tied around his neck, looking like Bob Crachet himself.

"And yet, you had some bad breaks and let a lot of easy ones get through."

"Mr. Chase committed twenty-seven errors last season," Harry said without looking up from his ledger.

"Was it that many?"

"I'm afraid so, Mr. Comiskey."

"How's the fever, Harry?"

"A little better. Thank you for asking. Sir, excuse the interruption, but should I pay the coal bill or the telephone bill this month?"

"The telephone bill. In case one of the players needs to contact us during the holiday season."

"Very good, sir." Harry began to cough.

"That sounds worse. You should be home in bed. I can plug away without you."

"We have ten more ballplayers to sign. I have to think of the team. Besides, you had to give up—forgive me for speaking out of turn."

"No need to go into my little trials and tribulations. I've taken one in the ribs for the club before. My family can do without Christmas one year, I suppose. So where were we, Hal?"

"Because of my sterling play you were about to offer me a sizable raise."

"I thought we were discussing your unusually high number of errors at first base."

"Hell, once upon a time you played the bag yourself, *Charlie*." That got his attention. Even Harry looked up. The ballplayers were expected to address the owner as Mr. Comiskey. Or, Sir. Certainly not Charlie. "I got to balls that most guys just wave at. Mind if I help myself?"

I reached across the desk to liberate a couple of Comiskey's expensive cigars from a humidor. I looked at him as I lit one up. He was probably making a mental note to replace the humidor with a cardboard box of White Owls before his next appointment.

"And another thing," I said. "Most of those muffs on my record were really sweet throws to your basemen standing out of position holding their dicks."

"Of those twenty-seven errors, Harry, how many were of the throwing variety?"

"Only seven."

"If I were you, Harry," I said, "I wouldn't lose this job. Where else can you get paid to pull numbers out of your ass? But come to think of it, a lot of mugs in finance could use a guy like you. How much are you making here?"

"This doesn't have to be such a contentious experience, Hal," Comiskey said. "We assess the objective facts then arrive at a scientific calculation. We only want to be fair to the player and the ballclub."

"The way I calculate things I'm in line for a raise of a thousand bucks, because I know for a *fact* that attendance picked up when I came to town."

"What was Mr. Chase's batting average in relation to the rest of the American League, Harry?"

"Unfortunately—"

"How many fannies did I put in the seats? That's the only number that matters."

"Let's just put all the facts on the table and sort through them," Comiskey said.

"All right. The fact is that you're the number two team in a two-team town. The fact is that getting me was the biggest boost for this franchise since you started to sell hot dogs. And the fact is that all those extra souls I brought out to the yard ate quite a few of those overpriced franks, not to mention soda pop, beer, peanuts, pies and chewing gum."

"Even if a certain number came out to see you play, the novelty will wear thin."

"So will the Rocky Mountains. Until then I want my share of the swag."

"Well, I have to be honest with you, Hal." Comiskey fidgeted in his high-backed chair. "I was going to suggest that in light of your difficulties in the field and somewhat disappointing year at the plate, *and* for the good of the club, that you accept a modest cut in salary."

"You can drop that idea right now."

"I could advance you a little something towards next year's contract in anticipation of you leading the White Sox to a world championship. I'm sure the money will come in handy for Christmas."

"I want to get paid for what I do in the here and now and not in anticipation of winning the World Series. Unless you spring for some more live bats in the line-up we don't have a shot, and I'm not going to let you hold the World Series we don't get into over my head when we talk money next winter."

"And yet," said Comiskey, leaning back to inspect the rain-stained ceiling, "I'd like to think that somehow we could manage to keep you at the same level."

"Mr. Comiskey, if I may suggest," said Harry. "It might be possible, if we're able to—"

"What, Harry?" I said. "Take in laundry? Maybe sell your blood?"

"I was only going to say—"

"Come off it. The world has changed. You know and I know that there are some real duffers signing for big money to play with the new boys in town."

The Old Roman almost burst a blood vessel on that one. "Any ballplayer who runs after a few extra dollars and risks the stability of the game itself, let alone his future in Organized Baseball, is nothing for a fool and a—a—a *damned* scoundrel!"

What we were talking about was the fresh competition to the majors, the Federal League, headed up by the oil tycoon Harry Sinclair who was determined to horn in on the action. Half the Federal clubs were already going head-to-head in big league towns: Chicago, St. Louis, Pittsburgh and Brooklyn. The Feds were eager to throw money at any established big league player willing to chance blacklisting by Organized Baseball. So far it was mostly guys on the fade, like Three Finger Brown and Joe Tinker. Most players were waiting to see if the new league would be able to make a go of it.

At first Ban Johnson and the owners tried to laugh off the Feds as just another pie-in-the-sky baseball league that would never play so much as an inning of ball. When real players signed for real money and construction began on real ballparks, Johnson changed his tune. He delivered sermons on the great institution of baseball and how the players owed allegiance to it, but it didn't take long for the players to see that they could actually sell their services for more money somewhere else. Just mentioning the Feds to Charlie Comiskey was enough to turn him as red as a fire engine.

He knew I could go uptown to the Federal League offices and in twenty minutes have a contract. So he collected himself, smiled and said, "You know something, Hal? I like the cut of your jib."

"All I like is the color of your money."

When we were through dickering I signed for $6,000, with the last $1,500 acting as a payment to reserve my rights for the following season. I let Comiskey insert his pet ten-day clause that allowed either party the right to terminate the agreement by giving ten days' written notice. What it meant to Comiskey was that if something happened to me, like I got hurt, he could chop me off the payroll. But I figured that Charlie and Harry would never be at a loss to find a way to fuck over an ailing ballplayer. Hey, it was a dirty business.

Chapter 46

For the 1914 campaign the White Sox changed some bats around but remained pretty much the same club that hadn't set the league on fire the year before. Since I was making the big dough, Comiskey blamed our poor showing on me. He had made an investment and figured I wasn't bearing the kind of return he had a right to expect.

One day I showed up late to morning practice. Nothing new there. But this time Comiskey was sitting in his private box with Harry Grabiner perched behind him. Even in an empty ballpark Harry wasn't good enough to sit next to the Old Roman.

Comiskey called out to me as I took the field. "So good of you to make an appearance, Mr. Chase."

"Wouldn't miss it for the world."

We took a little infield, knocked the pill around and worked out the kinks. Harry comes down to the railing and waves me over to Comiskey's box.

"I think you've lost your way, young man," Comiskey says.

"Yeah, how's that?"

"Plenty of fellows with just as much talent have caused a lot less commotion and are wishing today that they had toed the line."

"Save the speech for the Rotary Club."

"Harry, how late for practice was Mr. Chase this morning?"

"Sixteen minutes."

"Please deduct fifty dollars from Mr. Chase's next paycheck. I'm afraid you've forced me to be firm, Hal."

"Who do you think you're fooling?" I said. "You're just taking back that raise I got fifty bucks at a time."

"I was hoping you'd take this in the proper spirit."

"And thank you for fucking me?"

"That'll cost you twenty more."

"That totals seventy," Harry reported.

"How much extra to kick the little shit halfway across the diamond?"

The threat cost me five, but Comiskey refused to put a price on beating up Harry. I figured it was worth at least a hundred. But I didn't bother to find out. I showered, changed and caught the elevated to the north side to look up the Feds. They were outraged on my behalf, but frankly not overly surprised. They made it seem like the Feds were the enlightened champions of the down and out. Starving children in China, disease-ridden Africa, put-upon ballplayers—it was all one great mission to them. Federal League contracts, they pointed out, gave a player the right after only a couple of years to sell his services to the highest bidder. Right now we were nothing more than slaves to Organized Baseball and their reserve clause. In short, the Feds were put on earth to combat this last trace of slavery. Then, I suppose, they could get on to the problem of world hunger.

All I cared about was if the Feds' checks cleared the bank. For ten grand I said I would be willing to jump from the White Sox and take my chances with the blacklist. Ten per sounded just dandy to the Fed. What did I think about playing for Buffalo.

"Buffalo?" Anna said, when I broke the news. "I was just starting to make friends in Chicago. What am I supposed to do in Buffalo?"

"There's always Niagara Falls. I'll buy you a barrel."

So one fine June morning while the rest of the Sox are taking the field for practice, I pack my stuff and leave a letter on the training table for Charlie Comiskey, giving him ten days' notice of my intent to quit his employ. I didn't plan on waiting ten days, of course. The Buffalo ballclub was in town to play the Chicago Whalers in their new northside ballpark that would wind up someday being called Wrigley Field. I stepped right into the line-up, went two for four, then immediately skipped town before Comiskey even had time to meet with his lawyers.

To Comiskey, Johnson and the rest of the club owners, hanging was too good for the likes of Prince Hal. Comiskey went to court and got an injunction to keep me from playing for the Feds. To avoid being served papers I hopped a boat to Ontario, then joined my new team in Buffalo to take on Pittsburgh.

The baseball fans in Buffalo packed the yard to see their new star, the Prince himself, and I didn't want to disappoint, even though word had it that local authorities would serve papers on me as soon as I stepped onto the field. I hid in a shed under the stands while another player started in my place. When it came my turn to hit I popped out of that shed, swinging a bat to loosen up as I made my way down the foul line to home plate. The roar from the crowd got louder and louder as people figured out what was happening. The cops didn't catch on until the next inning, when they escorted me off the field. My new employers were happy enough, since I got them a good paying gate and a lot of publicity for the league. And getting yanked by the cops like that fired up the entire city of Buffalo, which always liked to think it was being picked on by bigger towns like Chicago.

I brought suit in Buffalo to vacate the injunction. The judge ruled that a ballplayer had every right to turn the tables on his employer and give ten days' notice. So the Old Roman was left holding a bag of air, and I went right back into the Buffalo line-up. Poor Charlie gave up a bunion and an onion for nothing.

That heated up the baseball war almost as much as the war that started in Europe, although in America the baseball skirmish seemed a little more urgent. With Prince Hal in the Federal fold, some of the other star players began to jump their clubs. Officially we were all banned for life, but that didn't keep the majors from trying to steal us back with fatter contract offers. Some of the big names, like Ty Cobb and Walter Johnson, got large raises just to stay at home.

What was hurting the Federal League was the inability to crack Manhattan. This time there was no Frank Farrell and his cronies who could cobble together enough land for a ballpark. The Feds had the Tip Tops in Brooklyn where they gave the Dodgers some trouble, but that was hardly the same thing. The Feds needed Manhattan. They accused Organized Baseball of acting like a conspiracy and went shopping for just the right courtroom to file suit. Finally they settled on a Chicago judge who a couple years earlier had made a name for himself by taking on Standard Oil itself. He had a hard name to forget—Kenesaw Mountain Landis.

Landis was a tough little rooster with a gutter mouth and reputation as a trustbuster, but what the Feds didn't take into account was that he attended White Sox games and liked things just the way they were. So as it turned out Organized Baseball couldn't have asked for a better judge to sit on the case. And that's exactly what Landis did. He sat on the case for a solid year, concocting one delay after another, while urging the parties to settle their differences no matter what the right or wrong of the matter.

In the end the Federal League owners either got paid off or the richest ones got what they wanted all along: a chance to buy into the established leagues. Weegman in Chicago bought the Cubs and Phil Ball bought the Browns in St. Louis. Federal League players were reinstated and divided up among the major league teams and signed to prewar levels. And forget about the Feds' idea of ballplayers selling their rights to the highest bidder after a couple of years. Wasn't that just a quaint notion?

The Prince, of course, was a different story. My rights were returned to Comiskey who had already made it known that I would never again have the privilege of wearing a White Sox uniform. He would have preferred to let me wither on the vine but knew that I'd go to court if I was the only guy to get blacklisted. And he might as well get something out the situation, so he rose above the insult and dealt me to a National League club that had been bringing up the rear for the past few seasons and was willing to take a chance on me.

"Cincinnati!" cried Anna. "What do they have in Cincinnati?"

"Beer and steamboats. And now the best ballplayer they've ever had."

Not many in Cincinnati shared my opinion about my abilities. I was thirty-four years old when I reported to the Reds in 1916. I was thought to be a washup, a guy you brought in late for defense, to pinch hit or maybe start a game to spell a regular. I admit I wasn't in the best of dispositions. I looked around and all I could see were crooks and fools running the game. During my Federal League days I had gotten the urge again to own a ballclub, to do things right. When I got behind the desk I wouldn't forget what it felt like to be on the other side, not like those ex-players Comiskey and Connie Mack, even the great Spaulding himself, who cared less about preserving the National Pastime than lining their own pockets.

Sure I had made a few mistakes along the way, but nothing compared to those crooks. I only hurt myself. Besides, the way they tried to kick me out of the game and sully my good name gave me every right to use all their rotten tricks to get what I wanted—the power to do some good in the world.

Chapter 47

I began the season on the bench with the Reds, playing behind Zip Moll-witz, a .260 hitter who was big and strong and if he didn't have to bend over too far could actually catch a ball at first base. He was popular with the fans, having been born in Germany. With all those immigrants in Ohio the club was always partial to Krauts like Heinie Groh, Buck Herzog or Peter Schneider. But when the European War became more of an issue in the States, those ballplayers were wishing they had been named Smith or Jones. At the moment, though, the country was still pretty much divided in their rooting loyalties between the Germans and the Brits and French. It took a U-boat sinking the *Lusitania* to change all that.

I didn't ride the bench for long. In the first inning of a game Moll-witz took exception to the umpire calling a strike on him. Zip grumbled something about the guy only lacking a cane and a tin cup, to which the ump replied that Zip should just swing the lumber and lay off the sub-marine tactics. Zip took the crack as a German insult and went crazy. If it wasn't for the intervention of the Brooklyn catcher, Chief Meyers, being an Indian and something of a neutral, there might have been some blood shed, and America could have gotten involved in the war a year early.

So Zip got himself tossed from the game and I inherited his two-strike count. I had nothing to lose so I hacked away and hooked a dou-ble down the left field line. One batter later I'm standing on third base when I notice that Chief isn't paying attention on his lob back to the pitcher, so I take off and swipe home plate on him. I got a couple more hits that day and pulled off some swell plays in the field, and just like that Zip and me switch positions. Now he had plenty of time on the bench to mull over the Belgian question.

I had something to prove, so I really bore down and got into a solid groove at the plate. Over the years I had my share of hot streaks only to have an injury hamper my play. This season everything went right for me. I had the batting average floating around the three-fifty mark all year long and found myself in the race for a batting title. Then the usual contenders, Daubert in Brooklyn and Hornsby in St. Louis, cooled off and I looked like a cinch to win the crown.

Prince Hal was a star of the game again, and don't think I didn't glory in it. With my reputation restored I could move on to bigger things. What the club needed was a new manager, and having experience under my belt I couldn't think of a better candidate for Gary Herrman, the new owner of the franchise, than yours truly. Not that I relished the idea of wet nursing the young players. It was just another way to get my foot in the door of ownership.

The season was nearing an end, and I was completely focused on winning the batting title when Herrman decided to get a head start on the next year and traded for a player to take over as manager. That was bad enough, but he couldn't have picked someone who'd aggravate me more. The guy he tabbed was Christy Mathewson, the star pitcher with the Giants, my chief rival for attention during my years in New York. And the biggest phony in the entire game.

After winning twenty games a season for a dozen years Matty began to drop more than he won, and it was obvious that he didn't have the knack anymore. Mugsy McGraw loved him like a son and decided to set him up in the managerial business by trading him to Cincy. Matty took over for the final stretch of games, and the two of us made an effort to get along. I had my batting title to worry about and he wanted to get situated.

I finished the season batting .339 and won the crown by twenty points. Charlie Comiskey could now officially stick it in his ear. I was the toast of the town again, even if it was just Cincinnati and everything closed down at night when I was just getting warmed up. For once I couldn't wait for the next season to begin so I could enjoy life as the reigning batting king. And I'd find the time to see about Christy Mathewson, too.

◈

Nineteen-seventeen was a pretty rough year for the world in general. It looked like Woodrow Wilson had kept us out of the European slaughter until he got himself re-elected. Now we were up to our ears in it. Any able-bodied man, especially if he was a fit ballplayer, was expected to enlist in the American Expeditionary Force and personally slit the Kaiser's throat with a Bowie knife. Even if you weren't going into the Army you were expected to act patriotic, like every day of the week was the Fourth of July. Pretty soon people couldn't resist accusing each other of being slackers who hindered the war effort. Everybody was trying to make hay out of the situation. Even Judge Kenesaw Mountain Landis got into the act, issuing an arrest warrant for Kaiser Wilhelm himself. Too bad the German emperor didn't turn himself into the Chicago police or we could have saved ourselves a lot of trouble. And, of course, the politicians were the worst of the lot. Everybody and everything, including baseball, had better toe the line.

The politicians didn't waste time in closing the racetracks to show how serious they were. Of course the French weren't about to stop horseracing and they were smack in the middle of the fighting. So it was like 1908 all over again, with the gamblers shifting their interest from the ponies to the ballpark. The politicians then started to consider other sacrifices that could be made for the war effort, and before long there's a clamor to close down baseball for the duration of the conflict.

Ban Johnson and the owners had to call on all their friends in Congress to keep the ballparks open, but they began to have problems keeping the clubs adequately stocked with players. Not wanting to be called slackers, a lot of the boys began to volunteer for the Army, or at least defense work. What made it insulting to Organized Baseball was that the steel mills and shipyards that took on the players for war work assigned them to their company teams. The guy might show up on the docks with a can of paint once or twice, but really all he did was play ball. It was just another league, and with a pool of talent getting better all the time. You didn't have to worry about being blacklisted by Organized Baseball. Hell, you were helping to win the war!

The owners kicked some about the industrial teams, but compared to the likes of Charles Schwab and Bethlehem Steel they were just bush leaguers who had to work hard to keep the politicians happy. To make it seem like Organized Baseball was part of the war effort the owners resorted to a lot of flag waving, war bond drives, free passes for the doughboys, and the playing of the national anthem before each game, not just the season opener.

The owners had to make baseball players seem like men who were involved in something more vital than playing a kid's game. To show we weren't just ballplayers but actually soldiers in disguise, they had us demonstrate drilling before the games. Of course there weren't Springfields to waste on marching ballplayers, so we had to shoulder baseball bats instead. It was embarrassing to be put through the paces like that, but attitudes changed when a competition was announced with a cash prize for the best team. Your average ballplayer doesn't like to lose at anything, or pass up an easy buck, so now the boys came out early to get in some extra drill work. They started to brag on which outfit had the best spit and polish and gave odds on who was likely to cop the big prize. What you ended up with was a bunch of obsessive drill teamers, working on their routines whenever they got the chance. So what if the batting average suffered—it was for the war!

Being older and married I didn't feel the heat to join the army, and I preferred to play in big league towns over joints like Norfolk, Virginia. Besides, I had a batting crown to defend and I aimed to defend it. It was a little different in Cincinnati anyway, what with the heavy German population that wasn't overly inclined to push their players into killing their relations overseas. Like all the teams we lost players and had to scramble to find replacements, but the biggest problem that spring training—at least for Christy Mathewson—was finding enough experienced bridge players to make up his foursome.

Chapter 48

M atty loved to play bridge, especially for dough, especially during spring training, and with the loss of personnel to the war effort there was only one man on the club who knew how to play: Jack Ryder, who he hired as his coach and crony. To fill out the foursome Matty drafted me, not because he liked my company but because he knew I'd be quick to pick up on any card game, and a hack pitcher named Mike Regan who was dumb enough to be beat and still come back to lose more dough. Most guys would have split up the inexperienced players, but not Matty. I knew it was a raw deal to get stuck with Regan, and the games, at least on my part, became real grudge matches. To get an edge I worked out some hand signals with Regan to tip off what cards each of us was holding. We started to win our money back and just as we were about to pull even Matty declared that bridge playing season was over. Time for dominoes. Of course what the guy never bothered to tell us was that you were *expected* to tip off your partner to what you were holding by the way you bid. Somehow he forgot to teach us that lesson.

So we head north to begin the regular season, and we're waving the flag and marching with bats on our shoulders and making do with whatever players we can find to fill out the rosters. After hearing a bunch of rumors, the Work or Fight order is finally announced and the season is scheduled to close down early. The owners have to beg just to be allowed to hold the World Series a month early in September. They were looking to be out an entire month of gate receipts while still contracted to pay us players for the full season. So how did they get out of the jam? At the end of August they released everybody, meaning that all the players in the bigs were free agents, able to sign anywhere we wanted for anything we could get. In theory, anyway. In practice, the owners refused to sign each other's property.

I had heard the rumors about the Work or Fight order and figured we would be out some pay, so I got in ahead of time and began to dump a few games. And why not? It was going to be a long winter. I sounded out some of my teammates to see if anyone was interested in having a little fun. Lee Magee, our second baseman, practically begged me to let him in. The guy had played in the league for a few seasons and all he had to show for it was an extra pair of pants. Even though I was more interested in pitchers I took him on.

We had something going on a game in Boston late in July but things weren't working out. No matter how many chances we gave the Braves, that second division club refused to win. Magee and me were kicking the ball all over the lot, striking out on rotten pitches, looking like real duffers. Even then we were lucky that Boston took the game into extra innings tied at two. In the thirteenth Magee came up to bat and, not wanting to strike out again, punched an easy roller to Johnny Rawlings playing at short, only to have the ball take a wicked hop and break the kid's nose and land Magee on first base. Our next batter was Big Edd Roush, a great young hitter and no fool, either. Edd got his pitch and slammed a ball over the center fielder's head that skipped all the way to the fence that was over 500 feet away in Braves Field. It looked like an easy inside-the-park homerun. It should at least score Magee, but he's got 500 bucks riding on the outcome and the chances that the Braves would have the spunk to come back in their half of the inning were pretty slim. Lee slows down, hoping that Big Edd will be hell-bent for the homer and maybe pass him on the bases and get called out. But Roush is wise and shouts at Magee that if he doesn't run faster he'll wake up murdered in the morning. So the poor guy is forced to score the run that cost him five C's.

The Reds already had an unhappy clubhouse, and that game pretty much cinched it. Some guys didn't like the fact that I was doing business, and others didn't like the fact I was doing business without letting them in it. Then Mike Regan, my spring training bridge partner, got called up to the service and really fixed things.

Being a good Catholic, Mike was terrified that he might die in battle with a mortal sin on his ticket and felt compelled to confess to Matty how he and the Prince had cheated him at bridge. Matty flew off the handle. He thought *he* had been cheating *me*.

Matty was just looking for something to fuss over. All summer long he had been acting screwy because of the war. I could see through the guy. I knew it really bugged him that here he was supposed to be this true blue American hero and now that the country was in a war he was getting shut out of all the glory. Now with American soldiers pouring into France the war wouldn't last that much longer. Matty knew a lot of influential people, of course, and wrote plenty of letters hoping to land a commission and get into the action while the Big One lasted, but there didn't seem to be much call in the service for ex–baseball pitchers pushing forty.

At the same time that Mike Regan broke down weeping and blamed his moral collapse on Prince Hal, Edd Roush and his buddies, all of them green to the ways of the world, complained that I wasn't playing on the level. Matty was wise to that, too, but he had been around the game long enough to know that the Reds were a dozen games off the pace so why raise a stink over a loss here and there?

So Matty got in a huff and suspended me because he said I was fixing ball games. But the real reason was for cheating him at bridge.

He didn't have the brass, of course, to tell me to my face. He announced it to the newspapers, putting on his righteous act, declaring that he was determined to drive the bad elements out of the game of baseball. That would be his contribution to the war effort.

Well, if he wanted a war so much, the Prince was always willing to accommodate.

Chapter 49

There was an unwritten rule in baseball that players don't hire lawyers. The club owners made it seem unsporting, not to mention unmanly, to have someone else do the talking for you. The owners hired lawyers, especially during those frequent baseball wars, but that was only to fight off the lawyers representing the cowards on the other side.

The first thing I did after Matty tossed me off the Cincinnati team and besmirched my name to the press was to scare up the slickest, black-leg lawyer I could find. His name was Alcorn. He looked like a dime store Romeo gone to seed. Pencil-thin mustache and greasy, combed-back hair.

As I told him the situation he became dismayed.

"Who do they think they are?" He shook his head slowly, looking less angry than generally ashamed for all of mankind. "The uncompromising gall, the smugness, the duplicity. And after the fine service you rendered to the ballclub. Mr. Chase, I want you to know that I don't really care if you *ever* pay me. I want to teach these people a lesson."

Maybe the shyster was serious, but he didn't get down to specifics until he had a hundred buck retainer safely tucked inside his vest pocket.

"So what do you think we should do?" I asked.

"Sue the bastards."

"Well, that's what I had in mind."

"But let's establish some ground rules," he said. "One, there is no such thing as *the truth*. The truth is what I make of the facts. That's my job. Your job is to come up with the facts. If necessary I can help you with that, too."

"I should be all right there."

"Two. I never want to know where you are, but I must be able to reach you at all times. Three. You are always the victim. *Always*. So be sure to act like one."

Alcorn then suggested that it would be advantageous if I wasn't around when the Reds tried to serve me papers, prefer charges and get me suspended from Organized Baseball. Buying time would be to our advantage. The longer things dragged on the less stomach the club owners would have to pursue a case against me, since they had enough trouble with the war.

Cincinnati didn't really have much of a case, no evidence, just the word of Christy Mathewson, and according to the newspapers, Matty had finally pulled the right strings and got himself commissioned in the American Expeditionary Force. Still, Alcorn preferred to have the guy in France before anything official happened in my case.

So Matty was off to the wars. I guess he missed taking to the mound and being the center of attention. Oh, I had the guy pegged. I knew what he was really after. Matty was looking to get himself killed in battle. He would lead some kind of hopeless charge against an impossible position and get chopped down as he waved the flag. He would then live forever. Statues of Matty the hero would occupy town squares everywhere. Even the pigeons would have too much respect to roost on his broad shoulders. And it wouldn't be just American town squares. All of France would embrace him. French school children would memorize his win-loss record. *Three years in ze row he won ze thirty games.*

Yeah, I knew he was trying to pull a fast one. He wanted to be good and dead before people got wise to him like I was.

But the AEF wasn't about to send a national treasure to the front lines. Instead Matty was assigned to chemical warfare training. He taught soldiers how to pull on gas masks, then escorted them into sealed-up rooms to give them a taste of it. Not exactly a star turn. Sort of like coaching first base. So it's autumn 1918, the Germans are falling back all over the front and it has to look to Matty like the odds are getting pretty long on grabbing a share of the glory.

Then one morning the nation awoke to learn that Christy Mathewson had been gassed in some tragic training accident and now lay close to death's door. Newspapers printed extra editions to keep vigil with a shocked nation. A raw recruit had panicked when his mask malfunctioned and would have surely died had not the quick-thinking and heroic Matty given up his own gas mask and hustled the boy out of the training room. There he was again, coming through in the pinch, despite sucking in a lungful of the chlorine that landed him in the hospital in critical condition. It was touch and go and when he finally pulled through, banner headlines announced the good news to a grateful nation that praised the Lord, lit candles and bought more newspapers.

I knew it was all a sham. Matty had tried to pull a fast one and botched it. The big dope saw his chance and sucked in that gas on purpose. To die a hero. He chickened out, didn't finish the job, and wound up surviving. A glorious charge is a lot better than a training accident but you take what you can get. And in a hundred years who'd remember the exact circumstances? A war hero is a war hero is a war hero. Right? But only if he died.

All Matty got was burned-up lungs and a ruined constitution. Sure, he became the object of pity, only that ain't hero worship.

◈

For most of Matty's short army career I was on the run from the process servers. When I skipped out of Cincy I wouldn't even tell Anna where I was going.

"Like I really care," she said.

I kept ahead of the private dicks the Reds hired, until I decided to make some dough playing semi-pro ball in Bayonne, New Jersey. Even using a fake name you couldn't keep a lid on the news that Prince Hal was playing for the locals.

Even then Alcorn was able to stall for a couple more months. It wasn't until January, almost six months after Matty made a splash in the newspapers with his charges against me, while he was recuperating in some hospital in France and the National League was thoroughly sick of the entire matter, that Alcorn reported that his client was ready to attend a league hearing on the matter.

Chapter 50

Ballplayers were expected to attend league hearings alone, but I showed up with Alcorn, a couple of law clerks and a stenographer. The National League was between presidents, a man named John Heydler was filling in, and I could see the wind drop out of his sails as my legal parade marched in.

The Cincinnati ballclub was surprised to be outnumbered. They presented a case, but without Matty they didn't have the juice to press the matter. They offered up Mike Regan fresh from France, who managed to survive the carnage he never saw. He was wearing his army uniform, as if that would make a difference, and told how he had been led astray by the smooth-talking Prince to cheat Matty at bridge.

"I have to chuckle," said Alcorn, only he wasn't. "Here you are, an *admitted* card cheat, trying to drag down my client to your own debased level. I'm only thankful that the loved ones of those valiant soldiers who paid the ultimate price are not here to witness this travesty. I warrant they'd rip that uniform off his back, Your Honor."

"I am not a judge, Mr. Alcorn," answered a weary-looking Heydler.

Next, Jimmy Ring, a young twirler for the Reds, was called to testify. His claim was that in 1917 during his rookie year he was brought into a game with the score tied and a pair of runners on base.

"After I finished loosening up," he said, "The Prince comes over and says to me, 'Listen, kid, I got some money riding on this one. There's something in it for you if you lose.'"

"And what did you do?" asked Heydler.

"Well, I lost. Cravath was so fooled by a sweet hook I slung up there that it was only by complete accident he got wood on the ball. It bounced off the fence and a couple runs come in."

"But you're saying you lost?"

"Toney took the loss. Hell, he put the runners on, didn't he?"

"Did Mr. Chase comment on your pitching?"

"That's just the thing. The next morning I'm sitting in the hotel lobby just watching the world go by, the way I like to, when Prince dropped fifty bucks in my lap, winked and kept right on walking."

"And what did you do?"

"Told Matty."

When Alcorn got his chance he asked Jimmy what Matty had told him to do with the money.

"He said it was probably a joke and to forget about it. So I figured I could keep the dough. Bought this suit. Pretty sharp, huh?"

"Do you get nervous when you pitch, Jimmy?"

"Nah, I don't hardly get the fidgets. I suppose I'm favored that way."

"Yet you're not a very good pitcher, are you, Jimmy?"

"I'm the best there is in the National League!" he said. "At least when I got all my stuff going."

"The fact of the matter is that you never do have all of your stuff going. The fact of the matter is that last year you won but three games and lost seven. Mr. Chase would have ample reason to think you might get the *fidgets*, considering your rather limited abilities, and so in an attempt to loosen you up he may have made a facetious remark. You laugh, he laughs, Matty thinks it's a joke, then you go and strike out the side."

"And I would have, too," Jimmy said, "if Cravath hadn't got that lucky hit."

The next up was Greasy Neale who claimed that one time when the Reds dropped a doubleheader to the Phillies the Prince bragged about winning fifty bucks on the afternoon.

Alcorn paced back and forth, just glaring at Neale with a look of complete disgust. Finally he spoke. "So they call you *Greasy*."

"Actually, that's an interesting story—"

"One I'm sure I don't care to hear. Your honor I have no questions for a man named *Greasy*."

Batting clean-up was Pol Perrit from the New York Giants. He said that the Prince once asked him which end of a doubleheader he was going to pitch so he could connect with a certain party to make sure the both of them got an early Christmas present.

"And what did you make of that comment?" asked Heydler.

"He wanted me to go easy."

"And what was your response?"

"I told him to get away from me before I took a poke at him."

Alcorn didn't take long to pull the story apart, getting Pol to admit that I liked to joke around.

"He wasn't joking this time," Perrit said.

"Why do they call you Pol Perrit? Is it because of your willingness to repeat everything the prosecution tells you?"

"This is a league hearing," Heydler said, "There is no prosecution."

"Nor is there a case against my client!" Alcorn cracked the table a good one with the palm of his hand.

Alcorn was just giving Heydler a taste of the business they could expect out of him in front of a jury of twelve gulls. Even before Matty's affidavit could be introduced or John McGraw called in from the hallway to vouch for his pet pitcher, we had them on the run.

Everyone figured I was guilty, but making a suspension stick would be a problem. It would only give baseball a black eye and the game had enough problems at the moment. Heydler issued a statement to the press clearing me of all charges and immediately reinstated me to the league. Cincy didn't waste any time, either, settling on back wages.

The Reds didn't want me back for the 1919 season, but I knew that there would always be some team in need willing to take a guy if there was a chance he might still be able to produce. As it turned out it was John McGraw and the New York Giants. He might have been willing to help run me out of the league but he was short a solid first baseman and put in a trade for my rights.

"Well, kid," I told Anna, who had been plenty miserable since we got back together, "It's back to New York."

"What's in New York?"

I couldn't have asked for a sweeter deal, because also joining the Giants for the season, fresh out of the hospital and signed by McGraw to be one of his coaches, was the great Christopher Mathewson himself.

Chapter 51

With the European war finally over, 1919 started off with plenty of optimism. That lasted a day or two. Then the peace talks in Paris stalled, the newspapers filled up with stories about the Allies squabbling over how to divide up the spoils and how much dough to squeeze out of the Krauts in reparations. And if they didn't get it they were ready to fire up the war again. After four years of this business, people all over Europe were starving to death, civil wars broke out in the countries that lost and labor strikes in the countries that won. The Irish were going nuts, the Italians were going nuts, the Austrians were going nuts, and the Russians were showing everybody the really up-to-date way of going nuts. Even in America there were strikes, and not just factory workers and miners, but city cops and firemen. Towns were being torched and looted by everyday people who didn't think they were getting their fair share of the pie. Politicians blamed it on socialist agitation, setting off a red scare. Women were getting the vote, the religious fanatics were about to take our booze away—everybody had slipped a cog. So it was kind of tough to go back to taking baseball seriously.

At least that's what the club owners were afraid of. They pushed back the start of the season and cut the schedule to 140 games. As it turned out Americans were eager for anything that would take their minds off the problems in the world. Nightclubs, movie houses, golf courses, bowling alleys—amusements were doing land office business. *Especially baseball.* But once the clucks in charge of the game chopped off the front end of the season there was no way to get back that month of gate receipts. Screwing the players out of a month of salary helped, of course.

It was hard to tell when it happened but professional baseball no longer had a seedy reputation. I suppose in comparison to the slaughter of a world war it came off as wholesome. And with all the troubles in the world, preachers and politicians had better things to flog than playing baseball on Sunday. Not only was baseball not considered much of a problem anymore, hell, it was part of the solution!

"It's all a crock," I told Anna.

"I thought you loved your goddamn baseball." We were together in New York, drinking too much and making each other miserable.

"You want to know what baseball is?"

"I have a feeling you're going to tell me."

"Baseball today is just another racket out to gyp the common man."

"And happens to pay you pretty well. Not that we have anything in the bank to prove it."

"Did I ever tell you about playing town ball?"

"Only about a hundred-million times."

"That was the real game. You played for the sake of your hometown. Not for some fat cat."

"Thank God your big brother John didn't live to see this sorry day."

"I'll drink to that."

"Here's a toast." She raised her glass. "Here's to Hal Chase! Here's to the Prince! Long live the Prince. He's no dope, he's no busher, he's nobody's sucker!"

"If only you could see yourself."

"Yeah, well at least I can stand to look in a mirror."

I smacked her across the face for that one but she was so drunk she only laughed at me.

"I hope you don't say you're sorry," she said. "That would be too rich. You could go on thinking how misunderstood you are. Well, you're not misunderstood."

So you see the world had gotten so rotten that even my own wife was turning on me. I knew I was just one little guy who couldn't fix everything that had gone wrong. But maybe I could at least free baseball from all the bastards that had gotten their claws into it, and give it back to all those people who still lived in the small towns and played the game for the love of it. I didn't quite know how to do it, but any trick, any lie, any scheme was fair in time of war. And I also knew it was what I had to do to set things right in my own life. To save my own soul, to save the game— I had to kill it.

Chapter 52

John McGraw was supposed to be really sharp, a Little Napoleon who ran his team with an iron hand. But I had him pegged as just another phony. His teams were generally feisty but they turned chicken in most of the big games and he turned out to be a sentimental pussy cat. Bone-head Merkle, the guy who cost the club the pennant in 1908—McGraw treated him like a son. And Snodgrass, who dropped that easy fly to blow the 1912 World Series—McGraw gave him a fat raise the next season. And now he was well on the other side of the mountain. Mugsy had been the toast of Manhattan for so long that now he was just a pudgy, soft-bellied little gump. People took to calling him the Little Round Man.

The Giants arrived in Hot Springs, Arkansas, for spring training, and I paid a visit to McGraw in his hotel room. He was dressed in a robe and sat on the edge of his bed nipping at a bottle of Milk of Magnesia. He was still nursing a boiling gut that was left over from the year before when the Giants stumbled badly and lost out to the Cubs for the pennant.

"What's on your mind, Hal?"

"I just want to get some things out in the open. I've been around the show long enough to have my own game. I like to think for myself. I don't need some coacher flashing signs at me."

"Finally." He looks to the heavens. "A ballplayer who wants to think for himself."

"So we understand each other?"

"You're on your own. Lord knows, first base is the least of my problems."

And as far as I was concerned McGraw was the least of my problems. I didn't need any distractions from the Little Round Man.

Christy Mathewson, though, was a different matter. He was still recovering from his war wounds when he finally caught up to the team. Coaches didn't have all that much to do but the way the guy looked you had to wonder if he was even up to that. His face looked bleached, his eyes had no glitter to them, and he had a cough that made you sick to hear it.

On his first day back with the Giants everybody offered their respects. Only after he was left alone did I pay a visit, acting like we were long-lost pals.

"Hey, Matty, I heard you the won the war all by yourself."

I reached out to pump his limp hand. He was lucky to manage something of a smile, let alone a grip.

"How have you been, Hal?"

"Swell. Couldn't be better. It's great to be young, alive and a Giant, right?"

Matty started to cough.

"You poor guy," I said. "What you need is some rest. We'll have plenty of time to catch up later. It'll be a long year. Yes sir, it'll be a long year."

I gave him a playful sock to the jaw then trotted out to take some infield practice. And the whole time I just stared daggers at the guy. Whenever he looked at me I gave him a little smile. He'd look away and cough some more and I had to laugh. I got to laughing so hard, I was doubled-over and holding my guts. I couldn't take the throws to first no more and everybody wanted to be let in on the joke.

Oh, I'd let them in on the joke, all right. I'd let them in on the joke.

Chapter 53

To the owners it was all about money and always had been. They'd do anything to make a buck. Bicycle racing gets popular, so run a track around the outfield. Attendance drops off, so turn the joint into an amusement park the way Van der Ahe did in St. Louis with his loop-de-loop. And now that they were stupid enough to cut out the opening month of revenue, the owners decide in 1919 to make the World Series a best of nine affair instead of seven. So much for tradition.

If the owners didn't care about the game, why should the players? We got cheated out of the last month's salary one year and the first month's salary the next, so a lot of the boys were willing to cheat the crooks that cheated them. Playing for the love of the game—that was for suckers.

Guys that used to spend hours in a hotel lobby strategizing about baseball now bellyached about the owners. And how eagerly they listened when the Prince preached the good word. Hadn't he shown up Cincy when they tried to kick him out of the game just for taking a little side action?

"You boys think you're the game?" I'd say to a circle of the hired hands. "Maybe you play it, but you ain't the real game. You're just chips that the real players toss across the table. Have you ever thought about how much dough the real players make out of you? And I don't mean grandstand admission or even the hot dogs and beer. I mean all the newspapers we sell. I mean all the Coca-Cola and Gillette razors and Bull Durham and Lifebouy soap we sell. Try to picture how the money just spreads out from the ball diamond like a spider's web. First they build a ballpark where the land is cheap, but because it's so far away they have to build a trolley line or a subway tunnel that, naturally, will require a little public assistance. Somebody's got to land that contract and pad the bill to the taxpayers, right? And since they spent all that money on public transportation they got to provide other reasons at the end of the line to give the suckers even more reason to ride. New businesses spring up, the price of land jumps, regular people can't afford to live there and have to move even farther out of town. The trolley line gets longer and branches to the left and the right. The city gets bigger, the population gets bigger, so factories come in to take advantage of all that cheap labor. Whatever they offer to pay, you better be willing to take or be ready to move back home to the country. But, hell, that ain't progress! And there's no home in the country to move back to, anyway. All of this is caused by money, the root of all evil. And where does that money start? From watching you boys hit a ball with a stick. But do you get your fair share? Why should coupon clippers and stock trading crooks get more than you do? The way I see it, a ballplayer deserves all the dough he can manage to cart home, and no need to apologize how he gets it."

Every time I delivered that little stem-winder I sowed a few seeds, and don't think the ground wasn't eager to receive. Oh, I never told anyone to look up a gambler and toss games. I didn't have to. Even to the players I corralled in my own deals I didn't say anything direct. I treated it all like a big joke. Wouldn't it be funny if we did this, wouldn't it be funny if we did that, and *somehow* we lost a game. Good thing we had some money down on the other side to win. God, it was all so funny.

But the point wasn't to help some boys scrape together the down payment for a store back home. I wanted to make all the suckers in America who were willing to lay down two-bits admission to the ballpark to be so thoroughly sick of all the rotten phoniness that they'd wash their hands of the game forever. Years later, maybe, we could start playing baseball again. In the small towns. In the sand lots. For the pure love of it.

Dropping a ball game here and there, and convincing others to follow my lead, wasn't likely to do the trick. That was just setting the stage for something bigger: the World Series. If you fixed the Series and America found out about it, now *that* would turn some heads. That would get some attention. But it had to be fixed just right, so ham-fisted that even the dumbest cluck in the yard could see through it, get disgusted and say the hell with the whole dirty business of big league ball. I wasn't about to become a ringleader of the players who actually went out to do the stupid deed. I was just going to plant the seeds, water them, and wait to see how my garden grew.

The Giants were supposed to be in contention for a World Series berth that season, and when I played on the level I contributed my fair share to the effort. The real surprise in the National League was my old club in Cincinnati. Maybe without the distractions of Matty and me they could concentrate better. They weren't really a great club, just a good-enough club in a mediocre league. The Giants hung around in the race but we knew early on we didn't really have the horses. In the American League it looked like the White Sox were returning to their 1917 form when they won the Series. Out of the gate they were the club to beat. And the club to bet on.

I knew that if there was any bunch of players who felt they were being clipped by their owner it was those Sox. You could always count on Charlie Comiskey to fleece his players—and he had some pretty good ones to fleece. Plenty in the fast company made more money than Shoeless Joe Jackson, but not many could clock the ball the way he did. After thirteen years on the mound Eddie Cicotte had to beg to get a bonus clause in his contract if he won thirty games. Guess who got a seat on the bench after he won 29? The only Sox player who had a good deal was the second baseman Eddie Collins, a college boy who signed an airtight contract during the Federal League war. He was no dope and rubbed guys the wrong way by letting them know it. His teammates called him Cocky and half of them hated his guts. The leader of that half was Chick Gandil. What he lacked in brains he made up in nastiness. To me he looked promising.

I had never played on the same club as Chick but over the years we got to be friendly. Fellow first basemen and all that. Chick had come up to the big show with the White Sox in 1910, then before I arrived in Chicago he got shipped out to Cleveland where he actually developed into a decent fielder with a fair stick. He didn't possess much flair around the bag but at least he wouldn't butcher the routine balls. Comiskey brought him back to the Sox in 1917 because what Chick had to offer was all the club needed. Or was willing to pay for. The guy found himself on a World Series champion, and while most players might count their blessings, not Chick. He wanted more dough out of his situation and had to haggle with Comiskey to finally squeeze three grand out of the old pawnbroker. In Cincy, a lot smaller town, that was considered backup pay.

Yes, Chick Gandil was a goat made to order. Waiting to be cut out of the herd.

Chapter 54

When the Giants and the White Sox crossed paths during the season I paid Chick Gandil a visit. I found him in the dining room of the hotel where the Sox were staying. No other club in the bigs was cheap enough to book that fleabag joint. Chick was just staring into a cup of coffee when I sat down across from him.

He looked up and grumbled, "Well, if it ain't my boyhood idol."

"The very same. You on the wagon or something?"

"I like coffee when I think."

"Then this really is an occasion." I ordered a cup from the waiter that came over. "So how's the Old Roman?"

"Peachy as ever."

"I hear if the Sox win another pennant you're in line for a big bonus."

"Fuck you, Prince."

"That's right, all you got in 'seventeen was a case of champagne."

"Flat champagne. A case of flat champagne."

"No wonder he got such a good price."

"I'll take beer this time."

"Don't forget Prohibition. Maybe Charlie will hand out turkeys to you like they do to bums down on their luck at holiday time."

"I'm glad you think it's funny," he said. "But some of us have already spent our World Series' share just to pay the bills, and hell it's barely August."

"Too bad you're have to face us Giants in October. You'll have to settle for the loser's share."

"Aw, who are you kidding, Prince? You just don't got the arms. It's Cincinnati and easy, too. But they don't scare us. Especially in a nine-game series."

"And that's why you're shelling your peanuts already?"

"Peanuts!"

"You know me. I got different standards than most."

"As a matter of fact I do know you, Prince. I hear you been conducting a little *business* this summer."

"I thought you were a businessman yourself, Chick, and here I find you hunkered over the joe trying to find a way to scare up a couple bucks when you're about to step into a gold mine."

"I told you I've already spent the winner's share."

"You know, if a smart operator were so inclined he could easily make ten times the winning share by *losing* the goddamn Series."

"What are you getting at, Prince?"

"I ain't getting at nothing. I'm just saying stop the griping and do something. There's always ways to make dough if you use the old noodle."

"Meaning the Series?" he said.

"That's just an example. I'm throwing out ideas. For instance, there's ways of getting dough out of the World Series other than taking the little Christmas Club check the National Commission sends in the mail. In theory. If you want to play around with ideas. You know me, Chick. I'm an idea man."

"Sure, Prince. There's nothing wrong in fooling around with an idea." He looks around the dining room a second, then lowers his voice. "But if you tried something, wouldn't people get wise?"

"If there's one thing I learned after fifteen years in this game is that nobody wants to get wise. For Christ's sake, Chick, people want to believe the game was invented in Cooperstown."

"Yeah, but how one guy could pull it off is what gets me."

"Who said one guy? For this kind of prank you need all the hands you can get. At least six, seven guys. At least two pitchers. Some of the better hitters on the club."

"Wouldn't it be more likely that somebody might spill the beans if there's so many in on it?"

"When you got that kind of dough on the line you don't want to leave anything to chance."

"What kind of dough are you talking about?"

"Hell, Chick, how would I know? This is all speculation. For fun."

"Sure, Prince, for fun. But supposing a bunch of players tried to pull it off, how much do you figure they could get away with?"

"I'd hope ten grand apiece."

"Ten grand!"

"And that's just to lay down. If they're smart and don't spend it before they got it, they could get the money out on bets, parlay it, and only God knows how high the kite will fly."

"What's possible, do you think?"

"The breaks go your way ... a quarter million."

"Jesus!"

"Do the arithmetic. It's possible if you do it right."

"But what's the right way ... just supposing you did it?"

"I don't know. I suppose you approach a high roller or two to see if they'll finance the deal. You get your money up front to get it out early on bets. Spread it around with different bookies to keep the odds high. Something like that."

"Yeah, but how do you lose the ballgames?"

"If you don't know how to lose a baseball game, Chick, I don't know what to tell you." I reach into my pocket for some change to pay my bill. "I gotta run, but one more piece of friendly advice. Forget all this. It's complete pie in the sky. Just a way to pass the time of day."

"Yeah, sure, Prince. I hear ya."

I left Gandil to order another cup of coffee and recall all the things I told him to forget.

Chapter 55

I found a business associate on the Giants that summer, Heinie Zimmerman, who was finishing up his career playing third base. We dumped the odd game and didn't bother much to look good in the process—Heinie because he was a fool and me because I knew nobody had the guts to say anything. McGraw was too busy nursing his bum gut to want the aggravation of trying to kick the Prince out of the game. He saw what happened the last time somebody tried.

About the only one who found the gumption to stand up to me was my wife. One day Anna said she had had enough. She wanted a divorce.

"Say it ain't so." I was lying in bed, shielding my eyes from the light flooding in through the curtains she had opened.

"I'm moving in with a girl friend."

"I can't say I'm surprised. You're not the first woman to run out on a ballplayer once he gets to the end of his career."

"I'm not running out on you," she said. "I'm running away from you."

"I was good enough to introduce you to society."

"That was more like a crap game you introduced me to."

I didn't fight it. If a woman doesn't want to stay with you, there's nothing you can do or say to keep her. It was just more of the same in my life. People let you down. They're all phonies.

The biggest phony of them all, Christy Mathewson, was always there for me to contemplate that summer. I could always count on him to wax me good, to keep me determined to rid the world of his kind. The guy continued to suffer from his lung condition, moping around the ballpark the same way Kid Elberfeld did with his supposed bum leg. Matty picked up a nurse on the ball club, Rube Benton, a pretty fair country pitcher who idolized him. Rube was always asking after Matty, fetching him water, taking him by the elbow if it looked like Matty was about to faint.

One afternoon in September Mathewson is feeling poorly and goes into the clubhouse to lie down. Then I'm tossed from the game for arguing over a third strike and get sent to the clubhouse myself. Matty was lying on the floor with his legs perched up on a milking stool.

"The blue-suited son of a bitch!" I screamed and threw my mitt against the wall. Then I sat on a stool next to him.

"Hey, Matty," I said, "Maybe we should go back to the days of one umpire. At least the two of them won't have to prove to the other how tough he is."

Matty didn't answer. He didn't even open his eyes.

"You ain't gone and died on me, have you, kid? We got enough troubles in this country without losing a genuine war hero."

"I can hear you. But if you don't mind, I'm not feeling up to conversation."

"My, he's even polite when he tells you to shut the hell up."

I pulled off my spikes and began to unbutton my blouse to get ready to take a shower.

"*Daddy, what did you do in the war?*" I said. "*Well, son, I showed the real soldiers how to put on their gas masks. We ate a lot of beans in France.*"

"What's going on in here?" said somebody. It was Rube Benton, his spikes clattering on the concrete as he entered the clubhouse. "Are you feeling okay, Matty?"

"Your beau is here for you." I pulled off my pants and stirrups.

"Did you say something smart?"

"Did you hear something smart, Rube?"

"Maybe you should take a shower before I punch you in the nose."

"It's just like in the picture show. He's come to save his man."

"I'm wise to you, Chase."

"Oh yeah?"

"I know about you and Heinie, and I know the difference between right and wrong. As far as I'm concerned, you're as wormy as they get."

"Geez, Rube, I guess you told me off. I think I'll go have a cry."

I tossed a towel over my shoulder and walked slowly to the shower.

I had Heinie Zimmerman approach Rube about dumping a game for five hundred bucks. When Rube laughed at him, Heinie offered six hundred. Rube just walked away. So I told Heinie to offer seven-fifty and the big lefty threatened to punch out Heinie's lights.

"We must be getting close to his price," I said.

"If you ask me, we're getting close to his boiling point."

"What's the matter, Zim, afraid the big hick might beat you up?"

Heinie was almost as big as Rube but pretty much a coward. He'd hit a guy if you held him down, but he wasn't the sort to do something on his own.

"Offer the dope a grand," I said.

"A thousand bucks! Jesus, we don't need him that bad."

"Who's in charge here?"

"You are, Prince, but a thousand is too much."

"We'll take that Sunday School shine off him."

"I just don't get it."

"Offer him the grand. If he doesn't take that, then he'll just have to accept the consequences."

"What's that supposed to mean?"

"He's married, ain't he?"

"Sure," Heinie says. "Hey, Prince, what's so special about Rube Benton? I thought we were only in this to make a little money on the side."

"He thinks he's better than us."

"He's a pitcher and we play the field. Where the fuck is the comparison?"

"He needs a lesson."

"It doesn't make any sense."

"You don't have to make sense of it. Just do what I tell you."

"Don't get sore, Prince. Jesus. A grand. Whatever you say."

Rube didn't take the offer, although he did take a swipe at Heinie, who was lucky to run away in time.

Then Rube's wife began to receive little poisoned notes in the mail. Hey, it's a crazy world.

Chapter 56

As the season wore down and the Giants were just playing out the string, McGraw confined me to the coaching box and Heinie to the bench. Mack never said anything, just eased us off the field. Heinie was upset that we were put out of business, but I didn't really care. I was more interested in what was happening in the White Sox clubhouse.

It was after a home game that our team trainer handed me a note from an old pal, Sleepy Bill Burns, asking if I could meet up with him for a drink at the Ansonia Hotel. Bill liked to think of himself as an operator, so I knew he had something on his mind other than drinking to my health. I had known the guy ever since he broke in as a pitcher with Washington in 1908. He was called "Sleepy" because on more than one occasion he got caught napping on the bench in the middle of a game. Sleepy never learned his lesson and kept nodding off. He never learned his lesson in anything. I faced him as a batter plenty of times and it was always the same pattern of pitches. I tattooed the guy so hard it was a shame to see Sleepy waived out of the league.

So we meet up at the Ansonia for a bite to eat and play catch up. It seems that he returned home to Texas to drill for oil. I was starting to think he was about to put the touch on me to invest in a potential gusher when for once Bill threw me a surprise pitch.

"Prince," he says, lowering his voice, "What would you think if I told you that the World Series could be swung to the short-ender?"

I almost laughed out loud. All those little seeds I tossed into the wind were taking root just the way I'd hoped. The big fix was coming back full circle.

I called the waiter over to get me a different fork. I knew that stepping out of the box was the way to handle a duffer like Sleepy. I waited until after the waiter was done before I answered. "To tell you the truth, I don't think it can be pulled off."

"Anything can be fixed. Everybody has their price. You taught me that one."

"One game, maybe. But the whole Series?"

"What if I said it was a sure thing."

"There are no sure things. Or didn't I get to that lesson?"

"What if I told you that Arnold Rothstein himself is bankrolling the operation? I made him a little proposal. The Series is already in the bag for Cincinnati."

"Jesus, Bill, that's different. If you got a big-time gambler like that on board I'd say you're sitting pretty." I began to take a sip of water but stopped. "But why are you telling me?"

"Actually Rothstein jumped ship. The guy's gone stale, he's slipping, he don't see this one. So I'm looking for investors."

Good old Sleepy, still telegraphing his pitches.

"Personally, my funds are all tied up at present," I said. "But if I come across anybody who might be interested in this kind of proposition, I'll be sure to get back to you."

"Sure, Prince, that's it. Send out some signals. I'm staying here at the Ansonia. And don't worry, there'll be a taste in it for you."

A taste? What did Sleepy think I was, a bellhop he could flip a quarter to? And the last thing I was going to do was line up backers for the guy. I didn't want my name connected to the business. I was just happy to see that matters were proceeding. With Sleepy Burns looking for payoff money door to door, I knew that the big fix would become the kind of secret that every bootblack and cabby knew about.

Then one morning I woke up nervous. All of a sudden I was full of doubts. What if Chick Gandil told Bill that the fix was my idea in the first place? Maybe Bill thought he was just the go-between and we were both playing it cute. I would come up with the payoff money and Bill would deliver it to Chick for the players. All that talk about Arnold Rothstein was hot air, or a threat that he'd turn elsewhere if I didn't come through with the dough. I just couldn't be sure where things stood. What if nothing happened? What if nothing went wrong?

Chapter 57

I sent a message to Sleepy that I wanted to talk. We arranged to meet at a ten-minute club, the kind of prohibition place where you have to order a watered-down drink every ten minutes or move on.

But Sleepy didn't come by himself. I felt a lot better to see he had a partner with him, Little Abe Attel. Abe had been a good prizefighter in his day, held the lightweight belt for a dozen years, and after hanging up the gloves went to work as bag man and errand boy for Arnold Rothstein. What I couldn't tell yet was if Rothstein was back in the picture or Little Abe was in business for himself.

"Champ, you know of Prince Hal, I'm sure," Sleepy said.

"Sure, who don't?" Abe didn't seem too enthusiastic to make my acquaintance.

Sleepy kept up the small talk for a while before he turned to me and said, "So I guess you had some luck?"

"I was going to ask you the same thing."

"Seriously, Hal, have you found any interest?"

"In what?"

"You know. Involving the upcoming ... situation."

"Oh, the situation."

"Yeah, that."

"Actually," I said, "no."

"Jesus Christ," says Abe.

"He's a kidder, Champ. You're just kidding us, ain't you, Prince?"

I just gave him a look like he was crazy.

"Didn't I tell you?" hissed Abe. "It's a shakedown. We don't need him. We never needed him."

"I just want to spread the risk is all," answered Sleepy.

"You're spreading the risk, all right."

What a relief it was to watch them bicker. "I can see this deal is over your heads," I said.

"And I suppose you're just the wonder boy to help us out of a jam?" Abe pulled open his coat so I could see the crosshatch handle of a revolver. "Let's get something straight, pal. The train has already pulled out of the station and you ain't on board."

"Sure, Champ. No need to flash the heat."

"Hey, I'm sorry, Hal," Sleepy said. "Things are a little tense right now. In a couple of months we'll all get together and have a good laugh."

"I don't think so," Abe said.

So I left. I could see that this pair was primed to butcher their end of the deal, so I turned my attention to the ballplayers.

The next time the Sox and Giants were in the same town, after the Sox and Cincy had both wrapped up their World Series slots, I went looking for Chick Gandil and found him in his team's hotel lobby reading a newspaper. I tapped him on the shoulder and the guy was so edgy he almost jumped out of his shoes.

"Christ, what do you want?"

"Calling in my marker, Chick?"

"I don't owe you any money."

"Just information," I said. "Come on, I know what's cooking."

"You and everybody's aunt, I guess. Well, I don't know nothing about dumping the Series if that's what you're talking about. Every year it's the same old rumors."

"Chick, you're talking to the Prince. I know what's up. Remember the idea didn't just come to you in a dream. All I want to know is how it's going to play out. Win the first, drop the second."

"I don't know what the fuck you're talking about." He tosses the paper and heads quick for the elevator.

I'm right on his heels whispering, "I ain't no goddamn busher. Either I get in on this deal easy, or I get in on it hard."

He steps inside the elevator and as the operator begins to close the doors Chick looks at me and says, "If you screw this up for me, Chase, I swear I'll blow your brains out."

I turn to leave, happy in my work, and I practically bowl over a gambler I knew from Boston, Sport Sullivan. The way he looked at me, hoping I wouldn't recognize him but knowing I did, said all I needed to know. The cockroaches were crawling out of the cracks for this one.

"Chick is on his way up to his room in case you're interested," I said.

"I beg your pardon?"

I just gave Sport a wink. "See ya in the funny pages."

Chapter 58

With the Giants out of the pennant race McGraw called it a year early and left Matty in charge the final few games. I knew I would be lucky to see any more time on the field. My last appearance in the big leagues was as a pinch hitter in Boston. I lashed a sweet double to knock in a meaningless run in a meaningless game. So much for fifteen years in the fast company, seventy-five-hundred at-bats, and who knows how many hours riding the rails, how many hotel meals, how many twisted ankles, plunked ribs, spiked shins and strained muscles.

On second base I knew this was the last time I'd ever stand in the middle of the diamond in the major leagues. It's not like there was an overflow crowd to witness the occasion, but I still took a moment to close my eyes and take it all in. I guess I wished it could last forever. The pitcher and batter would just go after it forever, one foul ball after another until the end of time. I'd never have to leave the field. I'd never have to pull off that uniform.

Three pitches later my teammate struck out. So much for a big rally, so much for immortality.

The day I pulled off that major league uniform for the last time, I didn't feel sad about it. I was too busy savoring all the good I was about to accomplish. The World Series was just a couple days off. I had set the bomb, lit the fuse, and now all that was left was to wait for the explosion. All those bastards with their mitts on baseball would be blown to Hell. In the spring, when the smoke cleared, the professional game would be dead or dying. People would figure it was all a Red plot. Politicians wouldn't be able to resist getting into the act and pass a law to banish professional baseball just like they had booze. So the Prince would have plenty of company in hanging up the old spikes.

Everybody's in the clubhouse making their good-bys and leaving for the year. I see Matty in the corner, slowly getting dressed, like each movement is pure agony. I take my time, waiting for everybody to clear out. Knotting my tie, I walk over to him.

"Gonna catch the Series, Matty?"

"I promised to cover it for the newspapers."

"Swell deal. You get *paid* to watch the World Series. Me, I'd have to pay double before they'd let me through the gate. If you had anything to say about it, right?"

"Have a good winter, Hal."

"No '*See ya next spring*'? I guess you figure the Giants won't have me back. And who wants to come back? The game's not the same. New York's not the same."

"It's still a great game," he said. "Just different."

"That's awful generous of you, Matty. 'Never is heard a discouraging word,' huh?"

"Christy, I got us a cab out front." Rube Benton was picking up a couple of suitcases when he spotted me talking to Matty.

"Don't you look the sport," I said. Rube was wearing a new suit, bow tie, straw boater and two-toned shoes.

"Are you okay?" he asked Matty.

"I'll be with you in a minute, John."

"Hold on, *John*, and I'll walk out with you." I took up my grip and gave Matty a pat on the shoulder. "You get well now, you hear?"

I followed Benton out of the ballpark.

"I got a tip for you, buddy," I said.

"Save your breath."

"It's a real peach. The Series is in the bag for the Cincinnati."

"I guess you'd be the one to know."

"If you're smart you'll get your money down quick."

"Get away from me." He stopped in the middle of the runway that led out of the yard. It was getting dark so at the end of the runway all you could see was a purple mist.

"What's the matter, Rube?"

"You're what's the matter."

"I ain't gonna rob you."

"Just walk on and keep away from me."

I laughed at him. "It's in the bag, pal. Wise up!"

I kept walking out of the ballpark, to be swallowed up by the purple mist.

Chapter 59

I headed back west, the World Series was held, the White Sox dumped it as ugly as you could please and the Reds pulled the surprise upset. The rumbling of dirty business began to appear in the newspapers, then— nothing. Not a damn thing. Chick had almost half the team in on the deal, the odds swung so far in favor of the Reds that you knew something had to be up, yet nobody wanted to face up to what happened. I should have guessed that nobody wanted to get wise. After a couple of days, once the shock of Cincy's win sinks in, it's just chalked up as another victory for the underdog, just like what Fielder Jones and his Hitless Wonders did to the Cubs a dozen years earlier.

God, I was sour. Was baseball so rigged, so crooked, that there was no way to bring it down? I had done my best, but the world didn't want what was right. The world wanted to wallow in the mud. If that was what it wanted, I thought, so be it. I washed my hands of everything.

I received a contract in the mail from the Giants for the next season that called for only a couple hundred bucks in salary. It was just their way to get rid of me without any legal problems. So I asked for my release and it came flying back in the mail.

I signed to play in the Pacific Coast League and didn't waste time the next season going into the game-fixing business, with no higher purpose than to realize some cold, harsh cash for myself.

What I didn't realize was that the seeds I had planted the year before just took a little longer to blossom than I expected. A couple of newspapermen kept snooping around, and by September of the 1920 season, when the White Sox were fighting Cleveland for another American League pennant, the story suddenly caught fire and spread out of control. A Chicago grand jury was impaneled to look into the matter, and people all across the country started to get upset over the Big Fix. Ban Johnson and the club owners were suddenly scrambling to defend the integrity of the game. Finally things were cutting my way.

Everybody ran for cover, blaming each other, and looking for scapegoats. Even Rube Benton got caught in the net after a couple of Braves players reported how he told them about Hal Chase bragging how he fixed the Series. That's what got me indicted. People wouldn't believed a mug like Chick Gandil could organize a job that big. Some kind of smart operator had to be behind it all, and that spelled the Prince, Hal Chase.

So one day I'm minding my own business, entering a San Jose movie house with a buddy's pretty young wife on my arm when I'm stopped by the cops, arrested and tossed in jail. I still had some friends in political circles, so California refused to extradite me to Chicago. I told the newspapers that if the grand jury wanted my testimony so bad it'd cost them transportation plus five hundred bucks. Since all Rube Benton had to offer was talk and no hard evidence to implicate anybody, they let me drop.

Just as I dreamed, Organized Baseball was taking a kidney punch. Charlie Comiskey tried his best to come off as the poor sap done in by his pampered, ungrateful and greedy ballplayers. He acted like the courageous Old Roman who was going to track down every lead on the fix for the sake of the integrity of the game, even if it meant breaking up his great ball club and losing a major investment in property.

But it was Ban Johnson who was really taking the hit. The club owners ganged up on him and decided that in order to restore public confidence what was needed was a baseball "czar" to replace the three-man National Commission that Johnson ruled for the last twenty years. What the game needed, they said, was a commissioner.

In order to whitewash the game the owners needed a well-known, respected and popular American to become the first commissioner. They considered ex–presidents of the United States, even a future president in Herbert Hoover who had done such a wonderful job during the Great War running Belgium relief. But in the end they turned to the judge who had made a name for himself by years of grandstanding in the newspapers and had done them such a swell turn in the Federal League lawsuit. They called on that snow-headed, hanging judge with the funny name, Kenesaw Mountain Landis.

The owners had no intention of giving Landis unlimited powers. All they really wanted was a figurehead, but they knew they were in a jam, he knew they were in a jam, and he drove a hard bargain. They gave him all the authority he wanted, then declared him to be the wisest man since

Solomon. And one good thing about Landis—he never was one to let the law get in the way of what he decided to do. All of the White Sox charged over the fix were found innocent in a trial—but that didn't stop Judge Landis. He banned them all from Organized Baseball for life. It was in the best interests of baseball, he said.

And the gulls fell for it. A few fallen apples had tried to ruin the pure game of baseball but the judge had tossed them into the fiery lake so everything was once again as it should be. And if that wasn't enough, the owners juiced up the ball again, brought in the fences to produce more homeruns and made a national hero out of a big lug like Babe Ruth. In no time baseball was more popular—and profitable—than before the fall. I could see it was all hopeless. America was being sold another bill of goods, just like all the nonsense about Cooperstown, and they loved it. They begged for more.

I never got charged with any wrongdoing, just got booted from the Pacific Coast League. Then the California State League. Then from every organized circuit in the country. I was pretty much banished to the desert of Arizona and New Mexico where I continued to play ball in the outlaw mining leagues with other outcasts and no-accounts. Even there I couldn't run away from the stain of the Big Fix. Forget Chick Gandil, Shoeless Joe or even Arnold Rothstein—for years people figured Hal Chase to be the villain. Everywhere I turned I could hear people whisper, "There goes the guy who fixed the Series." I was the fall guy. And when I no longer cared what anybody thought, when I was ready to take all the blame upon myself for the sake of attention if nothing else, people forgot me. Like I never had nothing to do with the fix. I didn't know which was worse: To be remembered for doing something rotten, or to be forgotten completely.

Chapter 60

At the age of forty-five I was still playing baseball, for a club in Douglas, Arizona, in a mining league. I'd lost my speed but kept my guile, so I figured I was still the best player that loop had to offer. I had taken to the Prohibition hooch awful hard and was pretty much just playing now for room and drink.

The owner of the club ran an auto dealership and lent us a couple of roadsters for traveling to away games. At the end of the season some pals and me got liquored up pretty good and drove into the desert without the lights on. I was sprawled in the back when we hit a rut, then a huge boulder, and I went sailing feet-first through the windshield. Cut up my legs pretty bad and I could hardly walk for weeks. I couldn't afford a doctor but I hoped to heal up in time for the next baseball season.

I begged off practice and didn't play at all until the opening game. In the very first inning I came up to the plate with nobody on base. It didn't take much doping out to get an edge on the kid pitcher toeing the mound. After watching a couple of sloppy hooks I laid for the straight one, got it and laced a ball into right-center for a sure triple, maybe even an inside-the-parker if the outfielders kicked the ball around. I was already planning to glance up before rounding second to see if there was a chance to score. The only problem was that the legs turned to jelly, and right out of the box I took a dive. It was like the ground jumped up and smacked me. I scrambled to my feet, trying to ignore the pain that's shooting up my tailbone, but only my arms cooperate and I wind up sprawled on the ground again. The crowd is shouting, the outfielders are still running down the ball, I tell myself to just take it easy and settle for the double. If I get up now I could waltz into second. Hell, everybody gets clumsy now and again. But it doesn't matter how much I try, the legs won't work. It's like a goddamn nightmare, a slow-motion nightmare. Just getting to my knees takes everything I have.

The pain is so bad now that I'm yelping like a dog and the entire time the old baseball instincts are screaming, *Go, go, goddamn it, go!* Now I'm willing to settle for the safety. Just get up and walk to first base. It'd be worth a few laughs over beer after the game. *Jesus, Prince, I figured somebody's husband shot you dead!* But first base looked like a life preserver that had been thrown out of reach. I couldn't even get to my knees now. It was all I could manage to crawl in that hot Arizona sand. The great Hal Chase, Prince Hal, crawling like a fool in front of seventy-five paying customers in the most rundown yard in the sorriest league in the entire country. The pill finally came sailing in from the outfield and thirty feet over the head of the cutoff man. The catcher finally had to run it down and flip the ball over to first base for the force out. The umpire didn't even bother to make the call. The crowd was stone dead quiet. There was just the desert wind rolling over me as I swam in the dirt not ten feet out of the batter's box.

My playing days were over but there was still the rest of my life to think about. I kicked around the southwest for another twenty years. I always had some scheme that would turn to shit. Down in Mexico I convinced some big-time bandit to start up a baseball league to challenge the gringo major leagues. Then his wife or girlfriend or some rival crook had him killed. I tried selling cars, peddled real estate, made a go at all kinds of business ventures, but none of them worked out. Mostly because of the drink. I became a carnival barker. I did some carpentry. I went into the hills with a complete nut case to try my hand at prospecting. When Roosevelt came into office I found odd work through the WPA. And all the time I was convinced that I was just waiting for a break.

One day I read in the newspaper that the Columbia University football team was training in Tucson to get ready for the Rose Bowl. The trainer was Doc Barton, an old pal from my Yankee days. I get this notion that Doc would be honored to lend me some money to finance whatever scheme I was brewing at the time. After all, hadn't I bailed out Doc on more than one occasion? And if I hadn't, he knew I would have. Besides, I would actually be doing him a favor to let him in on a surefire opportunity that would pay him back in spades.

I hitchhiked to Tucson, showed up at the football practice field and asked to see him.

"Doc's busy, old-timer," says this peachy-cheeked kid.

Well, I raised bloody hell until they brought out Doc. He looked like a few years had passed but still seemed pretty fit. I gave him the old smile and held out my hand.

Doc's jaw drops. "My God it *is* Hal Chase."

He didn't shake my hand, just laid his arm over my shoulder, sat me down and went to get me a drink of water.

I couldn't remember the last time I bothered to look at myself in the mirror, but I caught my reflection in the glass frame of the football team's group picture that was hanging on the wall. I looked like a goddamn wreck. I thought I was dressed good enough to talk business when really I was wearing nothing but rags. My hair was filthy and matted. I probably smelled like a garbage scow.

Doc came back with the water and we chatted about old times for a few minutes. I didn't even bother to put the touch on him. Then he said that he had to get back to practice. He reached into his pocket for a couple of dollar bills that he began to stuff in my breast pocket.

"Don't do that," I begged. And I meant it.

"It's just a loan. You'll pay me back when you can." But we both knew that we'd never see each other again.

I drifted back to California where one of my sisters took me in. My health was shot and after years of boozing and not eating too good I developed beriberi of all the goddamn things.

And that's how I wound up here in the county hospital, a charity case, bending any ear that will listen. I can't walk no more. Can't hold much food down. I know I won't be going back to my sister's place. I talk about the old days, those clean hits and those miracle plays with the leather, and wonder how my life got away from me. You try to do your best. You try to bring a little light to the world, to leave it better than the way you found it. Only nothing ever changes. Nothing ever will. The game goes on without us.